NEVER AS GOOD AS THE FIRST TIME

Mari Walker

St. Martin's Griffin ⚞ New York

Walker

This is a work of fiction. All of the characters, organizations, and events portrayed in this novel are either products of the author's imagination or are used fictitiously.

www.stmartins.com

Library of Congress Cataloging-in-Publication Data

Walker, Mari.
 Never as good as the first time / Mari Walker.—1st ed.
  p. cm.
 ISBN-13: 978-0-312-37542-3
 ISBN-10: 0-312-37542-5
 1. Single mothers—Fiction. I. Title.

PS3623.A35955N48 2008
813'.6—dc22

2007048876

First Edition: April 2008

10 9 8 7 6 5 4 3 2 1

In loving memory of my father and mother, Horace and Lillie Mae Walker. Mama, thank you for the gift of reading, and Daddy, thank you for the gift of storytelling.

And in memory of my sister, Deborah Lynn Walker—Debbie, this is for you!

ACKNOWLEDGMENTS

Wow! Here I am. The dream has finally become a reality! For those who think dreams don't come true, let me assure you that they can and do, and that with God, all things are indeed possible!

I want to thank God first, because without Him, nothing can be created. Thank you for always being in my corner and loving me no matter what.

I would also like to thank my agents, Elaine Koster and Stephanie Lehmann. Elaine, thank you for giving me a chance. Stephanie, thank you for reading, re-reading, and reading again, and for the constant feedback. To my editor, Monique Patterson, thank you for believing in my work and for helping me shape and mold it into the best that it could be. And to Monique's assistant, Kia DuPree, thank you for all you do! And for just being a listening ear.

To my beautiful children, Dawnesa, R. J., and Kevin, thank you for being my first and best readers, for all your encouraging words, and for being honest enough (and brave enough!) to tell me when something "just didn't sound right."

Bri, Mani, Quinton, Malachai, Kemari, and Dyla, you are my heart! Lucy and Brittany, much love. My brothers and sisters; Babysister, Larry, Cheryl, Nat, J. R., Ralph, Mattie, Roy, Vickie, Johnny, and David. To Gary Smith, my brother, my friend, thank you for giving me a shoulder to cry on, loving counsel, many,

many prayers and (almost) never being too busy to answer my cries for help. Toia Walker, thank you for everything—you know my struggles better than anyone! I will never forget your undying loyalty and support. Lil Eiland, my sister/cousin; I love you, girl! Shirley Hayes, what can I say? You know! Mike, Erica, Russell, Tonya, Jason, Elizabeth, LaToya, LaKitia, Arelle, Monica, Jomial, Murphy, Shennell, Cierra, Deja, Emari, Aaron, Nicki, Damon, and Mark. To Pat Nedd, Alorian Honeywood, Cindy, Mark and Dana Cummings, Katherine Genovese, Larry and Patricia Howard, Lil Carter, Mary Morris, Rose Oberholzer, Valerie Winston Banks, Mildred Galloway, Bob Ostrander, Monica and Terrell Guidry, Mama and Pop Knox, Gene and Sandy Bennet, Betsey Davis, the Armstrongs, Julian and Pam O'Loughlin, Fela Riley, Melissa Smith, Sherelle Brown, Alana and Les, and the Reeds.

To all my family and friends! It is impossible to include you all here, but please know that a name missing from this page is in no way missing from the gratitude I feel in my heart.

And finally, a very special thank-you to Pastor Tyus Nedd, my pastor, mentor, brother, and friend, for never allowing me to give up on my dreams.

In the beginning, Cain slew his brother Abel and destroyed his ability to think and reason, forever preventing him from being all that he was meant to be.

Many centuries later, coCaine slew the brothers' Ability and destroyed their thinking and reasoning, forever preventing them from being all they were meant to be....

PROLOGUE

The room was dark and I was on my hands and knees, naked, digging at the floorboards with my bare hands. The lone thought in my mind was finding a rock that maybe someone had hidden in the little crevice where the board and the floor met. I couldn't get it out of my head that there could be a little piece of crack hidden there. I knew that it had once been a crack house before I had moved in and there had to have been a lot of ballers and shot callers in and out of here night and day for years. They could have hidden some. Some long-neglected corner of my mind knew that I was being ridiculous and that I wouldn't find anything. A long-forgotten, faraway voice that sounded like mine was telling me to stop, to get up off my hands and knees, but that driving, all-consuming need to have another blast, to have "Scotty beam me up" just one more time was keeping me captive, naked on my knees.

I raked my hand across the crevice one last time and felt something sharp slice across my fingers. I snatched my hand back and peered at it in the darkness, trying to assess the damage. The pain was immediate and intense; I could feel the blood starting to trickle down my fingers from the open gash across the tips. I had been right about one thing, it had once been a hiding place for crack. I had just found the still sharp razor blades embedded in the crevices that had once protected it.

I sat there on the floor for a long time, still naked and bleeding, not really caring if it stopped or not; in fact, an idea was forming in my head that bleeding to death wouldn't be such a bad idea. I could get a razor blade from the medicine cabinet in the bathroom and open another gash on my wrists and let the blood from my fingertips mingle with the blood from my wrists and together they might drown the life out of me. But that nagging little voice would not be stilled. That voice of reason that had once been mine. And for about the hundredth time it was asking me what was I doing here. What in hell had brought me to this? I started to cry. *Dear Jesus, where are You? Help me! Oh God, please help me out of this pit I've dug for myself!*

But I was down so deep, I wasn't sure that even Jesus could reach me.

Part One
SINKING SAND

1

Getting divorced is never easy. Even if the person that you're divorcing is someone that you've grown to despise. Being in church doesn't protect you from it. Even being married to a minister doesn't protect you from it. Even if everyone in your whole church is praying for you, it's still hard going through a divorce. Because in reality, no matter how many people are *there* for you—your church, friends, family—when you go home at night, you're still alone.

I had two older brothers, one older sister, and two younger sisters, but ever since our dad passed away of liver failure a few years back, we had become more like people who happened to share the same blood than a family. Dad had been the one who kept our family grounded and had been the one to organize the family gatherings. And he wouldn't ask us *if* we were going to participate, he would just tell each of us that he was cooking out or whatever and we were *expected* to come *and* bring a dish. Dad's cookouts had always been such fun that we all hated for them to end. Mom would be slammin' in the kitchen, cooking her special macaroni and cheese, green bean casserole, greens, baked beans, and potato salad. Our neighbors would wander over and ask what time the fun was going to start, once they got a whiff of Mom's cooking and Dad's barbecue. Especially once they got a whiff of Mom's homemade pecan pie and peach cobbler.

Most of the time, Mom would just follow Dad's lead. She was like a lot of Southern women of her generation, raised to love, honor, and obey their husbands without question. At least, that was my mom's idea of being a perfect wife, which is why Mom was so lost when Dad died. She no longer had anyone to follow. She wasn't equipped to take over and hold the family together once Dad was gone. Mom kind of went into a shell and retreated to the four walls of her home, rarely venturing out on her own. And even if the rest of us managed to get a cookout or something organized, Mom almost never came.

"Now, y'all know I don't feel like bein' bothered with all that noise and stuff," she would say. "Just bring me a plate by when y'all get done. That'll be fine."

So with no family cookouts or any other real family gatherings to hold us together, we began drifting apart. Not that we didn't still love one another, we did. We just got so busy doing too many of our own individual things and not enough family things until we had become almost strangers as time went on.

Sitting in church Sunday night (on Sundays, we usually had at least two services, a morning and a night service), thinking about family problems instead of listening to the pastor's voice speaking the word of God to my soul, naturally led me to thoughts about the problems between me and my soon-to-be ex-husband, Ian. I wondered what had brought us to the brink of divorce. To be totally honest, I was also wondering why in the world I had ended up marrying Ian in the first place. He wasn't exactly the type of man I had pictured myself going out with, much less walking down the aisle with. So what had happened?

He wasn't at church with me, although if we had still been together he would've been. We had been separated for months now. I hadn't been happy in my marriage for quite a while. The bad times had far outstretched the good until it got to the place that bad was just about all I could remember.

Ian had been driving this old beat-up maroon-colored '72

GTO when we had first started dating. The passenger side door was bashed so far in, I didn't see how in the world anyone could ride in the car with him. From the looks of it, I thought he would have to be riding around with the Jaws of Life in the backseat to get that door opened. He was always telling people that he was going to go to the junkyard and get another door and put it on himself, but he never did. I remembered thinking that I needed to wear jeans or something when we went out, just in case I had to climb over the driver's seat to get in. Wearing a dress and climbing wouldn't be cute.

When Ian parked and stepped out onto the sidewalk, I rolled my eyes and sighed when I saw the way he was dressed. Just watching him made me ask myself again what in the world had made me say that I would go out with him. He had on these lime-green high-waisted pants that made his arms seem far too long for his short trunk and, because he was bowlegged, gave him the appearance of a monkey. So in my head, before our first date, I had nicknamed him "the orangutan." I still called him that whenever I was mad at him.

My thoughts about Ian were suddenly interrupted when Mr. Wilson stood up to testify about how glad he was to be saved, sanctified, and filled with the Holy Ghost, and how the Lord had kept him on his journey for most of his ninety-two years. I marveled, once again, at how spry he was at his age. The man still walked everywhere he went, even to church. We had all offered Mr. Wilson rides whenever we'd see him strolling around town, but he always turned us down.

"You know," Mr. Wilson would say, "the good Lord done woke me up this morning in my right mind and started me on my way! I'm on my journey and can't stop now! He gave me two legs to walk and feet to carry me through and I'm gon' use them as long as God gimme strength!"

Mr. Wilson usually launched into his favorite song while testifying, as he did now.

"I shell fall asleep one day fa-rom this earth, I shell pass away and be redeemed, I shell reach the golden sand. I shell see His blessed face! God who had kept me by His grace! When I wake uup in glory by and byyyyyyyy! I'll awake—wake, wake uuuuuuuuuup in glo-ory and by faith I shell sing a redemptions stooooory. . . ." He sang with his eyes closed, keeping his hands prayerfully clasped in front of his chest (only peeking out every now and then to see if the congregation was loving his song as much as he was).

And then Mr. Wilson caught the Spirit as he usually did before he finished his testimony, and began to sprint around the sanctuary, as though the years couldn't hold him back. I couldn't help but raise my hand and wave it in his direction and yell, "Go 'head, Mr. Wilson!" as he tore around the sanctuary like a miniature whirlwind. I had a big smile on my face as I watched Mr. Wilson, and prayed that the strength in his heart would be equal to that of his legs. But then suddenly, without really meaning to, my thoughts turned back to Ian.

Even when I had first seen Ian in church, I could see that he wasn't my type at all. I had never had a romantic thought in my head about him. He was married, for one thing, and too short, for another. He was only about five seven but would tell everyone he was five nine, as if saying it would make him miraculously grow the extra inches.

Ian had deep dimples in both cheeks, the kind that showed even when he was just talking. He could sing like Peabo Bryson and played the lead guitar. Ian was also a minister, but I remember thinking that when he preached, there was something off about it, somehow it was not quite spiritual. I thought this even more after I heard him preach the sermon about "The Little Drummer Boy" one Sunday morning. He had the nerve to say that story was in the Bible (lucky for him he didn't try to name which book, chapter, and verse it was in!). I still had to stifle the laughter that welled up inside me just thinking back to that day.

"Ohhhhhhh yaaaaaaaaaawwwwwwwl!" Ian had begun. "*Dmp!* Don't ya'llllll *dmp!* see that little bitty boy! *Dmp!(clap!)* Oh Lawd, ha' mmerrrrrrrcayyyyy! Don'tcha see that child walkin' unh! He walkin' up to the manger! *Unh dmp!* He walkin' with that drum in his handsah! *Dmp!(clap!)* He walkin' upta the child. Mary's baby-*ump!* the Lamb of God! *Ump!* Slaaaaaain ah! *Dmp! (clap!)* I said slaaaaaaaaaain! *Dmp!* GREAT God from a Burnin' World! Don'tchaya'll see that Little Drummah Boy! Ohhhhhoh Lawday! He marchin' right on up to that manger! Yes, he is! And he begin to play. He played for you! And don't ya'll know he played for me . . ."

And on and on he had gone, lying in the name of the Lord. I had to get up and leave the sanctuary because I was about to laugh in the man's face!

I knew that day, minister or not, that the man couldn't possibly be reading the Holy Scriptures and not know that "The Little Drummer Boy" story was nowhere between those pages! I didn't really care for him as a person or as a minister after that.

After a while though, he and his wife got divorced and Pastor Greathouse made it known that she thought Ian and I would make a good match.

"Samai, honey," she had told me soon after Ian's divorce, "a good Christian man is hard to find. Ian is a good man, and you know you have a child to take care of. Ian is a hard worker, too. You might want to take a good look at him!"

I trusted my pastor's judgment. *Maybe I should take her advice?* I had thought to myself. I was young, so what did I know about these things? A woman of God couldn't be wrong about one of her "sheep" could she? I convinced myself to take another look at Ian. If the pastor thought he was a good guy, maybe I was missing something.

I don't remember how we started talking, but Ian had asked me out one Sunday after church. Maybe our pastor had put a bug in his ear, too.

"Hey, I was wondering," he began gazing into my eyes most sincerely, "I was wondering if you want to go to the movies or something with me sometime."

Despite the pastor's recommendation, with Ian standing in front of me, I still wasn't really attracted to him. I didn't like that I wouldn't be able to wear heels if I went out with him. It would make me taller, and I didn't like being taller than my date.

"Now, you shouldn't have to study that question all like that. I didn't ask you to marry me or anything, now did I? And I ain't speakin' Chinese. All I asked you was would you go out with me sometime," he said, grinning hard so that his dimples made two deep holes in his cheeks. Those dimples were cute!

I smiled back at him but I wasn't quite ready to commit, although my pastor's words still rang in my ears. I didn't know why I was hesitating; it wasn't like men were lined up, beating down my door to take me out, or anything. So what right did I have to be being so choosy?

"Well, we'll see. There's nothing wrong with friends going to a movie," I said.

"That's right," he agreed. "Friends do things together all the time. I can't see a thang wrong with it."

So when he came to pick me up for our date, I was amazed to discover that the passenger door opened quite easily. I ain't gonna lie, I did buckle up my seatbelt extra tight because I wasn't going to fly out of that car if a sharp turn made that raggedy door pop open!

Ian took me out to the usual dinner and a movie. It turned out that he was pretty funny and for some reason, he didn't look so much like an orangutan after our date. I'm ashamed to admit that I *almost* found out what a good lover Ian was not long after. Somehow, being in church and Ian being a minister didn't stop our hormones from almost getting the best of us. I guess the pastor hadn't thought about *that* one when she made her thoughts known about what a good match we would make.

I started thinking now, as the women's choir sang "There's Not a Friend Like the Lowly Jesus," about the final straw that had caused

Ian and me to split. It was so stupid, really, compared to all of the stuff that I had taken off Ian over the years. That final thing really paled in comparison.

We had been looking for a new house. One of the reasons was that our family had grown to five members, me, him, our two sons, and my daughter, who I'd had while I was a young teen and un-married. We were really six if you counted his daughter, Dasche, by his first wife. She didn't live with us full-time, but she spent a lot of weekends and vacations with us.

My husband hadn't wanted to go house-hunting with me. He said that he trusted my judgment and I knew what he liked, so any-thing I picked out would be fine. After weeks of searching, I'd found someone who could not only get us into the house that I chose, but who could get us into it for the same mortgage payment that we had now. That in itself was a miracle, because the house that I had cho-sen was a far cry from the small two-bedroom (three if you counted the attic that served as the boys' room) ranch with the smallish yard that we had now. The house I had picked out had a yard dou-ble the size of the one we were in. It was a split-level stucco, which was still very popular, had a sunken living room, a huge kitchen, finished basement, had a private patio with a built-in barbecue grill, and the entire backyard was surrounded by a privacy fence. It was love at first sight for me. The only thing that bothered me slightly was the fact that all of our neighbors appeared to be white.

It's not that I really cared. It only bothered me because my husband was from down South, and was a little old-fashioned in his thinking. I knew that it might be an issue for him. Sometimes white people made him more than a little uncomfortable, which I really couldn't quite understand because Ian had some white friends. I had my fingers crossed that he would like the house so much that our neighbors wouldn't matter. Besides, it did have that privacy fence.

I couldn't wait for Ian to get home from work so that we could go see the house. We went on a weekday and none of our neighbors seemed to be out and about, which I thought worked out great for the moment. It would give him a chance to judge the house on its own merit and not because of who our neighbors happened to be.

"Oh yeah, babe! This is it! Look at this room here," he said, cupping his hands against the window to block the sun's glare and peering inside. From that vantage point there was a smaller room to the left of the living room.

"Look at this, baby!" He grabbed my arm and pulled me in front of him, again blocking the glare so that I could peek in.

"That room's perfect for my music room, Samai. Yeah, this is it!" He grinned broadly showing his dimples, pulling me close and hugging me from behind.

I could tell Ian loved the house. He went on and on about how great it was and asking when the Realtor could let us in to see the inside. I told him I had seen the inside earlier and described it to him. He was still grinning from ear to ear when I finished.

"The agent said that he can't come back out to show you the inside until Sunday," I told him.

"That's okay, baby. We can come over here right after Sunday morning service." He winked at me and gave me another hug and a peck on the lips.

All the way home he talked about how much he loved the house and how he couldn't wait to move in and how we needed to get boxes to start packing and on and on and on. . . .

By the time Sunday afternoon rolled around, it was a bright sunny day and all the neighbors were out in full force, mowing their lawns or lounging on lawn chairs, sipping lemonade or some other concoction from their iced glasses. I realized immediately that I had made a huge mistake choosing Sunday for Ian to see the inside of the house. He would never move into any neighborhood that had this many white people living so close. My hopes were quickly dashed that the house would ever truly be mine. As soon as he saw all our prospective neighbors, his whole attitude and demeanor changed.

"I don't like it," he said and I could tell he was upset.

"Why not?" I challenged him. "You seemed to like it well enough when you saw it a few days ago! You were the one wantin' to go get boxes and start packin' everything, remember?" I stared at him with my arms folded across my chest and waited for his reply.

"Well, I ain't goin' in! You can forget that!" He said with that stubborn, mean look of determination on his face that he always got when he had made up his mind about something. And when he got that look on his face, there was no use trying to change his mind about anything. My heart dropped to my shoes. The real estate agent was already there. He had pulled into the driveway, gotten out of his car, and was standing near the hood waiting for us to get out of our car and join him.

I pleaded with Ian to just come in and look at the house. "Ian, please, please don't do this! The Realtor is here and he has already shown the place to me. Look, we're already here, what harm can it do for you to just go inside and look around?"

He didn't answer me, he just hardened his face, sucked his teeth and pinched his lips together and I knew in my heart that any further pleas would do no good. But I couldn't stop myself.

"Looking doesn't mean we have to take it, Ian. If you do this, the man will think we're not serious about finding another house. He won't want to work with us anymore," I said, trying to appeal to the side of him that wanted a new house. I was feeling bad that the real estate agent had altered his schedule just to accommodate us and now this. But Ian stubbornly refused.

Too ashamed to face the Realtor alone and come up with an explanation for why my husband refused to look at the inside of the house, and why the agent had come out for virtually nothing, I told my husband to take us home.

We fought like cats and dogs all the way home. Ian was really angry, he was even cursing, and I was so furious, I was saying things that I had never dreamed of saying to him before.

"When we get to the house, why don't you just leave? I don't need this kind of crap! I'm sick of this! You said that you would like anything I picked out, remember?"

"Yeah, I don't give a damn what I said! You should have had sense enough to know that I wouldn't want to live around there. You knew I wouldn't like it, that's why you picked it!" he shouted back at me.

How ridiculous was that? "Why would I do something stupid like that? Why would I purposefully pick out a house that you wouldn't want to live in, Ian? What an idiotic thing to say. I don't want a new house, too? That's just simple!" I was really angry by then. "I'll tell you what? Why don't you just get the hell out of the house and out of my life! Hunh? Why don't you do that?"

Ian's face turned dark and I could see the vein in his temple begin pulsating in and out as he frowned. "You want me to leave? You want me to leave? You got it, bitch!" He screamed back at me and I was shocked that he called me that name. I was stunned into silence after that but he kept shouting, letting bile spill from his minister's lips.

"Every time I look around you startin' shit, just like my moms used to do with Pops. All night, every night all I heard was her mouth belittling Pops, till he started believin' all the bullshit she spit at him! And when she was done with him, her ass would start in on me. Always callin' me stupid and good-for-nothin'! I can't even remember that woman ever tellin' either one of us she loved us! And you act just like her! You got the *nerve* to say you sick a' me? I want to vomit every time I look at you! You look like somethin' that's been hawked up and spit on the ground, you stupid, scarred, scabby slut!"

First I'm a "bitch" now I'm a "slut"? And a "stupid, scarred, scabby" one at that? Hot tears of hurt and shame immediately filled my eyes and spilled over onto my cheeks. I couldn't believe that he had even resorted to making references to the scars I had gotten from a car accident long ago. It wasn't my fault that his mother had treated him so shamelessly and hurt him so badly that every time we had a disagreement about something, he would launch into a bitter tirade against her. The problem was, his mother wasn't present during our fights, so he spewed his venom out on me. Who was this man sitting beside me driving this car? Was this the father of my two sons, stepfather to my daughter, a preacher, calling me these filthy names? I know I had said some things that weren't right, but I didn't deserve that.

"You can dry up them crocodile ass tears, too! 'Cause that shit don't mean nothin' to me, you hear? You the one started this shit so don't try to put on that poor pitiful act now!"

The tears and the pain I felt from Ian's hurtful names and the other things he was saying shut me down, and I couldn't say another word. All I could do was keep on crying silent tears.

When we got home, he immediately threw some clothes and personal things into the trunk of the car. When he was breaking down his amp and packing up his electric guitar, I wasn't so sure I wanted him to go, despite all the names he had called me. But he hopped in the car and roared off so fast, I didn't have time to say anything.

Once Ian had left, the house felt odd and eerily quiet. My mother had taken the kids home after church and I had to go and pick them up. On the way to her house, I thought about all the terrible things Ian had said about his mother and me. I found myself imagining, once again, how life without Ian would be. I had been entertaining thoughts about becoming a single parent a lot lately. Thinking about how things were becoming more and more strained between us and the fights breaking out over the smallest things all the time, before I knew it, I had convinced myself that this separation was for the best.

I was sitting in church still not listening to the sermon and thinking these thoughts when all of a sudden this feeling just came over me. It was the loneliest feeling I had ever had in my life. It wasn't just emotional; it was a physical loneliness and a longing that hurt all over. I was overwhelmed with this feeling that I would never again feel my husband in the bed next to me. Never again feel him on top of me, caressing and kissing my breasts and nipples in that special way that he had. It was the "never feeling him on top of me" part that seemed to hurt the most, and bring the most desire and the most emptiness at the same time. And on top of all those feelings, I was ashamed, too, because I was sitting here in church thinking these thoughts instead of listening to what "thus saith the Lord." And you shouldn't be thinking these kinds of thoughts, even about your soon-to-be ex-husband, while you're sitting in church and the preacher's message had half of the congregation on their feet shouting and doing a spiritual dance.

But being ashamed didn't make the thoughts go away. They were there and so were the feelings I had about wanting to make love to my husband. Soon, I was so miserable sitting there that I began to cry. It was just silent tears at first and they were falling slowly enough that I could catch them in my hands and quickly wipe them away. Before I knew it, the slow trickle became a steady stream wetting my face, and the more I tried to hold back the tears and not cry, the more they came.

One of my friends, Bennie, a deacon in the church, came over and put his arm around my shoulder.

"You OK, sis?"

What did he do that for? The dam broke and the tears let go in a torrent. Not only that, but my body started to tremble and shake as the wave of loneliness overtook me, and I got up and ran into the bathroom.

I cried and cried for the longest before I could finally make myself stop. I blew my nose and dried my eyes, composing myself as best I could, taking a quick look at myself in the bathroom mirror. Other than having bloodred eyes from all of the crying, I wasn't bad looking for a twenty-eight-year-old woman with three young kids to raise.

My short dark hair looked coal-black shiny, and thanks to the girl who did my hair, it looked healthy and cute. My eyes were cat-shaped and my brows had a natural arch that most women had to go to a professional or spend tortured minutes plucking theirs to achieve. I was a good-hearted person who would give her last to anyone who needed it, so why was my life such a mess? I blew my nose one last time, opened the bathroom door, and there was Bennie.

"What's the matter?" he asked. "Are you OK?"

I said, "No!" And the tears started trickling again.

Deacon Bennie drew me close, giving me a much-needed hug as he spoke.

"What's bothering you, sis? You can tell me, and if I can help you, you know I will."

I trusted Bennie. He was known around church for keeping confidences, but I was too ashamed to admit that my thoughts about not being able to have sex anymore had brought on the flood of tears. So I told him the other thing that was bothering me.

I pulled away from him and said, "Well I guess the whole church knows by now that me and Ian are separated. Bennie, I haven't worked in over six years! I don't have any skills, and I only have a couple thousand in the bank, and that won't last long with the kids and me, between paying rent and buying food. What am I gonna do?"

This was not a lie. It was a major concern of mine, it just didn't happen to be the concern that had me crying like a baby at that moment. The deacon reassured me that he could help me with that.

"Look here," he said, holding my shoulders firmly so that I had to look him in the eye. "That's an easy fix. The warehouse hardware store where I'm working has me pulling overtime to the tune of fifty or sixty hours a week and they're looking to hire some more people. Now if you ain't afraid of long hours and working hard, I know I can get you an interview with my boss."

I blinked back the tears and managed a smile. "For real?"

"Yeah, just make sure that you come down there no later than ten tomorrow morning and I'll set everything up."

I thanked him and gave him a big hug. He hugged me back. As we broke apart, the deacon put a finger under my chin, making me have to look him in the eye once again.

"Don't worry so much, Samai, the Lord is able to supply your every need. Remember that," Deacon Bennie said with a smile. He gave me another quick hug before he walked away.

That night before I left church the pastor came up to me and asked me if I was all right. My eyes were red, but I wasn't crying anymore—though her question had me again on the verge of tears.

"No, pastor, I'm not OK, can I talk to you for a minute?"

"Of course you can. Is it about Ian?" she asked.

I nodded, the tears choking off my speech and threatening to spill over again. The pastor led me back to her office to talk. Even though she was a woman, I hesitated. I couldn't find a way to put into words how I missed the *sex* with my husband but didn't really miss the *man*. How could I explain that the love I had for Ian had all but died, but the physical desires remained more alive than ever?

"I don't know where to begin . . . I have these feelings and thoughts about sex and they just pop into my head at the strangest times. Like tonight during service, I started thinking about the last time Ian and me had made love. I-I mean, not just thoughts, the feelings came with the thoughts and I don't know what I'm going to do with these feelings now that Ian and me are separated." The words tumbled out in a rush.

Pastor Greathouse took my hand. "Samai," she began. "It's perfectly normal for a woman to miss her husband. Especially if the two of you have had children together. Not to mention the fact that he has taken care of all your material needs as well. I know it's hard being separated from him. You must miss the companionship the two of you shared. . . ."

My pastor was getting it all wrong. Strange as it seemed, I was adjusting to my new life without Ian. After Ian had been gone for a couple of weeks, I realized that I had been walking around holding my breath while we had been together. Like Terry McMillan had said in one of her books, I had been waiting to exhale. Ian had subjected me to so much cruelty over the years. Now that he was gone, I had a better idea of just how mean he had been.

Like the way he would walk around the house for days, maybe even weeks if I had made him angry enough, giving me the silent treatment. Most of the time, he wouldn't even tell me what I had done wrong to warrant such treatment, leaving me to guess. The worst part was, he would never make up with me until *he* was ready, turning his back to me if I reached for him in bed. But then, one night without a word of apology, he would reach under my gown and begin fondling me. He didn't care if I responded or not, he would roll over on top of me and hump until he was satisfied and then roll back off me. It was a double slap in the face, because usually, Ian would be so gentle and loving when he wasn't angry. He could be an unselfish lover, making sure that I received pleasure as well as giving it. His silent cruelty was one of the main reasons my love for him had died. But even if it wasn't completely dead, it was buried so deep beneath the pain he'd inflicted that I didn't think I'd ever be able to resurrect it again.

Oddly enough when the intimate thoughts would overtake me, it wasn't Ian's cruelty that would come to mind. It was the gentle, loving, and at times, heated lovemaking sessions that tormented me the most. They kept popping up unexpectedly, warming my lower parts unbidden. How could I make my pastor understand these feelings, when I couldn't quite understand them myself?

"No, pastor, it's not that at all. I can't honestly sit here and tell you that I'm sorry Ian is gone, or even that I miss the companionship or whatever. I know that it will be hard to take care of the kids and things without him, but Ian and me were fighting so much toward the end that it's almost like a relief that he's not there anymore. Pastor, like I was saying before, I miss the love-making. The desires are still there. They didn't go away when Ian left. Sometimes, I need relief so bad, it's all I can think about. Now I know that the Bible teaches us that we're not to have these kinds of thoughts outside of marriage, but Pastor, two months ago these thoughts were OK, you know? I had a husband and I was married and having sex was OK and now all of a sudden it's not, but the feelings won't stop. I miss it! I miss it so much! What should I do?"

I poured everything out, not leaving out one bit of my sexual desires and feelings. Since I was a Christian and everything, I couldn't very well go to a bar and hook up with some stranger and take him home to get my physical needs met. I sincerely didn't know what I was going to do.

After listening to all I had to say, the pastor merely took both my hands in hers and said, "Just pray, Samai, the Lord knows what you're feeling and He will take care of those desires. You just have to lean on Him and trust Him, and pray He'll see you through! Do you believe that?" she finished, patting the top of my hand. Then she sighed, and leaned close to me as if she were about to unleash a big secret. One that single Christian women had been using down through the ages to help them with their sexual frustrations.

"You know, dear heart, sometimes the Lord will send you a dream so that you can, you know . . ." She looked around before leaning in even closer and whispering, "Release yourself, if you know what I mean." She leaned back in her chair, patted my knee, and gave me a knowing nod.

I just stared at her. I knew that she meant well, but what she had said hadn't helped. It made me feel worse, because I thought if the pastor only knew how hard I had prayed every night since the separation for these feelings to go away. Since they hadn't, maybe there was something wrong with me, with my faith. Maybe I wasn't being as sincere in my Christian walk as I thought if I could let such feelings overwhelm me. What she'd said had merely rein-forced those doubts.

I didn't tell her how her words made me feel, I just thanked her, gave her a hug, and left.

The next morning, after I had gotten my mother to watch the kids, I went to the address that the deacon had written down for me the night before. The name of the place was Mr. Custom's Warehouse. I had worn a nice dress, one of the ones I would wear to church. I soon felt uncomfortable and overdressed, though, because the man who was interviewing me, Mr. Kolaskos, had on jeans and a plaid shirt with the sleeves rolled up.

"Hello," he greeted me as he entered the room. "My name's Craig Kolaskos, I'm the general manager here."

He extended his hand and I took it before answering, "I'm Samai Collins."

"I know, Bennie Howard's told me all about you. He's one of the best workers we have here, always on time, never misses work! I like that a lot. I hope that you're the dependable type, too," he said, handing me an application and some other forms to complete. He excused himself while I went to work filling them out.

When he came back, I handed all the paperwork to him and he spoke as he looked it over.

"What we need is someone who can be flexible enough to work any shift. We have a lot of work to do here before the grand opening, so we have mandatory overtime as well. You can work as many hours over as you like, after you work the minimum number of overtime hours we set. Does this seem like something you can handle?"

I quickly reviewed my options in my head. I really didn't want to work on Sundays, but if I told him that he might not hire me. And I did need the job. Badly. I wasn't thinking that when I came down this morning that I would get hired on the spot! I wasn't prepared for this. I figured that my mom would babysit the kids for me while I worked, since she wasn't working. But since I hadn't asked her, I couldn't be sure. My mind was racing. I didn't have much time to make a decision since Mr. Kolaskos was waiting on my answer.

"Yes, that sounds fine to me," I finally answered.

"Great! Then I'll see you in the morning, 8:00 A.M. sharp!" he said smiling and extending his open palm for a handshake. He also handed me two bright yellow, polo-type T-shirts with the name of the store printed on the pocket.

"That's your uniform. You can wear khakis or jeans with them, dark blue or black only, no skirts or shorts, since you'll be climbing ladders to restock merchandise when you work overtime."

He shook my hand again and said, "Welcome aboard! I look forward to working with you. See you tomorrow at 8:00 A.M. sharp." He repeated the time again, which wasn't necessary.

"OK, I'll be here, and thank you!" I said.

"You betcha," he said as he turned to walk away.

That next morning, I was early. I never liked being late to anything and work was not going to be an exception. I was scheduled to start my training on the cash register. The woman who would train me was an older woman. She looked about forty-five years old or so. Her name was Loretta James, and she was a grandmother who was raising her daughter's kids by herself, she told me after we were introduced.

"My daughter Jillian, Jilly I call her, she got some real problems," Miss Loretta said, as she opened up the little compartment on the register and dropped in a new roll of tape.

"She got herself hooked up with some no good, wannabe drug dealer and now both him and her done got hooked on that mess."

Miss Loretta's caramel-brown skin had not one wrinkle until she frowned as she did now talking about her daughter. "Called me up from the children's services one mornin' and told me that if I didn't come and get the children, the state was goin' to be my grandkids new mama."

I noticed that her eyes were tearing up a bit, so I decided to change the subject.

"Miss Loretta, how long you been working here?" She looked at me from the corners of her eyes. I saw that the hand that she was using, trying to feed the register tape through the holding bar was trembling slightly, so I reached over and gently took it from her. As I began threading the tape for her, she smiled slightly and nodded.

"Thank you, Samai," she said. "I been working here for about three years now. I had to hurry up and find a job to take care of those two grandchildren of mine. I hadn't worked in about ten years. I worked hard all my life so that I could retire a little bit early and still have a little life left to enjoy before I leave this world. But you know, sometimes, the Lord got a different road for us to take. I retired at fifty and enjoyed myself a little while before the Lord saw fit to let me raise my grandkids."

I looked at Miss Loretta. Wow! If she had retired at fifty and hadn't worked in about ten years, that would make her in her sixties! She was tiny, only about five one at the most and small-boned. She had the reddish brown coloring of someone who probably had some American Indian mixed with her family. Her hair was twisted in a long silky, slightly crinkled, blue-black braid that fell to the middle of her back before curling up at the ends and nestling against the curve of her spine. She sure didn't look nearly that old. Didn't really act it either from what I could see.

"Miss Loretta, that was good of you to take your grandchildren in like that. I can only hope that I would have the same strength of character that you do if that ever happened to me," I said and I meant every word of it. "It's not easy raising children, and when yours get grown, I can't even imagine what it would be like to begin again. I know you have to love those children a lot though, or you couldn't have done what you did. Even so, I know it still had to be a tough decision for you to make."

Miss Loretta chuckled. "You got that right! I almost ran down the street screamin' and pullin' out my hair at the thought of havin' those little tyrants around raisin' sand all the time!"

I laughed with her.

"No, not really," she continued once we managed to stop laughing. "I could never even think of my babies bein' with total strangers, so I didn't hesitate." She smiled and clasped her hands together. "But truth be told, I can't for the life of me understand why they own muhtha wouldn't feel the same way!"

I nodded my head in mute agreement, and Miss Loretta said that we needed to get on with the training.

I was a quick learner, and Miss Loretta was a good teacher, so by the third day of training, I was working the register alone.

They had these new devices that would scan the bar code on a sticker that was on each of the items for sale in the store, and the price would just pop up on the screen and keep a running tally of what each item cost. It would even add the tax for you at the end of the sale, so the job was pretty simple. You just needed to know how to count change back from whatever amount was given to pay for the purchase and how to process personal checks and credit cards if the customer chose that payment method.

The job kept me busy and the days went by pretty quickly. I was working twelve to thirteen hour shifts, because the warehouse was open twenty-four hours. And like I said before, Lord knows, I needed the money.

I generally took lunch and breaks with Deacon Bennie. He was a very nice guy and a really good friend. He was tall, and although we were both in our late twenties, he looked older because his hair was thinning on top. A few men had started shaving their heads completely bald to look sexy, but Bennie either hadn't thought to do that or didn't want to. Personally, I thought it might make him look closer to his true age, instead of five to ten years older, and

more attractive if he had. Don't get me wrong, he wasn't bad looking by any means, he was a good friend and I was very fond of him,
but that is all we would ever be. Friends.

We were laughing about some of the people who came into the
store, and some of the things people were buying. Ceiling fans had
just come on the scene and everyone and their brother had to
have one.

I was doing some calculations on a sheet of paper to see what
my check would look like with all the overtime. According to my
math, even after taxes, I would have nearly eight hundred dollars
for one week's work.

I decided that I would take the kids to see a movie on Saturday
if I didn't have to work. They would like that. I thought that the
boys had said they wanted to see that new movie with Michael J.
Fox in it called *Back to the Future*, or something like that. Yeah, I
would make it a good outing to help them get their minds off not
having their dad around much.

There it was again. That thought about Ian had touched off
that feeling of complete sexual need and loneliness again. I
couldn't stop thinking about the last time we had made love. How
he had laid me down on the living room floor, slowly removed my
clothing, and kissed me deeply, as his hands squeezed and caressed
my breasts. Usually after the kissing got us hot and bothered, he
would move down to my breasts. He told me that he loved the way
sucking, kissing, and licking my nipples would drive me crazy. He
said he thought that I loved that almost as much as him being inside of me, and he was right. I had always loved the sensations that
filled me when my breasts were fondled, and they were super sen-
sitive to the touch of his warm lips and tongue on my nipples. I
could swear I had an orgasm if he did it just right. . . .

"What are you thinking about so hard?" my friend asked, draw-
ing me away from the pleasant daydream.

I looked at Bennie and blinked. "Hunh? Oh, just thinking
about how I was going to spend my first check and what I was

gonna do with the kids this weekend," I lied, suddenly glad that my friend had interrupted my thoughts. I was also glad that he wasn't a mind reader. Where were all of these thoughts coming from? I was a Christian woman soon to be divorced and I had to find some way to banish these unholy thoughts!

"Well, you better be thinkin' about gettin' back to your job before you're late back from break, otherwise, this might be the only check you can plan on gettin' from here!" he joked.

I looked at the clock on the break room wall. Oh my goodness, I had less than a minute to get to my station. That wasn't good. I started gathering my things, but my friend shooed me away.

"You better get goin', I'll clean this up for you," he said.

I smiled at him, mouthed "Thank you," and did a very fast walk back to my station. I made it just in time.

2

It was a beautiful, clear, bright blue Sunday morning and very slow at work. I found myself longing to be out there enjoying the day, instead of being stuck behind the register.

There were only about two or three customers in the entire store. I was bored and beyond that, it felt funny not being in church. This was the first time I had missed a service on a Sunday in more than eight years and I couldn't shake the feeling that I was doing something wrong.

I was feeling guilty that I hadn't told the boss that I absolutely couldn't work on Sundays like Benny had done, and as he had instructed me to do as well. I had started to mention it to Mr. Kolaskos during our interview before he hired me, but, I was afraid to tell the boss that I couldn't work on Sundays after he had asked me if I could work any shift. I thought that, despite Bennie's reassurances, Mr. Kolaskos might not have given me the job. I regretted not speaking up now.

Church was the only life I knew, really. My mother and father were pretty strict, so I had never really partied or gone out to nightclubs. That was why everyone was shocked when I had taken a trip down to Indianapolis to visit my eldest sister, Aubrae, and her new husband one summer, and come back pregnant. My mother had never quite forgiven me for becoming a teenaged parent, though she tried to pretend she had. After that she wouldn't allow me to get as close to her as she did my sisters. My getting pregnant was something that she took very personally. As far as she was concerned, I had brought disgrace on the family. I thought it was just one more thing she added to her list of reasons I wasn't as good as my sisters.

I smiled bitterly and shook my head as I thought back over that summer. I can't lie about it, I went buck wild that week I was there.

My brother-in-law had this fine cousin named Monte and along with Monte's sister Reena, and another cousin Marcia, we went out every night, drinking Boone's Farm wine, and partying with their friends. My sister didn't say much because she thought I was young and just trying to have some fun that summer. Aubrae probably never would have believed that Monte and me were even thinking about having sex. I wasn't thinking that we would either, but one night we had a little bit too much wine and had a little too much time alone, and it had just happened.

Standing at my register waiting for a customer to come through, I was mentally going back and forth, between the summer I got pregnant and the church service that I was missing that day. A man walked into the front lobby. I noticed that he looked like a guy named Zane Blackmon, who I had had a major crush on during high school.

Zane was the kind of guy that I had always lit up around—tall, light-skinned, with black curly hair. If I had ordered him to fit my specifications of a boyfriend and had him tailor-made, I couldn't have done any better. He had to be around six four, with big brown eyes that were fringed with really long, thick, dark eyelashes. I had met him when I was in tenth grade and he'd once sat in a seat directly behind mine in study hall.

When he walked into the hall that day, my heart had skipped a beat. But I didn't dare speak to him because I wasn't the most popular, or one of the prettiest, or one of the finest dressers at school—we had too many kids in our family to feed and clothe for that. But I was one of the smartest when it came to books and learning things. I loved to read any- and everything, and that translated into good grades.

Zane was extremely handsome. All of the girls (and some of the female teachers, too!) couldn't help but do a double take whenever he walked by. He wasn't one of the best dressers, either. He always looked like he was wearing someone else's clothes since they didn't quite fit—always too big. But with his looks, no one really cared.

He took a seat behind me and it was hard to concentrate. He was laughing and joking and doing everything except studying. I just kept on reading my book.

Then I started feeling little pieces of something hitting me and then my book. I picked one up. Someone was throwing little wadded up pieces of what looked like chewing gum wrapper at me. I felt my body grow tense. I thought it was Zane and that he was trying to draw attention to me. And that him and his cohorts would start making fun of me. I decided to do something to stop it before it could get started.

I turned around, planning on fixing him with one of my most evil stares, but when I looked at him, he gazed up at the ceiling and started whistling in an exaggerated way. I kept staring at him as mean as I could, and he gave me a wide-eyed innocent look.

"What?" he asked with an amused look on his face.

I tried to hold my stern expression, but he looked so cute feigning innocence that my lips quivered as I tried to hold back a smile. I turned back to my reading.

Pretty soon I was being hit with little pieces of paper again. I quickly turned and this time he was smiling at me as he threw up both his hands.

"Why you keep lookin' at me? I'm not doin' nothin', I swear!" He made a "cross my heart" gesture with one of his hands as he spoke. His friends started laughing.

I just stared at him and curled my lips up at the corners in what

I hoped looked like a smirk. I shook my head, still trying not to smile.

"What, you don't believe me or somethin'? Aw, now you done hurt my feelings! I'm telling the teacher!"

He raised his arm and started waving it in the air.

"Teacher! Hey, teacher!" he said, assuming a hurt expression. I was laughing by then and his friends were cracking up, giving each other five.

"Oh, you think it's funny hurtin' somebody's feelin's, hunh?" He was laughing, too.

The study hall teacher was walking up the aisle and I went back to reading my book in earnest.

Zane got a detention. He protested, but I could tell that he didn't really care. I glanced up from my book in time to catch the teacher's stern look and warning.

"You're a good girl and a good student, Samai," Mr. McMahon said. "Don't let this character get you into trouble!"

Neither myself, nor the teacher, had to worry about Zane being a bad influence on me. Laughing and joking in study hall was as far as our relationship ever went.

I was still staring at the guy who had come into the store. He really did look like Zane, only better. He had on a red turtleneck sweater and a pair of khakis that I thought made him look sexy. Yeah, he looked like Zane all right, but I couldn't be sure. He was too far away. A customer had walked up to my register, but I was so busy staring at that guy and trying to figure out if he was who I thought he was, that I didn't notice.

"Miss?" the customer said.

"Oh, I'm sorry," I said and began to ring up the items. I had a little rush of customers after that, so needless to say, I lost my view of the one I thought might be Zane.

After the rush slowed, the lead cashier came and told me that

I was relieved to go to lunch. I kind of didn't want to go right then. I was anxious to see if I could get a closer look at that guy if he decided to buy something and came to check out. But I didn't have any control over the lunch schedule, so I had to go.

I really wasn't hungry, so I went outside and sat in my car to listen to some gospel tapes to try to soothe the guilt I felt about missing church. I chose The Winans and as they sang "Tomorrow," I glanced at the time on my car clock: 12:05 P.M. The preacher had to be up in the pulpit beginning her sermon by now. I wondered what her topic would be for the day. I let my thoughts go through the order of service and replaced the Winans' tape with Commissioned's song "There Is No Excuse." I didn't really know why I needed to hear that song right then. Maybe it was because I felt I really had no good excuse for not telling Mr. Kolaskos that I couldn't work on Sundays. Before I knew it, lunch was over and it was time to get back to work. I locked my car door and walked across the parking lot and through the front of the building.

As fortune would have it, at about the same moment, the guy who I had thought was Zane stood at one of the checkout counters finishing up his purchase just as I walked in. He started walking toward me and our eyes met.

"Hi, Zane," I said on an impulse and I was nervous that he wouldn't recognize me.

He smiled as he approached me. "Yeah, hi! How you doin'?"

We had passed each other by then and I had to look over my shoulder and so did he.

I said, "You don't remember me!"

"Yeah, I do. Hold up," he said. As he turned back toward me, I turned to face him.

"No, I can't talk to you right now, I have to get clocked in before I'm late," I said, continuing toward the employee area, walking backward.

He stopped in midstride and, if I'm not mistaken, I think he looked a little disappointed.

"OK, it was nice runnin' into you—I guess," he half-smiled at me before turning and walking away. I watched him for a brief moment, smiling to myself. The way his eyes had lit up I knew that I must have looked good to him. I wondered if he thought I looked better than I had in high school, too.

I was back at my register, still smiling about my chance meeting with Zane. It had been more than a few years since I had last seen him. All sorts of thoughts were filling my mind. I wondered if he was married and if he was, was he in love? Was he going through changes with his wife like I was with my husband? Was he on the brink of divorce like me?

I tried to steer away from those thoughts and keep my mind on my job, but it was hopeless. The attraction was still there. Just that brief encounter with Zane had me messed up and fantasizing. Daydreaming that we had gotten together in school and that my children had been his. Most of all, I was wondering what my life would have been like if I had married him. I was sure that if I had, I wouldn't be going through what I was now.

I was thinking these thoughts and ringing my customers through, when all of a sudden, I saw him standing behind the next person in line.

Zane was in *my* line! My mind started racing a hundred miles a minute wondering what I was going to say to him. I knew one thing, I had to give him my number. Give him my number? *Girl is you crazy? You are married. He could be married. You are a child of God. You need to get a grip!*

When Zane reached my register, he was holding a screwdriver. I looked at him and he looked at the screwdriver and we both laughed.

"No, now I know how this looks. See, I know you think I'm just usin' this screwdriver as an excuse to come through your line but I need it to put together the ceiling fan I just bought."

We both laughed again. Our eyes met and my heart thumped.

"OK, look I ain't gon' lie to you, we both know I don't really need this thang." Zane laid the screwdriver down on the counter. "I wanted to ask you for your number so I could call and talk to you later on."

My line was starting to get kind of backed up and the lead cashier was heading my way. I didn't have time to think. I tore a scrap of register tape, quickly scribbled down my name and number and handed it to him. He glanced at it briefly before stuffing it into his pants pocket.

"I'll call you tonight. What time you get off?"

"Ten o'clock," I said as I reached for the next person's item.

"OK, I'll talk to you later," he said and gave me a smile and a wink.

I know that it sounds too stupid, but I melted just like butter. I couldn't stop smiling, even as I furiously scanned items trying to get my line down.

When I took my break, I had another attack of guilt. Here I wasn't even divorced and I had given my phone number to another man. God was surely not pleased with me. I started thinking that I had made a big mistake. I didn't want to start up a relationship with another man. Maybe what I needed was just to talk to my husband and explain what I was feeling. We weren't divorced yet, so it wouldn't be a sin if our talking led to lovemaking. It was perfectly legal in the eyes of God and man for a married couple to engage in sex.

I made up my mind and hurried to the phone and dialed my soon-to-be ex-mother-in-law's number before I could chicken out. Ian answered the phone.

"Hello."

"Hey, Ian," I said, trying to sound casual and upbeat although that was the last thing I was feeling. "Are you busy?"

His tone changed immediately when he heard it was me. "What do you want?"

I tried not to let his tone affect me. "Well, I was wondering if we could get together after I get off work and talk," I said, feeling foolish.

I heard him snort before replying. "Talk for what? I ain't got anything to say to you. As far as I'm concerned you ain't got nothin' to say that I wanna hear. So why do we need to meet?"

He was being as cold as ice. Same old Ian. Still unwilling to allow me to be the one to make up with him. In my mind's eye, I could see the look on his face, a hard sneer that I had seen too many times before. It was hard to believe that I was talking to my husband, a minister. I tried to speak, but my throat had become dry and I couldn't make a sound. And anyway, every answer that I played in my head sounded dumb.

I heard Ian suck his teeth as he always did when he was mad before he said, "Just like I said, nothin'!" And I heard a loud *click* in my ear.

I held the receiver for a beat, staring at it. I was so humiliated my face felt hot as fire. I couldn't believe he had spoken to me that way. I had thought that after months of being apart, Ian would miss me—just a little. I guess I thought wrong.

"It's really over," I said out loud as I placed the phone on the hook. I felt more alone than ever, but I vowed to never call Ian again for anything that wasn't related to our sons.

By the time I left work, I didn't know what to feel. A lot had happened in the span of a few hours. I went to my mother's house to pick up the kids, but she had given them a bath and put them to bed, so I told her that I would pick them up in the morning.

I took a hot bath when I got home and fell across the bed. I hadn't realized how beat I was until my head hit the pillow. I fell asleep almost instantly.

I thought I heard church bells ringing in a dream, but it was my telephone. I was still half asleep when I reached for the receiver that was on my nightstand.

"Hello," I said, trying to wake up.

"Did I wake you? Were you asleep?"

My heart leaped so hard, I thought it was coming through my chest! It was Zane. I looked at the red numbers on the digital clock beside the phone. Two o'clock in the morning! I wanted to be upset, but considering who was on the other end, I wasn't. Not much anyway.

"Isn't everyone at this time of the morning?"

"Well, I meant to call you earlier, but I had a little drama that I needed to take care of."

"What's wrong?" I couldn't help asking and at the same time was puzzled about the kind of drama that could keep him up this late.

"Ah, nothing major, I'll tell you all about it sometime. So, are you in bed?" he asked and for the first time, I noticed how sexy his voice sounded. I laid my head back on my pillow and held the phone to my ear.

"What are you wearin'?" he whispered before I had a chance to answer his first question.

"Why do you want to know what I have on?" I asked, smiling slightly to myself. I could tell that he was smiling on the other end, too.

"I just want to be able to picture you in my mind while we talk. That's all."

What I had on was one of Ian's old T-shirts and nothing else, but I wasn't sure that I wanted to give him that picture.

"I have on what I always sleep in . . . a granny gown," I lied.

I heard him groan. I guessed he was disappointed, and since I was feeling a little naughty, I added, "But I'm not wearing panties."

"Now you're talkin'." He seemed to perk up again. "Can I talk dirty to you?"

I was a little uncomfortable with the conversation, but I didn't want him to hang up.

"I don't know, I haven't really had anyone talk dirty to me before."

"What? You gotta be jokin'," he teased. "You mean to tell me that you ain't never had phone sex?"

I hesitated, trying to figure out what the right answer should be. I wanted to keep the conversation going without sounding too lame, yet I didn't want to try to be something I wasn't. I thought about his reaction when I had told him the lie about what I was sleeping in and decided that the truth was best.

"No, no I haven't," I said and he let out a whoop.

"Hot damn! I gots me a virgin on the line. This is gon' be fun as hell!"

"What?"

"Now you know I can't wait to get you naked and spread you like a turkey wishbone and eat that pussy!"

"What?" I repeated, and if I had been as fair-skinned as Zane, I know that I would have turned all shades of red at that moment. As it was, my face felt hot as fire. I know that he was trying to get the phone sex started but I definitely wasn't expecting that one. No one had ever spoken to me like that before, not even Ian.

"Don't talk like that to me! That's rude. You don't even know me. You don't know anything about me!" I wasn't worried about him hanging up now, I was about one second away from hanging up myself.

"Hold up, hold up now. That's what I'm trynna do . . . get to know you. Ain't that pussy a part of you?"

I hung up.

The phone immediately started ringing again. I stared at it. I knew that it was Zane and part of me still wanted to talk to him, but not the phone sex jazz. I wanted to talk about who he was and what he had been doing since we had left school and if he had a wife and kids. I couldn't understand why he didn't want to know those things about me, too.

The phone was still ringing. I didn't want him to think that he could talk to me like he had, but I did want to talk to him. Maybe I could give him another chance. The phone stopped ringing just as I reached for it.

I sat on the edge of the bed for a few minutes thinking if he called again I would answer. I stared at the phone willing it to ring. It didn't so I lay back on the bed, drifting back to sleep imagining what I would say if he called back.

I was dozing when the phone rang again. I picked it up on the first ring. Before I could say anything, he was speaking.

"Hey, I apologize if I offended you. Are you mad?"

I smiled. "Well, not mad, just not expecting that kind of talk. You don't even know anything about me and vice versa. Can't we just talk about simple things like where do you work, and do you have kids, and things like that for now?"

"Ba'y, we can talk about whatever you like. What you want to know about me?"

"How about are you married or do you have a girlfriend?"

My question was greeted with silence on the other end. He didn't answer for so long that I wasn't sure if he was still there.

"Helloooooooo, are you there?"

I heard him sigh. "Yeah, I'm here. What if I was to answer yes, would you hang up and not talk to me anymore?"

That wasn't a good answer, but I decided to give him the benefit of the doubt.

"I'm not sure that I wouldn't speak to you again."

I almost told him that I was married but separated, but the timing didn't seem right. I wanted to hear what his status was first. "I'm just not sure what there would be to speak about . . ."

"Oh, what the hell, I might as well tell you then . . . yes, I'm married. And the reason I called you so late was that me and her are separated but she came over to where I'm stayin' and wanted to talk. But it was a disaster because I ended up sayin' some things she didn't like, and she said some things that out and out pissed me off, we got into a physical altercation and she left. . . ."

He spewed all these sentences out in a flood without taking a breath and at the end he blew out his breath loudly. I didn't say anything; I was trying to figure out how I was feeling about all he had just allowed. What exactly did he mean by "a physical alter-cation"?

"Look, I don't want you to think that I'm some kin'a woman beater or nothin'. She was the one doin' all the swingin' and slap-pin' on me. I just was mainly trynna keep her offa me! I would never really hurt a woman."

He paused and I still didn't comment. It was a lot to believe seeing that I didn't know the man that he had become, only the boy that he seemed to be years ago.

"OK, now that I done spilled my guts, you ain't gon' say nothin', right? You just gon' let me wonder what the hell's goin' on in your head?" His voice sounded a little edgy, but I was thinking it was just his nerves.

"Zane, since we seem to be turning this conversation into true confessions I might just as well tell you that I'm married, too. My husband and I have only been separated a few months now, but he made it pretty plain that he's not interested in reconciling, at least not right now anyway. And the longer I'm away from him, the more I'm wondering if there's any point in delaying filing for the divorce. The only reason I'm holding off is because no one in my entire family has ever gotten a divorce. Not for generations. Even though some of my relatives had pretty bad marriages and proba-bly should have. In my family once you get married it's for life, good, bad, or indifferent, if you make your bed hard, you lay in it, I guess. I mean, I'm starting to enjoy my freedom and he did keep a pretty tight rein on me, didn't like my friends or want them around. He was very controlling and he could be abusive, too," I finished, surprised that I had told Zane all that. I suddenly won-dered if I had said too much.

"Yeah, women can be controllin' and abusive like that, too. Or try to be anyway. Some women don't know how to let a man be a man," Zane said.

"What do you mean?" I asked, unsure of how I felt about his last comment. I heard him sigh before he answered.

"Well, you know, they won't allow a man to have any say in anythang in his own home. Like he is suppose to just work, bring home his money, turn it over to her with a smile on his face and listen to the status quo. Be a damn sex machine in bed, 'cause if she don't come at least two or three times you ain't been on your job, and shit. But if she don't feel like givin' up the pussy when *you* want it, it's suppose to be cool. She on her period, or got a headache, or she too tired and shit, and you suppose to be like 'OK honey, it's all right that you done had a headache for two muh-fuckin'weeks and I'm gettin' so backed up that my balls is turnin' blue' and that type shit. You go on to sleep and I'll just get myself off.' I mean, shiiit how come your period keep you from givin' your man some head? If that ain't bein' abusive, I don't know what is!"

At the moment it felt as if Zane were talking to himself more than he was me. And his language! I was beginning to think that Zane didn't realize how offensive his language was. He must be used to talking this way, to everyone, women included, foul language and all. All the cussing and sexual references ruffled my feathers, but I wanted to continue our conversation. I figured I would explain to him later how his choice of words made me feel.

"There I go, spillin' my guts again. I guess it ain't no secret that I ain't had none in a while."

I decided to change the subject. "So do you have any brothers and sisters?"

"Yeah, I got one brother named Damon, two sisters, Cocoa, well her real name is Collette, but everybody call her Cocoa, and Michal. My father's dead and my mother lives on the north side by herself. She got a boyfriend, I guess you could call him, named Mr. Calvin. My sisters are married and . . ."

Good, I finally had him telling me about himself and his life and off the sex talk. As I listened, I started asking myself what I was getting myself into.

We ended up talking for four hours straight! About his family and my family and his kids and mine. He was really very funny and easy to talk to. He never cleaned up his language much, although I did finally speak up and tell him that I wasn't comfortable with it.

"Shit ba'y, this is me. It's how I been talkin' all my life. I don't mean nothin' by it. I'll try to watch what I'm sayin' but I ain't makin' no promises," he had said.

We agreed that we needed to talk face to face, but we didn't make a date or anything. He said that he would call me back on Friday and we would talk about it then. It was only Monday morning. Friday seemed like a long time to go without talking to him.

3

Ian had decided that he wanted to pick up the kids every other weekend, which was fine with me. What he really said was that he would be picking up his *sons* every other week. He didn't include my daughter Jadyn, or his daughter Dasche for that matter. I remember thinking that seemed strange, because for six years, he had been the only father my daughter had known and they seemed to get along fine. So it was kind of strange that he was leaving her out and almost ignoring her. I guess that should have given me some real concerns, but she wasn't his biological daughter and she was twelve years old now and she didn't seem to care one way or the other.

Friday was to be Ian's first entire weekend with the boys since our separation, although he had been picking them up on his payday and taking them to get their hair cut or shopping and things. Our sons, Ian Jr. and Devon were six and four by then. They were happy that they were going to spend some time with their dad.

We called Ian Jr. "E." He was dark skinned like me and had a stocky build, even when he was just a little thing. He was quiet and *all* boy. He didn't like to be held, or kissed, or cuddled. If you kissed him he would scowl and wipe his face hard and say, "Mens don't kiss mens!!" Where he got that from, we never really knew because neither his father nor I had ever told him that. It was just how he felt I guess.

Devon was the complete opposite. He was skinny, all legs and arms. He loved being hugged and climbing into your lap to give big wet sloppy kisses to show his love. Devon would leave his mark when he kissed you and it was usually the other person wiping their face after a "Devon kiss." But you better not let him catch you wiping it off. He would laugh and quickly cover your face with a lot more kisses and say, "Don't wipe off my sugar!"

I had packed their pj's, toothbrushes, some extra clothes, and underwear. Ian was to bring them home after church on Sunday. Jadyn was going to her Aunt Denise and Uncle Lee's for the weekend. So I was going to be totally free for the first night in years.

When Ian got off work, he came right over to pick up the boys that afternoon. I had just gotten out of the shower and E had let him in. I was in my bedroom drying myself with a towel when Ian opened the bedroom door. I quickly wrapped the towel around myself.

"What do you think you're doing? I ain't got no clothes on!" I had shouted.

He stood there with his hand on the doorknob and our eyes met. I suddenly felt very odd. It was one of those moments where everything seems to be going in slow motion. Here was the man who had shared all my most intimate moments for the past six years, had been my lover, my companion, had seen every inch of my body, had even been in the delivery room when both of our sons had been born. Yet, in that instant as I stood there hiding behind the towel, everything changed between us. I had drawn a new line in the sand. In that moment we both understood there would be no more shared intimacy between us. He gave me a sad smile.

"Sorry," was all he said as he closed the door.

I put on my robe and hurried out to say good-bye to my sons. They both were holding on to a favorite toy. E had his little hard, blue football under his arm. Ian's mom had given him that football for Christmas one year, and he loved that thing. He, bathed, ate, and even slept with it. Which I couldn't really understand, because there wasn't a soft spot on it. Devon was holding on to his well-worn teddy bear, which my mom had given him. Devon ran to me first.

"'Bye, Mom," he said, and threw his arms around my neck and gave me a kiss as I stooped down.

"'Bye, son. Aren't you gettin' a little big to be carrying Bear-bear around all over the place?" I teased him.

"No, Mom, not yet! I'll tell you when," my little four-year-old told me.

E said, "'Bye, Ma." And didn't grimace or wipe his face as I kissed him this time.

"Y'all be good and I'll see you Sunday afternoon."

"OK," they both said and headed out the door. Ian handed me some folded bills, mumbled something, and left. I wasn't surprised when he handed me the money, he had been giving me $200 every time he got paid. I guessed he didn't want me to have to take him to court to get child support.

I had no idea what to do with myself after the kids left. I didn't really have any girlfriends who were single, except for my cousin Phyl, and she was never at home. She had too many men to juggle to stay in one place for too long. And I didn't know if any of my married friends would be available. What I should do is find out if there was a Friday evening service at church that I could go to, to make up for not being there last Sunday. And according to my work schedule, I wouldn't be there this Sunday, either. Yeah, church is where I needed to be to get my mind right and to make sure I stayed connected to the Lord. I really did love church and being a Christian. It was just that I had a feeling that something was changing inside of me, but I didn't quite know what. I didn't want falling away from the church to be part of it.

I decided to call Deacon Bennie and ask him if anything was

going on at the church, but as my hand touched the receiver, it started to ring.

"Hello?"

"What's up, darlin'?"

It was Zane! I had forgotten that he was supposed to call tonight. The sound of his voice made me smile.

"Hi," I said.

"If you ain't doin' nothin' tonight, I thought I could come by so that we could finish our conversation," he said.

I thought about what he was asking. There was no sin in having a friend over to talk.

"OK," I said.

"OK, see you in a little while," he said.

4

When Zane pulled up in the driveway, I must admit that I was more than a little nervous. I had put on a pair of jeans and a tank top, but I still had my feet shoved into my house shoes. I thought about leaving them on, but decided that would seem too casual and opted to slide my feet into a pair of flat sandals. He knocked on the door. I took a deep breath and opened it.

Zane looked even better than he had in the store. He had trimmed his mustache and his hair, which was freshly cut, sported short shiny black curls. Thick dark eyebrows framed his big brown eyes and made his eyelashes appear that much longer. He had on a white dress shirt that was open at the neck, with the sleeves rolled partway up his arms, which gave it a casual look. It matched well with the pair of straight-leg jeans he was wearing. I noticed he was slightly bowlegged and that only made him more attractive.

Zane stood at the door with one arm behind his back and what appeared to be an overnight bag slung across one shoulder.

"Hey, miss lady," he said as he bent slightly at the waist and kissed me on the cheek. "These are for you."

As he brought his hand around his back I could see that he was holding a bouquet of beautiful yellow roses.

"Beauty for beauty," he said as I took them from his hand.

"Thank you! That was so thoughtful of you! But you didn't have to bring me anything."

I hesitated slightly, uncomfortable about the bag, suddenly recalling what he had said he couldn't wait to do to me the first night we had talked. "What's in there?" I asked, feeling a little awkward and motioning toward the bag with the flowers.

Zane looked puzzled. "What? This?" He reached his hand up and took the bag from his shoulder. "Oh, I thought you might want to listen to some music, so I brought a few of my favorite jams along with me." He eyeballed me for a moment and suddenly grinned. "Why, what were *you* thinking I had in here?"

"Never mind," I said turning and walking into the kitchen to get a vase for the flowers. "The flowers are really pretty," I said, needing to redirect the conversation.

"Oh, that's just the beginning, I got a lot more surprises for you," he said making his voice slightly louder to reach me in the kitchen. When I walked back into the living room, he was still standing in the doorway.

"Oh, I'm sorry, come on in."

"I was startin' to think that you only wanted the flowers and not me," he teased.

He took a seat on the sofa as I arranged the roses in the vase.

"Make yourself at home, please," I said to him. "Can I get you something to drink?"

"A glass of ice water would be nice," he said as he sat back and spread his arms across the back of the couch. I brought him a tall glass and he promptly drank it down almost in one swallow!

"Damn, I was thirsty!" he said and we both laughed.

"You want some more?" I asked, still smiling.

"No, I'm fine for now. Come sit down," he said, patting a place beside him. I thought it would be awkward as I sat next to him, but we started talking like we had known each other all our lives. We talked about the time we first met in study hall and how he ditched his detention with Mr. McMahon and nothing ever happened to him. We talked about his marriage and my marriage. He seemed to get a little sad when he was talking about his wife. Soon to be his ex, too, according to him. We went back to talking about school days again and wondering what the different people from school were doing now.

"Remember when crazy-ass Dougie Mason thought he was some kin'a freakin' circus performer and he climbed the telephone pole by the lunchroom and tried to balance on the telephone wire like he was some kin'a tightrope walker or some shit, and his dumb ass fell? I think dude's head bounced two or three times when he hit the grass!"

It really wasn't funny but the way Zane was telling it made me chuckle.

"We all thought that he was seriously hurt and we all ran over to him and he got up and said 'ouch' and started rubbin' his head and shit and everybody busted out laughin'. Yeah, and the lunchroom teacher, what was her name? Miss ahhh Miss ahhh . . ." Zane was snapping his fingers between the "miss" and the "ahh"s, like the action would help his memory.

"Miss Trottman?"

"Yeah, old lady Trottman, she was a ugly, skinny-ass bitch, wa'n't she? But anyway, she called an ambulance and his crazy ass didn't wanna go to the hospital."

"I remember," I said.

"That sucker was lucky he had a rock head 'cause that shit woulda killed anybody else!"

We were both cracking up. Then Zane stopped laughing and gazed deep into my eyes. My heart started trying to beat out of my chest again, right before Zane slid closer. Before I could think about it, Zane pulled me close and kissed me.

It was a surprisingly sweet kiss, and while it was totally unexpected, I welcomed it. I had often imagined what kissing Zane would be like, back when we were in school. Now it was as if I were living my dream. It felt good to be held and kissed again. At that moment, I didn't care if it was right or wrong.

5

The weekend went by much too quickly and I was back at work before I knew it. Zane had stayed a couple of hours on Friday. We talked forever about everything under the sun and kissed again before he left. It turned out that the music he had brought with him really set the tone for the evening. He had everything from George Benson to Sade. We had a very nice evening. Before he left, he invited me to a party at his house the following weekend. He told me that his best friend, Quin, was moving to Detroit and he wanted to throw him a going-away party.

I was still confused about the timing of everything. Why couldn't we have done this while we were in high school? Everything was so much more complicated now. I liked the way he made me feel, the way we seemed to click, and we had been totally comfortable with each other right from the start. But neither of us really had a right to do what we were doing. We weren't divorced yet, and I was a Christian and I knew that any kind of romantic relationship with another person while you were married was wrong. And it didn't matter how long you were separated, either. Married was still married. The rational part of me knew all this, and that part of me also knew everything that I was risking, but this other part of me wanted to follow my heart.

. . .

My mother had always said that I wore my heart on my sleeve. When I had asked her what that meant, she'd said that everybody could see into my heart because I let whatever I was feeling show on my face. I guess she was right, because when Miss Loretta got to work, she asked me what was the matter with me.

"Girl, what's on your mind this morning? You seem like you wrestling hard with somethin' or other," she said with a smile on her face. And before I could say anything, she went on. "You and that almost ex-husband of yours must'a got together and had a little pillow talk last night, hunh?" she teased, poking me with her elbow and cracking herself up.

"No, Miss Loretta, didn't nothin' like that happen." I hesitated for a moment, trying to decide if I should tell her about Zane. She hadn't been working the day that he had come into the store and I had given Zane my phone number, and I hadn't bothered to mention it to her.

"Well, if Ian didn't finesse you outta your draws, then what is it?" she asked, still teasing, but I thought she sounded genuinely concerned, too.

"OK, look, Miss Loretta. There was this guy I knew in high school, right? And he came in here one day when you were off work. Well, you know I been tellin' you about how things are between me and Ian. And how I keep having these day dreams and feelings about having sex with Ian—"

"And I done told you that *that* is perfectly normal," Miss Loretta interrupted me. "Just because your mind is satisfied that you and Ian don't belong together don't mean that your body going to agree with it right away. No way! Honey, Miss Bessie got a mind of her own," she said referring to the pet name that she had given women's privates. "Shoot, Miss Bessie even try to rise up on me every now and then, too!"

I started laughing. "Miss Loretta, you know you need to quit!"

"I don't need to quit nothin'! You know Joe been dead five years now, but child, even before that he wasn't no good for Miss Bessie! Sho' wasn't!"

Miss Loretta leaned close and whispered in my ear. "His thang wouldn't get hard if you put it in a pan and deep fried it!"

I laughed out loud and Miss Loretta tried to shush me.

"Be quiet girl, we at work, we ain't at no party. The Lord gon' deal with you for the way you got me talking anyway!"

"No," I said between the laughter. "No, he gon' deal with *you* for sayin' what you just did about your poor dead husband!" I started laughing again.

"Hush, girl! I done told you now. You gon' mess around and get yourself fired if you don't quit this mess!"

Our supervisor looked over at us, so I pretended to straighten the items near the register, and Miss Loretta started counting down her cash drawer, so that it would be ready when the doors opened. I never did get to finish telling her about Zane.

6

Zane offered to pick me up for his friend's party, but I decided to drive. For one reason, I hadn't gone to very many house parties in my life (OK, I hadn't been to any!) and I wasn't sure that I would fit in, and if I got to feeling really uncomfortable, I would be able to just leave if I wanted. The other reason was since Zane was the one hosting the party, he couldn't very well leave to take me home before it was over. So I would have to close the party down with him, and who knew how long the party would go on. I wasn't trying to spend the night at Zane's.

When I got to Zane's house, there were already a few people there. He said he needed to explain some things to me, so he took me back to his bedroom and closed the door.

"Look, I just want you to know up front that some of my friends be gettin' high. I ain't goin' into the particulars about what kind of high they prefer, but you can believe it's some of everything. Now, I know that probably ain't your thang . . ."

"Gettin' high? What do you mean, gettin' high?" I had begun to shed my jacket, but shrugged it back up on my shoulders. "Look, Zane, maybe my coming here with you wasn't such a good idea after all. I mean, I like you and all, but if you have people around you getting high, I need to leave. And since you told me that, let me just ask you. Do you get high, too?"

"Look, Samai, you got the wrong idea. It ain't even like that.

Just because I have friends that do certain things, doesn't mean that I automatically do those things, too, now does it?"

Zane must have sensed that I wasn't feeling right about the whole situation, because he put his arms around me and began rubbing my back.

"Samai, you gon' have to learn to trust me, OK? I'm not gon' put you in a situation that could hurt you. Now, I understand that this kind of thing might be new to you. But this is me, ba'y. I throw parties like this all the time. I also understand that you been in church mosta your life, and shit, and I respect that. See, I think that it's OK that you go to church and I don't, as long as we each respect where the other is coming from, we could see what will develop between us."

Respect notwithstanding, I still wasn't sure that Zane was a man who I needed to go any further with. I pulled away from him.

"How, Zane? How can we do that? You said it yourself . . . I'm in church and you're not. I don't party and you do. Neither one of us gets high, at least that's what you tell me, but you have friends who do . . . Zane, this really is not my—"

Zane pulled me close and kissed me. It was a deep passionate kiss that made my head spin. When he took his lips away from mine, he stepped back a little and held me in place with his hypnotic gaze.

"Look, Samai, I'm feelin' you. I ain't makin' it no secret that I want to get to know you better. I'm really diggin' *us*. And I know you must be feelin' this, too, or else you wouldn'ta let me kiss you like I just did."

Zane's last remark rang so true, there was no denying it. I could only blush and continue to stare into his eyes. "Yes, I feel something, there's no doubt about that. I'm just not sure if the timing is right . . . I'm just not sure about any of this," I told him truthfully.

"That's OK, we can talk about it, but ba'y, can we talk about this later? I do have guests to attend to and I do need your help. Just stay with me this one time and if you don't like it, if you can't handle it, we'll deal with it. Is that cool?"

I thought about what Zane was asking. Fixing those beautiful brown eyes on me the way he did was making me weak in the knees and my heart began thumping loudly. I felt my resolve melt away.

"OK, Zane. What do you need me to do?"

Zane smiled and gave me a wink. "Thanks, ba'y. Let's do this. All I need you to do is to stay upstairs with the ones that just wanna drink a little beer and wine and listen to some good music. Those muhfucka's idea of gettin' buck wild is drinkin' a shot of Tanqueray straight, so I know you'll be safe with them. I'm gon' be bouncin' back and forth between the basement and the living room, to make my presence known and shit but if you could keep the folks up here entertained, that would be great."

"Me?" I started to panic a little. "Zane, now how do you expect me to entertain *your* friends by myself? I don't know them, or anything about them? What am I gonna talk to them about? How am I gonna—"

"Hold up. Now just calm down. I don't expect you to keep long conversations goin' or anything, even though, you know good and well you ain't got no problem keepin'a conversation goin'. The only thing I need you to do is, you know, keep the ice buckets filled and keep the liquor flowing . . . mingle a little bit, you know? Just do what you ladies do at parties—show off how pretty you look and shit . . ."

I still had my doubts about all this. Zane could tell I wasn't comfortable with his request, because he pulled me into his arms again.

"Look, ba'y, like I told you before, I know this is all new to you, but if we gon' be a couple, if you gon' be with me, this is all part of it. Just trust me, OK?"

A couple! Me and Zane a couple? I hadn't thought about that one. I wasn't even divorced yet, and I wasn't sure about being a couple with anybody. But Zane's touch made me feel so warm and secure. I could feel the muscles in his arms ripple as he tightened his embrace. How could I resist? "OK, Zane, I'll try. But if I need you . . ."

"I'm just a holla away! Don't worry ba'y, you'll be fine, you'll see."

At first, everyone started out in the same room, laughing, listening to music, and just chatting and catching up on the happenings of the week. Zane took me around the room with him and introduced me to everyone. I was surprised at how friendly everyone seemed. Before I knew it, I was so comfortable with Zane's friends that carrying on conversations wasn't the strain I had imagined it would be. I actually loosened up and started having a good time.

Eventually though, as the evening wore on, some of the couples and a few others began to migrate to the basement to do their thing, while the "regulars" remained upstairs.

I stayed upstairs as Zane instructed once the separation took place, changing the music, refilling drinks, and replenishing snacks. They were dancing and singing and having such a good time, it appeared they didn't even notice that some of the guests had moved downstairs. And even though Zane had said that he didn't think it was a good idea for me to come down, after a while, he raced upstairs to get me.

"C'mere, ba'y, I want you to see somethin'. It's some funny shit!" he said, taking me by the hand and practically dragging me down the steps.

"But what about your friends? I thought you wanted me to entertain them."

"Oh, they'll be all right for a few. You'll be back before they even realize you're gone."

There were only about five or six people down there at the time, some standing, some sitting in chairs, and one on the floor, on his hands and knees, apparently searching for something.

"Be quiet and watch," Zane whispered in my ear. "We got some new carpet cleaners here."

He sat down on the couch, pulling me down beside him, and

poured two glasses of wine, one for me and one for himself. I couldn't help but notice that all the guests had these queer vacant expressions on their faces, and their eyes were glazed over.

There wasn't much conversation going on. They all were gathered around Quin, the friend that the party was for, and seemed transfixed by what he was doing. Quin was seated at this table and in front of him there was a large, shiny, silver platter piled high with a mound of white powder. He was also holding a small vial with some liquid in it over an open flame from a Bunsen burner, gently moving the vial around in slow circles. All of the druggies were staring at the vial as if they were in a trance. A couple of them excused themselves quickly, saying they had to use the bathroom.

At first Zane had told me that Quin wasn't supposed to be leaving until 8:00 P.M. the following day, but then he said that Quin had changed his mind and was supposed to be leaving after the party. I'd asked Zane why Quin was taking the bus instead of flying to Detroit and why he had changed his mind about when he was leaving. It didn't make much sense to me to try to make it anywhere on time after partying.

"Who knows? Even Quin don't understand half the shit he does," Zane told me. "And as for takin' the bus instead'a' flyin', I guess he think that anything carrying somethin' as big and heavy as his ass is bound to fall out the sky!"

Zane's focus shifted back to the guy who was on the floor looking for something. He leaned over and whispered in my ear. "Watch this, ba'y," he said and threw something on the floor by the "carpet cleaner." Carpet Cleaner immediately picked it up, examined it closely, and then threw it back down. Zane kept throwing small pieces of paper on the floor, and each time the guy would pick it up and examine it, before throwing it back on the floor. He would sometimes pick up the same piece two or three times, carefully scrutinizing it again, sometimes taking it in his mouth as if to taste it, before tossing it away.

Zane was thoroughly enjoying the show, chuckling to himself. "Crazy geeker," he said under his breath as he rose from the couch addressing the guy on the floor.

"OK, my man, if your cash is low you gots to go!" he quipped and a few guests tittered. The guy protested, offering Zane the solid gold necklace around his neck.

"Man, why don't you hold this until I get paid on Friday? Give me $100 till then, and if I ain't back here on Friday, it's yours!" he said, a hint of desperation in his voice.

Zane snorted. "Oh, I need you to tell me that? Hunh, bitch? I *know* the shit is mine and you know this shit ain't worth no $100, neither," Zane said, holding it up to the light. I could see that it was real. Real gold had a soft finish, not the glitzy shine that fake gold had, and as thick as it was, it seemed that a hundred dollars would be a steal.

"Man, that necklace cost me $1,200! I'm only asking you to let me hold a hundred till I get paid on Friday!" Carpet Cleaner seemed more desperate now.

"I ain't got that much," Zane said thrusting the necklace back toward him. "So like I told you before, see ya!"

I took a good look at Carpet Cleaner for the first time. He was dressed really well in a black soft leather jacket and cream turtleneck sweater with jeans and matching casual shoes. He looked as if he had just stepped out of a magazine. I couldn't understand why he would be crawling around on anybody's floor. Zane's words made him go into panic mode. I didn't know how to feel about this new, tough side of Zane that I was seeing for the first time. Part of me knew I should be totally turned off by it. That I should get up, get my jacket, and just leave. I knew that there was only one reason that I didn't. Zane.

I had to admit that I was totally fascinated by him. He was gentle and at the same time strong. I could tell he wasn't a man who would let others scare him away from the things he wanted out of life. He would stand up for himself, for me, if it came to that. I loved the tenderness I felt when he held me. Not only that, his kisses held the promise of something more. More than the way he made me warm all over just being in his presence. More than the way his kisses made me dizzy. I wouldn't lie to myself about wanting, no *needing* to find out what the *more* was. So I squashed the feelings that I had about this whole scene being wrong and not for me. And I stayed.

"OK, OK. Damn, man, how much you got?" Carpet Cleaner asked, looking desperate and slightly angry.

Zane looked him up and down and the dark expression on his face turned stormy.

"Nah, man, I don't like your attitude. You act like I *gots* to do this. I'm doin' yo' ass a favor, not the other way around. You betta recognize!" Zane was getting angry, too.

The two of them stared at each other for a few ticks before Carpet Cleaner backed down.

"Aw, it's cool, brotha. I know I'm ass out right now. Whatever you can do, it's tight."

Zane took the necklace, pulled out a wad of cash from his pocket and peeled off three twenty dollar bills. The guy took it and mumbled something before darting back to Quin to trade for some of what Zane's best friend had been heating up in the little vial.

Quin looked like he was enjoying everything that was going on and didn't look as if he were even thinking about leaving any time soon.

Zane came and took me by my hand. "Come on, darlin', you look like you ready to go back upstairs."

As I rose to follow Zane, I glanced at my watch. 11:30 P.M. I wondered if Quin had forgotten that his bus was leaving at midnight but when I mentioned this to Zane, he just shrugged it off.

"Ba'y, trust me, that nigga ain't goin' nowhere until that table is empty!" he said, nodding his head toward the pile of white powder in front of Quin.

7

Weeks went by and I hadn't been to church since the night I'd broken into tears and Bennie said he would help me get a job. Zane and I had been talking to each other on the phone every night and seeing each other on the weekends when the kids were gone.

After attending Quin's going away party, I knew that Zane was in a different world than I was, but strangely enough, I wasn't turned off by that party, or even the side of Zane that I had seen that night in the basement when he had confronted the carpet cleaner. Somehow, I was more attracted to Zane than ever after that night.

Every day I was feeling less and less guilty about missing church services. It used to be a normal part of my week, planning what the kids and I were going to wear to church and things. Now the only time the boys went was the weekends they spent with their dad. Jadyn was still going every Sunday with her aunt Denise. I was the only one who seemed to be heading backward.

Zane had come to my house only once while the boys were there. I was intentionally limiting his interaction with my children, because I wasn't sure where our relationship was going. I didn't want them getting attached to Zane, only to have him disappear. I needn't have worried about that, though. It seemed that Devon took an immediate dislike to Zane, coming and sitting between us on the sofa and frowning whenever Zane tried to talk to him. He would ignore whatever Zane was saying to him and try to climb onto my lap. E was indifferent toward Zane, not really showing whether he did or didn't like him. He just came and took Devon by the hand and took him back to their bedroom to play while Zane was there. I didn't know why Devon had decided that he didn't like Zane; Zane was crazy about kids.

There was another time Devon was sitting next to me when Zane called. Right after I said "Hello" to him, Devon started pulling on my arm and asking to speak with him.

"Mom, is that Mr. Zane? Hunh, Mom? Is it, Mom? Can I speak to him pleeeeeeeease?"

Devon had the sweetest voice and the cutest little look on his face.

I was both amazed and amused that Devon wanted to speak to Zane after showing that he obviously didn't like him. I thought that he'd had a change of heart and quickly told Zane that Devon wanted to speak to him.

Zane seemed amused, too.

"He does, hunh? Put the little man on the phone, then."

I handed Devon the phone.

"Mr. Zane," he began in his sweet little boy voice, "I don't like you likin' my mom!" Devon growled, his voice suddenly changing into the best imitation a four-year-old could give of an angry man.

I took the phone from Devon and told him that he shouldn't speak to adults that way. Devon ran to his room. I couldn't help but laugh when Devon was out of earshot. It was so funny that he was trying to protect me from something he didn't understand. My little bodyguard would never change the way he felt about Zane.

The time had come for me to make a decision. Zane had wanted to make love to me almost from the first moment we met. But I wasn't ready to take that step, because I still had a grip on my

Christianity and I was trying to hold on for dear life. Although we hadn't moved much beyond deep long kisses, just being around Zane, laughing and talking with him, and having him hold me on his lap had somewhat diminished the feelings of utter loneliness and the sexual tension I had felt when Ian and I had first separated.

Ian had finally filed for the divorce about a month after he had come to pick up our sons for their first visit, and since I had no plans on contesting, it was probably going to be final in another month or so.

I didn't know what was going on with Zane and his wife. The only thing I knew for sure was that when he'd come into the store that day, he had already moved out and was staying with one of his sisters. He rarely spoke of their relationship and what was going on, and I didn't ask. I was happy with the time we were spending together and how being around him made me feel.

I knew that I wouldn't be able to hold Zane's sexual urges at bay for much longer. Already our kissing had progressed to where I had allowed him to remove my blouse and fondle my breasts twice.

"Girl, you know you got some pretty knockers!" he had said the first time he saw them.

I could tell he was getting frustrated at not being able to "get me naked and screw my brains out." But I wasn't ready to leave all my morals for a few moments of pleasure. I wanted to wait until my divorce was final. I was playing a game with myself though, because I was already compromising my morals and Christianity just by carrying on with Zane. But each time a thought like that would pop into my head, I would just make myself think of something else.

8

The annual Cincinnati Jazz and Rib Festival was coming up and Zane asked me if I wanted to go and spend the entire weekend with him. I had never been to anything like that before, and I was excited to see what it was like. Zane had gone two years in a row, the first time with his wife, the second time with his sisters. He had nothing but good things to say about it.

"Mannnnnnnn, the music was good, the food was good, they was sittin' up in the stands smokin' so much chronic that you didn't even need to light up, you could damn near get a buzz just by breathin'! And the atmosphere was off the hook! Niggas was standin' up, rockin' the house and havin' so much fun, none of those muhfuckas was even thinkin' about startin' no shit. Which was great, 'cause you know most of the time, niggas be trippin' offa dumb shit!" he had told me.

It so happened that the festival was going to be held on Ian's weekend with the boys. I told him that I was going to go out of town to visit my sister Aubrae in Indianapolis, and could he bring the boys home around seven instead of the usual four. I told him that so I wouldn't have to go into what I was really planning. I just didn't see a need to make things more difficult than necessary. Even though I really didn't have to answer to Ian for anything anymore, I didn't want to give him a reason to get an attitude and come up with an excuse not to take the boys that weekend.

. . .

Jadyn was going through some changes. She was almost thirteen and entering into that stage where she had gotten her period and broken out in pimples, all at once. Her hair, which had always been so long and pretty, had been ruined by a woman who I had taken her to to get a Jheri curl, a hairdo that was popular with all the girls. The woman didn't do something right and Jadyn's hair had become really brittle and started breaking off the day after. So she was dealing with newly damaged hair on top of everything else. She had put on some weight, too.

Jadyn, who was usually fun and outgoing and never afraid to stand up to anyone, was suddenly shy and introverted. I should have known, as her mother, that something serious was going on with her, but it was a time of change for all of us, and none of us were really ourselves. I just thought she was going through the normal process that all teenagers go through.

Ian's behavior toward her was getting more strange, too. Like barely saying hello to Jadyn when he came to pick up our sons. He never would look at her. I could tell that it bothered her and a couple of times I even mentioned it to him. He just said, "What am I supposed to do? I do speak to her. She's not really my daughter and we don't have a real relationship anymore." I was glad that Jadyn hadn't been around to witness Ian's cold response.

I should have checked him behind that right away but I decided not to say anything. I just felt that I couldn't make him have a father's love for Jadyn if he really didn't and trying to force the issue would only make matters worse. Still, I couldn't help but wonder how a man could be a father to a child for six years and act so unattached to her that way.

Jadyn was spending most of her time at her grandmother's or at her aunt Denise's house lately, though, so her contact with Ian was limited. She had already gotten her aunt Denise to approach me about letting her go live with her and her uncle Lee so that she could attend a different middle school than the one that was in our neighborhood. I was thinking it over. I really wasn't sure I wanted to do that. I loved my only daughter with all my heart, and she helped out a lot babysitting E and Devon after school until I got off work. She was growing into a mature young lady and very responsible for someone so young. But I wanted to give her every opportunity to succeed, and I was thinking that maybe not having to see Ian every week and be reminded that her real dad wasn't around, might be good for her. I was also thinking that she should go to school where she would be happy, as that might improve her grades. I hadn't decided to let her go, but I guess I was trying to convince myself it would be good for her. Summer was just beginning so I still had a little time before I gave her my decision.

9

I was very excited about going to the jazz festival and spending the weekend with Zane. It would be the longest time we had been able to spend together so far, so I decided that I was going to go all out for this date. I was going to get my hair dyed, and I was going to go to a mall and let one of the cosmetic counter girls show me how to apply makeup correctly. I hadn't worn makeup much since Ian and I had been married, and really not much before then since I had been so young when we'd gotten married. Ian said that he thought all women looked like clowns wearing makeup and he couldn't stand it. I remember once when I had put on some lipstick, just a little bit, he had started making sarcastic remarks and telling me how stupid it looked. That's why it hurt so bad and caught me completely off guard when he came home from work one day, raving about how pretty this woman at the bank looked in her makeup.

"Man, you know I hate to see women in makeup, but this woman, whooowee! When I went to cash my check at the bank today, this woman that was workin' the drive-through was lookin' *good*! She had on lipstick, eye shadow, and her skin looked so pretty, she was gorgeous!"

Now, he would have thought that I was wrong if I would have hauled off and smacked the *hell* out of him, and that's just what I felt like doing. But I was so hurt that I could only stand there with my mouth open and stare at him. He was smiling so hard, both of his dimples were showing, as he walked away toward the bathroom to get out of his work clothes. I was glued to the spot where I had been standing when he came in. Here was my husband raving about a perfect stranger and how good she looked with her face painted and not once did he refer to her as looking clownish, when he never missed an opportunity to express how disgusting I, or the women at church, looked when we wore even a tiny bit of makeup.

But more than that, he had the nerve to come home from work and let that be his greeting for me as soon as he hit the door. Not a "hello," much less a "how was your day?" I thought that the Bible said that we were to greet one another with a kiss?

So I was really anxious to see how much better I would look with my makeup applied just right. I was also interested in finding out if Zane would think that a woman wearing makeup looked like a clown.

The hair dying part was just to give myself a different look. My cousins had been dying their hair red, blond, auburn, and everything else since high school. Even my younger sister Lynn had experimented with color a time or two. I had never been that adventurous. I was also planning to buy myself two new outfits and a few new gowns to sleep in. The ones I had were old and not pretty at all. Ian didn't care about lingerie like most men did, preferring to have me sleep naked more than anything else. The couple of times that I had worn something pretty to bed he would just grunt, "You know I don't like to feel nothin' but skin layin' next to me." So after hearing that more than a few times, I gave up trying.

I made an appointment at Mr. Levon's House of Style, which was the place that my cousins and their friends went to get their hair done. Their hair always looked good, and I wanted something special, so I decided to go there, too.

"Girl, when you make your appointment, don't let none of them other broads touch your hair. You ask for Levon, and if he can't take you on the day you want, then you ask him which day you can get. Cause girrrrrrrrrrl, he is da bomb! As you can see," my cousin Phyl had said, patting her hair as she did a slow 360-degree turn, finally striking a pose. She knew her hair looked good.

So I took her advice and made sure that my appointment was with Levon, and when he had finished and showed me his artistry I did a double take. It didn't look like me being reflected in the silver glass. Levon stood behind me, and he was smiling. En Vogue was all that I could think of. My newly red-streaked hair looked amazing. He had given me a side swooped bang that was long, past my chin and flipped on the end. He had flipped the back as well, and I was so pleased that I tipped him ten dollars.

"So, miss lady," he said, stuffing the bill inside his smock and reaching for his appointment book. "What day did you say that you wanted your next appointment for?"

I looked puzzled. "I didn't."

"I know, *I'm* asking, 'cause I know you are going to want to keep your new look going, and sugar, *you* know and *I* know that you can't work the magic that Levon has. 'Cause if you could, you'd be standing here and I would be sitting there!" he said, staring directly at me.

We both laughed, and I made an appointment for two weeks later.

On Friday, Ian was going to pick the boys up from Mom's as soon as he got off work. Jadyn was spending the weekend with her friend Diamond. The only thing I had to do was go home, take care of a couple of last-minute things, double-check my bags to make sure that I had everything packed and ready to go, and wait on Zane.

10

Zane arrived at my door about an hour early, I guess he was just as anxious as I was to get to the festival. When he saw me with my new outfit and new hair, he let me know that he was pleased.

"Hel-looooo! I'm likin' that! Who did your hair? It looks good, ba'y! Where did you get that dress? Umph! Umph Umph! You lookin' mighty tasty, lady!" Zane said, not giving me a chance to respond to his barrage of questions. Circling my waist with his arms, he lifted me off the floor until we were face to face and began planting big sloppy kisses all over my face.

I was laughing. "Stop it, Zane! Stop, you're messing up my makeup and hair!"

"Hey, that sounds like a personal problem to me! I *told* you, you look good enough to eat, didn't I?"

After a few more kisses though, he lowered me back to the floor, and held me at arm's length, admiring me. One of the outfits I had bought was a canary yellow linen dress that stopped just about an inch or two above my knees and fit my curves perfectly. I chose to accessorize with yellow, red, blue, and green striped mesh wedge-heeled sandals. The matching belt accentuated my tiny waist and curvy hips. I wore those same colors in a beaded necklace, matching bracelet, with large gold hoop earrings. And from the way Zane couldn't take his eyes off me, I knew I had achieved what I was striving for: to blow his cap back!

"It's hard to believe that three kids came out of that body!"

I smiled. And for a second, I wondered why my husband had never given me these types of compliments.

We arrived in Cincy about ninety minutes later, checked into our room and grabbed a quick dinner, because Zane thought all the barbecue would be picked over by the time we got to the concert.

"The food *is* good, the only thing is, you got to get there real early to get some decent ribs. Last year, we call ourselves gettin' there early, like a half hour before the show, and wound up with some ribs so tough, I damn near felt like I was eatin' one of my shoes or some shit!"

Zane ordered lobster almondine and white wine. I had the lobster and crab alfredo, my favorite dish. I was happy to see that Zane was a seafood lover, too. We were pretty quiet during dinner; Zane kept staring at me and when I'd look up and catch him, he'd give me a wink that made me blush, and I'd glance back down at my plate. I got the feeling that it wasn't just the "tough ribs" that had Zane buying me dinner. I felt that he wanted to set the mood for later.

We still made it to the concert in plenty of time. Zane had gotten us really good seats for the show. Luther Vandross, Con Funk Shun, and Anita Baker were among the scheduled performers that first night.

Luther was on first, and after the introduction, you could hear the music to one of my favorite songs of all time begin while he was still off stage. Then you could hear Luther's mellow voice thumping out the beat before you actually saw him and as soon as I heard the first notes I was on my feet yelling, "Sing, Luther!" and swaying to the beat.

Zane stood up with me. Luther appeared onstage with the first words of his forever hit.

I had closed my eyes still swaying to the words. The man had sung my feelings in that first verse. That is exactly how I was try-ing to tell everyone that I felt after Ian left! I listened and he sung my truth some more.

I don't know if Zane knew or could somehow feel where this song was taking me, but for some reason, he reached over and pulled me close to his chest and held me tight. I let my head rest there and Luther sang.

Zane put his mouth close to my ear and started singing with Luther on the next verse.

> Pretty little darling, have a heart, don't let one mistake keep us apart,
> I am not meant to live alone, turn this house into a home.

Zane turned my face to his and kissed me deeply and Luther and everybody else went away for a heartbeat.

The concert just kept getting better. After Luther sang a few more songs like "Never Too Much," "Don't You Know That?," and "The Rush," Anita came out and rocked the house with "Sweet Love" and "No One in the World." By the time Con Funk Shun hit the stage I didn't have a voice left. They were the last act and they closed the show with "Love's Train" and "I'm Leaving Baby." I couldn't remember the last time I'd had so much fun.

We couldn't stop talking about the concert, and how we thought that they should've had that show on Saturday, because we didn't think anybody would be able to top the show that we had seen tonight. Babyface, Frankie Beverly and Maze, and DeBarge had their work cut out for them. Zane was driving with one hand and holding my hand with the other. I can't explain why the feel-ing of his hand holding mine seemed to be the most important thing at that moment.

Our room was lovely. Zane had booked a suite at the Hyatt Regency, which featured a living room and a kitchenette! It was like we had our own apartment for the weekend. I must admit, I was pretty tired and ready for bed. I had been wondering how this part would go all day. When we had checked in, I saw that there was only one bed, so I knew that Zane would make his move for sure tonight.

He said that he was going to take a shower, so I took out my bag and got out my gown. Gown? That was a joke. I had felt pretty bold when I picked it out, and very confident that Zane would like it. But as I looked at it now, I was too embarrassed! It was this black lace nightie with red satin trim, and matching panties so sheer that it wasn't hiding nothing. I looked at the "gown" again and shook my head at myself.

I took out the second set of sleepwear that I had brought. It wasn't any better. It was a very light-colored purple silk top that was split down the front from neck to navel and held together at the throat by a single tie, every bit as see-through as the black one. My choice of gowns revealed all; I couldn't lie or play games with myself any longer. I wanted Zane to seduce me, and I would be disappointed if he didn't.

I closed my eyes, and threw them both up into the air, whichever one I caught first would be what I wore. It wouldn't make much difference either way.

11

Zane came out of the bathroom smelling fresh and clean, with the subtle scent of cologne that smelled tangy sweet, spicy, and oh soooooo good! He wore a robe, and I didn't think he had on anything else, but before he could drop his robe, I grabbed my towel and walked to the bathroom, hoping it didn't look like I was running.

I chose to take a bath, because I thought a shower would mess up my hair. So I poured in a capful of White Linen foaming bath that I had bought at the mall and turned both water taps full force. The force of the water hitting the bath bubbles caused it to release its fragrance into the air. It was a fresh clean scent, and I was happy that I had purchased the lotion, the matching soap, and the perfume to go with it.

"Mmmmmmmmm, I can smell that out here!" Zane said. "It smells good."

I could hear the television in the background and was glad that he had turned it on. I don't know why the TV being on made me glad; maybe it was because I thought it might delay the inevitable.

The purple nothing gown had won the toss, so after I had lotioned and perfumed myself, I slipped the top over my head, and stepped into the panties. When I opened the bathroom door and stepped out, Zane sucked in his breath.

"Hellllllloooo," was all he said, but his eyes were gleaming. He was lying in bed and I could see from his bare chest that he had discarded the robe. He pulled the sheets back and patted a place beside him in the bed, his eyes devouring me. I hesitated for a moment, but when he patted the bed beside him again, I took a deep breath and joined him.

Zane immediately drew me on top of him and began kissing me. I had known that he was a good kisser, but the kisses he had given me before were nothing compared to this. He was doing something different with his tongue and I felt that he was pouring all the pent-up passion he had been feeling into each kiss. Each one was more intimate and probing than the last. When he pulled his warm lips away from mine, my head was actually spinning.

He rolled over and took the top position. Then he began to kiss my ears, neck, and throat before undoing the single tie at the neck of my nightie, baring one breast. He took the nipple in his mouth and began slowly rolling it and laving it with his lips and tongue. He was taking his time, not rushing at all, and he drove me to such frenzy on that one breast, I almost cried out for him to stop.

"We don't want this one to get jealous, do we babe?" he asked, his voice hoarse with desire. He bared my other breast and flicked the nipple with his tongue before taking it into his mouth to ravage. He was teasing me so unmercifully, that I was squirming and making noises and moaning and my hips seemed to have developed a mind of their own, bucking up and down on the bed.

"What's the matter, ba'y?" he asked between licks and sucks. "Hmmmmmmmmm?"

I couldn't speak. This was all new to me, Ian had never spoken to me during our lovemaking, I didn't know if I was supposed to answer Zane or not. I felt a little awkward and embarrassed.

"Oh, you're not going to answer me, hunh?" Zane teased and began kissing my lips and exploring my mouth with his tongue again, at the same time pulling off my nightie.

His warm hands made me tremble. I felt the heat as he slowly slid the sliver of material down over my hips. In my head, the words of a song came unbidden. "Feel me . . . I want to feel the fire . . ." The words of the song faded as quickly as they had come as Zane did something that no one had ever done before. He dropped his head low past my stomach, and taking my thighs in his hands, spread them apart wide. But what he did next was even more shocking and thrilling. He began kissing and licking my most intimate parts, just as he had been doing to my breasts moments before. It felt electrical each time his lips and tongue touched that part of my body. And then I could feel his fingers opening me up more and his tongue touched my "jewel," which sent a hot electrical jolt to my brain. I flinched, but his hands held me tight in the position and he was licking me slowly and circling my love button with his tongue. He was using just the tip of it at first, I thought, and then he made his tongue flat and licked from the bottom to the top always making sure to touch the spot that was electric, sometimes sucking and licking it at the same time. I had never felt sensations like this before. I couldn't stop my hips from moving and I took my hands and held his head there because I was afraid he would stop and push me to insanity's brink with the desire to finish, to get to the unknown place he was driving me toward with the motion of his tongue.

I was moving my hips frantically and thrashing my head from side to side and it just kept feeling better and better until the feelings spread all the way to my teeth and made them tingle. My body was flushing and I was getting warmer and it was all centered on that spot that he kept licking and sucking and flicking with his tongue and all of a sudden I felt my whole body blossom like a flower opening, and my entire being became a ball of pleasure so intense that my body went rigid, and still he kept licking until I couldn't take the touch of his tongue any longer and my hands that were afraid to let go only seconds before started pushing him away.

He lifted his head and, with one fluid motion, placed my thighs on either of his shoulders and pushed himself inside me. The sensation was so intense coming on the heels of such utter pleasure that I wanted to scream and laugh and cry all in the same instant. And as he stroked me, deeper and faster and harder, I bit my knuckles to keep from crying out.

Zane bent down and began whispering in my ear, his voice husky with passion, never missing a stroke. "Aw, baby, ah, Samai, Samai, you got some good pussy, baby . . . this pussy is sooo . . . good this pussy is too good baby . . . You gon' make me . . . Ah, baby, Ahhhhhh, Samai! I can't hold it . . . Mmmmphhh! Are you there, baby? Are you with me, baybee? Hunh?"

I still couldn't speak, the pleasure was too intense. I could only moan and whimper and cry out when he went deep. Zane had amazing control, just as I thought he was peaking, he would drop his head down and bury his face in my intimate parts and lick and kiss me there some more. He did this several times, keeping my legs on his shoulders, he would straighten and plunge deep inside me and stroke me hard and fast and pull out and bury his face and sit up and stroke me and he kept changing back and forth like that and it felt so good, that I started talking to him. I couldn't stop myself!

"Ohhhhhhhh, it's so good baby please don't stop! Yes! Give it to me give it ALL to me. Oh it's so gooooooooood! Pleeeeeeeeeeeease," I heard myself saying and I was shocked! I had never ever spoken during lovemaking, but I didn't care; I had never felt such pleasure before, either. And my words and passion drove Zane into such frenzy, he started pumping his hips faster and faster. "You want it, baby? You want it, baby? Here ITTTTTTTTT ISSSSSSSSSSSSSS!"

And as we both exploded in a super orgasmic mix, the walls of the room melted away and I felt myself move beyond the stars, become one with the universe. . . . As I clung to Zane, my last thought amid all of the pleasure was, "I am hopelessly, utterly lost, I'm lost, I'm lost . . ."

Zane continued to amaze me all during the night with his

stamina and control. We were both so exhausted the next day that we slept until two o'clock in the afternoon. And when Zane woke, he reached for my hand and, chuckling, placed it between his legs so that I could feel that he was ready for more. . . .

We spent the entire next day in bed, only getting up to shower, order room service, eat, and make love some more, completely missing the second show and everything in between. We had become lost in the wonder of each other's bodies. We were almost like newlyweds on a honeymoon, and only God and me cared that we weren't. Well, God cared anyway; my mind wasn't feeling anywhere near spiritual at the moment. I felt extremely relaxed and comfortable lying in Zane's arms, and I was thinking about all of the possibilities that a relationship with him could bring. I was riding on a wave of joy, happiness, and utter ecstasy and didn't realize that lurking just beneath the wave's calm, gentle flow, was hidden all the terror, danger, and destructive force of a tsunami.

12

The weekend went by much too quickly, and on the drive home Sunday morning, Zane seemed strangely distracted. I couldn't quite put my finger on it, but something was different. He still drove with one hand and held on to one of mine with the other as he had on the way down, but something in his attitude had changed. It was very subtle really and only slightly tugged at my subconscious. I was still basking in the glow and warmth, as they say in books, from our marathon lovemaking session and felt that giddy feeling that we had been joined and our souls had knitted. I wasn't getting quite the same vibe from him. Oh, he was still attentive and when our eyes met, he still smiled and winked at me, making me look away and blush. But still, his mind seemed in a totally different place.

When we got to my house, I thought that he was going to come in for a while, as he usually did when we came home from a date. Instead, he walked me to the door, gave me a kiss on the cheek, and said that he would call me tomorrow, mumbling something about being really tired and needing to get some sleep before work tomorrow.

"It's your fault I'm feeling so bad," he said. "You drained me drier than a man's mouth who ain't got a drop of water in a hot desert, girl!"

He gave me a hug and another peck and then you would have thought he was a nacho the way he dipped!

I can't lie, I was so disappointed, a lump got caught in my throat. And on top of that it was only two o'clock in the afternoon, how much sleep did he need? Anyway, I had gotten used to him calling me every night before I went to sleep, almost from the first time he called me. It was going to be strange going to sleep tonight without his voice being the last thing I heard.

I had five more hours to kill before Ian dropped the kids off. I spent some of the time doing a few loads of laundry, and getting the kids clothes ready for the week. After I was done with that, I decided to run a nice bath and soak some of the soreness of the weekend away, while I read one of my favorite author's stories. I loved the feel of the warm, soapy water surrounding my body and it instantly relaxed me and took away the stress I was feeling over Zane's abrupt departure. It was so soothing, that I dozed off before I could pick up my book.

I dreamed that I was in a field of beautiful yellow roses. I was smiling and slowly walking through them, stopping every now and then to bend down and inhale the sweet smelling fragrance. The beautiful blossoms surrounded me as far as the eye could see. I saw Zane and heard his voice calling me at the same moment. He was on the other side of the field and had his arms stretched out to me, beckoning me to come to him with a big grin on his face. I started across the field toward him, but even though he was standing still, I couldn't reach him. I was walking steadily in his direction, but the gap between us never closed. Then suddenly, the space between us disappeared and he was only a few steps away from me, but Zane was no longer smiling. I took another step toward him and felt myself sink. Looking down, I discovered that I was up to my knees in thick mud and I couldn't move, and all the roses had disappeared, their sweet fragrance replaced with a different odor, one I had never smelled before. I couldn't tell where the smell was coming from but it was strong and sickly sweet, and so thick, it was making me dizzy. I reached my arms toward Zane, wanting him to help me, but he was preoccupied burning something and was not focused on me. I soon realized that whatever Zane was burning was creating the stench, and I was sinking lower and lower. . . .

I had sunk so low in the tub, the water had gotten up to my nostrils, causing me to wake up. Lucky for me it woke me up before I drowned myself. What a weird dream. I was one of those people whose family members usually called to interpret the dreams they have, because I'm usually pretty good at it. I knew immediately there was a message, but for some reason, as scary as it was, it wasn't revealing its mystery to me.

The phone started ringing and I thought it might be Zane, so I jumped out of the tub and put on my bathrobe. I nearly slipped and broke my neck trying to get to it before it stopped ringing.

"Hello?" I said, hoping that Zane's voice would be the one that returned my greeting on the other line.

"Samai, what you doin', girl?"

"Oh hi, Miss Loretta," I said trying to disguise my disappointment.

"Well, I was callin' to let you know that I cooked some ribs, potato salad, greens, macaroni and cheese, cornbread, and a lemon pound cake, and I wanted to know if you and the children wanted to come over for dinner."

I hadn't eaten breakfast, so Miss Loretta's menu was making my stomach growl and my mouth water. But I really wasn't in the mood to go out. I was still sore from the weekend's activities and the kids wouldn't want to go out, either, since they had been gone all weekend.

"Miss Loretta, you know that I would be over there before you could get the dial tone from me hanging up the phone, but the kids aren't even home. You know this was Ian's weekend to have them, and anyway, I'm kind of tired myself. So can we get a rain check on your fabulous dinner?"

"Now, you know good and well you don't even have to ask that question. You and your children are always welcome. So if you change your mind when they get home, just give me a ring."

"I will, Miss Loretta, and thank you!"

"You're welcome," she said before hanging up the phone.

13

Jadyn made it home before the boys did. "Hi, Mom," she said when she came through the door; she seemed really excited about something.

"Guess what, Mom?"

"Hey, what you so happy about?" I asked walking into her bedroom with her.

"New Edition is coming to town, and Aunt Denise bought me a ticket. She said that she's taking me to the mall later this week to buy me a new outfit! Mom, I can't wait! I can't believe New Edition is really coming here!" She sat down on the edge of the bed and flopped back on it raising her arms above her head and smiling.

New Edition was the new group, kind of in the same league with the Jackson Five, from my day. It was one of Jadyn's favorites. I looked at her, loving how happy she seemed, and how grown-up she was becoming. It seemed like only yesterday that I was carrying her around inside of me. It amazed me that it would soon be thirteen years ago. I had already had the "talk" with her about boys, and sex, and that the onset of her cycle meant that she could now get pregnant, and she had to be careful. I told her that it was best not to have sex while she was so young, and that boys would tell her anything, including how pretty she is, and how much they love her, to get her to have sex with them. But I also told her that if she just felt that she was going to have sex, it was better to be protected at all times, so if she got to that point, she should tell me so that we could get her on birth control. I told her I hoped she wouldn't feel ready for a long time. I liked to think that Jadyn and I were very close and that we could talk about anything. We even had had the talk about good touching and bad touching when she was just a little thing. I had heard the horror stories about stepfathers, and I wanted to be sure that she knew that no one was allowed to touch her body or invade her space. Not her stepfather, not any of her uncles, not even her grandfather. And that if it happened, she should never be afraid to tell me. I didn't know then that there are some things that happen to little girls that they don't tell anyone, not even themselves.

"Mom, what do you think I should wear?"

"Now Jadyn, you know I'm not up on all of the latest fashions for you young people. I think you look good in anything you wear. Your Aunt Denise has really good taste in clothes, you know she will have you lookin' da bomb!"

Jadyn started laughing, "Please, Mom, and don't ever say that around my friends. Nobody my age is even usin' that now. That's lame."

"Oh, excuse me," I joked.

"Did anyone call me?" she asked, then added after a beat, "Oh never mind, I forgot that you went out of town this weekend. How was it?" she asked, smiling.

"I had soooooooooo much fun. Luther came on singing my favorite song—"

"'A House Is Not a Home,'" Jadyn said, finishing my sentence. And we both laughed again. Then we sat on her bed and traded stories about her weekend, and my wonderful weekend, leaving out the sex, of course.

I decided to make my world famous lasagna for dinner. It was a dish that all the kids loved, although cooking was never something

I would put on my list of favorite things to do. I did like making lasagna and it showed, because it was one of the things I made really well. I asked Jadyn to make the salad and get the garlic bread out to thaw.

When the boys got home, Devon ran to me and gave me a hug and a kiss. E said "Hi, Ma," and allowed me to kiss him. And they both said hi to their sister. Devon called her "Seesa" because, when he was smaller, he tried to mimic his older brother who called her "sister" and "seesa" was what came out and it stuck for a while.

We had a great time at dinner with the boys telling funny stories about their grandpa JR, Ian's stepfather, and Jadyn told funny Uncle Lee stories. Suddenly, it seemed the kids were adjusting well to Ian being gone. I hoped that we would always be happy like this.

14

Not only did Zane not call me on Monday, following our glorious weekend, he didn't call Tuesday or Wednesday, either! By Thursday, I was killing myself with fantasies about what he must have been doing. I started thinking that maybe our time together had made him miss his not-quite ex-wife, or that maybe she came over and he was now thrilling her in the same way he had me. Or maybe I hadn't satisfied him as well as he had me and on and on into infinity.

I had pretty much made up my mind that I was going to call him if he didn't ring my phone by Friday, and when I got him on the line, I was going to tell him off and dismiss him before he dismissed me. I wasn't going to let him have the pleasure of knowing how frantic he was making me feel.

The days dragged by at work. Not only was Zane not calling, but I was also starting to feel down in spirit as well. I hadn't been to church at all in months, and now I was beginning to feel strange about going. I didn't know how people would look at me after having been gone so long, and I didn't know how God was planning on dealing with me for all the things I had done, not the least of which was committing adultery. I hadn't even asked Him to forgive me for that yet.

I just knew that if I went to church, our pastor, Sister Judith Greathouse, would model her sermon on my transgressions, only thinly disguising it as something else. Everyone would know that her message was directed toward me. And after giving me a good preaching lecture, she would call me to the altar and have a couple of the nosy old sisters in the church come up and lay hands on me and pray the demons out. She would probably take the bottle of olive oil that she kept on a shelf built into the pulpit and use it to draw an oily cross on my forehead before grabbing my head and praying the spirit back into me until I spoke in tongues and started crying or something. And then I would leave church feeling guilty, go home, and think of how I was going to get Zane to call me.

Anyway, I didn't want Pastor Greathouse counseling me on my behavior when she had eight children of her own who attended her church, five of them ministers and three of them deacons, and as far as I could see, none of them was trying to live the life of a real Christian. So what she needed to be doing was to straighten out her own children first before she tried to start in on me.

I immediately felt guilty for having such mean thoughts about my pastor. She didn't deserve that. I was just taking things out on her because I felt guilty about not going to church anymore. I was also mad and upset about Zane not calling me, too. I guess it was really starting to get to me.

That's what I had reduced my service to the Lord to. Some kind of ritual that I acted out in my head in the worst scenario possible to convince myself that I didn't need to go to church anymore.

I didn't even have Deacon Bennie at work to talk to anymore, to try to counteract these negative thoughts about church. Less than a month after he had helped me get a job there, he'd quit the warehouse once he'd passed the exam to become a police officer. I hadn't talked to him since.

. . . .

By Friday, Zane still hadn't called me, and despite my previous resolve to call him, I decided against it. If someone didn't want to be with you, there was nothing to talk about. I had learned that from Ian. I wasn't about to put myself out there like that again.

Instead of sitting around waiting for him to call, I decided to take the kids out for pizza, and then to the arcade to play games. I asked Jadyn if she wanted to come along. She said no, that she wanted to go over to visit her grandmother. So I dropped her off on the way to the Pizza Play Palace, where the boys had said they wanted to go.

Pizza Play Palace was this huge buffet-style pizza place where you served yourself. They had every type of pizza you could imagine, including dessert pizzas. They also had a bunch of games for kids of every age to play, not just an arcade. They had a roomful of balls and a tunnel with padded walls for kids to crawl through, among other things. So after the boys had stuffed themselves full of pizza, I bought twenty dollars worth of tokens and told them that after those were gone, we were going home. I also told them that they shouldn't try talking me into buying any more, and if they whined, we wouldn't be back for a long, long time. I wanted them to have fun, but I wasn't trying to go broke feeding those arcade games, either.

As they took off to the video games, I followed closely behind so that I could keep my eyes on them. You never knew when a pervert might show up and try to steal your child.

I was standing beside them watching to see which one would be the first to win the game when I saw him.

Zane was standing over by the cushioned tunnel, with a little girl that had her hair in two long braided ponytails, and a tall light-skinned woman with green eyes, which looked amazingly similar to the little girl's. The woman had her arm around Zane's waist and they were watching the little girl. I guess Zane must have felt my eyes on him or something, because almost at the exact moment I took in the cozy little scene, he looked right at me and our eyes met. He didn't miss a beat with the woman he was with, he just looked away and kept saying whatever to the woman.

I did likewise; I kept laughing and joking with my sons and watching them play. Devon had spotted Zane and surprised me by running over to him before I could stop him. Zane saw him coming and as Devon reached him he swung him up over his head.

"Hey, little man, what's up?" Zane asked with a smile, right before Devon clasped his little hands together, made a fist and brought them down as hard as he could on top of Zane's head.

I ran over and retrieved my son, apologizing as I did so. Zane had a stunned expression on his face, and E, who had misunderstood the situation, thought that Zane had tried to hurt his little brother and promptly punched Zane in the stomach. Zane groaned before grabbing his stomach and bending at the waist.

I took both my sons by the hand, and led them away as quickly as possible. I didn't know what Zane was going to tell the woman he was with, and frankly, I didn't care.

15

By the time we got home, the phone was ringing off the hook. I knew that it was Zane, but I really didn't want to talk to him. I ran the boys' bathwater and laid out their pj's. I made sure not to put too much water in the tub, because they would have it all over the floor, and left them alone to take their baths.

E had told me he was big enough to wash himself when he was just a little thing, and after checking him over that first time, he had done such a good job that I left him alone. Ever playing the big brother, E made it his job to teach Devon how to bathe himself, too.

The phone must have rung a thousand times between the time I got home and the time I got the boys settled and into bed. Finally, I picked it up.

"What?" I said into the receiver. I knew it was Zane.

"Now you just gon' act all evil and shit without givin' me a chance to explain?"

"Explain what, exactly? You don't owe me any explanations about spending time with your wife, I knew you were still married."

I wasn't really angry about that, I was angry about him making me wait and wonder what was going on with him and not being man enough to come right out and tell me he was going back to his wife. I was also angry that he had made this decision after I had given it up to him, but I wasn't going to give him the satisfaction of knowing this.

"See, now you done jumped to all kinds of conclusions. Two and two is four all over the world, but you done added two and two and come up with five," he said.

"Look, I don't feel like sittin' here listening to your smart-ass answers," I said.

"Hold up, did I just hear you say *ass*? I believe that's a curse word. Have you or have you not been gettin' after me for cursing since day one?" he asked, his voice sounding both amused and sarcastic at the same time.

I wasn't in the mood to laugh at his jokes. "What the hell ever," I said.

"If you just calm down and give me a second to talk, I can tell you what's goin' on. Now that wasn't my wife that you saw tonight, that was my sister and my niece. And the reason why I haven't called you is that all hell broke loose when I got back. My sister said that my wife called my mother and told her that she was pressin' charges against my ass for domestic violence, and somehow, she found out that I took you out of town with me, and she was at my sister's house when I got back, cryin' and carryin' on about she still love me and everything, and wanted to try to work things out. When I told her that I wasn't sure that was the best move for us to make, she went off on me, talkin' about she knows it's because of you and how she knows all about us and she was pissed because me and her haven't even filed for divorce yet. Then she said that she gon' save us both some grief and have me put up under the jail for the shit that went down that first night I called yo' ass—"

"You never did really tell me what happened. You just said that she was the one throwing punches and scratching you, and you were basically holding her, to keep her from touching you," I interrupted.

"Yeah, that's true, but what I *didn't* tell you is that she told me to my face that she was fuckin' somebody else and I smacked the shit out of her, and since she really fair skinned, she's lighter than

I am, it left a big bruise on her face. I swear to God, ba'y, I been with a lot of women and I ain't never hit no woman before, but she was all up in my face and I kept tellin' her to go on, and then when she said what she did all raw and shit, I just had backhanded her, before I knew it. That's when the tussle started and she was tryin' to hit me and shit, and a lot of stuff got broken in the apartment, and one of our neighbors musta heard all the noise and called the police. I got taken to jail and she been holdin' that shit over my head ever since. There ain't no excuse for what I did, but when I think about it, it's one of the reasons I don't feel me and her should get back together."

I was thinking about what he was saying to me, trying to decide whether to believe him or not. The part about hitting his ex wasn't sitting well with me at all because I don't think that a man ever has the right to hit a woman. Well, not unless she has a gun or knife or some other weapon and his life is threatened, but other than that, if they are just in a heated argument, I just can't see why a man would hit a woman. He knows already that he can beat her, so what is the point? I feel that a man who can't manage his anger is a man who can't manage any area of his life very well, either.

"Why did you slap her? Why didn't you just walk away?"

" 'Cause I felt disrespected."

"So you mean to tell me in all of your time with her that is the only time she made you feel disrespected?" I was thinking about how he swore that he had never hit a woman before that. "None of your other women made you feel disrespected? And suppose someone else, another woman in your life makes you feel that way, are you gonna backhand her, too?"

"Didn't I just tell you no? I guess it was because she's my wife, and it's different when your wife gets in your face and tells you she's—"

"Well, in my way of thinking, I would think that would be all the more reason *not* to hit her."

"You're not a man, so I don't expect you to understand. But can I finish my story? I don't wanna argue with you, I miss you."

I wasn't in the mood to hear about his feelings for me. Reality was closing in on me. He was still married and so was I. Technically, there was no need to talk about feelings that we couldn't do anything about.

"Finish your story," I snapped.

I heard him take a breath, before he went on. "Well, I told you that she was over Cocoa's when I got back from the concert last weekend, and how she said she is gon' have me put up under the jail, and she was steady goin' off and shit, and then I told her that wasn't solving anything, and could we sit down like two rational sane adults and talk about what was really botherin' her. She broke out in tears and starts boo-hoo cryin' and everything, so my first instinct is to, you know, offer to comfort her. So I put my arms around her until she stopped cryin', and she looked so miserable and shit that I kissed her. And we ended up back at her place and we had sex but—"

I couldn't take any more of his explanations so I hung up the phone. I don't know what goes through a man's head, thinking he can talk to you about making love to another woman after he has recently made love to you like there wasn't going to be a tomorrow. It doesn't matter that it is his wife or whomever, a woman just does not want to hear that mess.

The phone rang and I picked it up.

"Are you gon' let me finish this or not?"

I hung up.

The phone rang. I picked it up.

"Would you quit actin' like a spoiled-ass brat for a minute and listen?"

"I'm not actin' like a brat!"

"It's *spoiled-ass* brat, and yes you are hangin' up the phone and poutin' and thangs."

I didn't say anything, but I didn't hang up the phone, either.

"Now, like I was sayin', we ended up in the bed, but nothin' felt right, and all the time I was doin' her, I was thinkin' about you, and my shit wouldn't stay hard, and she felt it, that my mind wasn't on her. But she didn't trip this time, we just laid there talkin' about everything and we knew that our marriage was over. The reason I didn't call you is I got confused and nervous and thangs because of how the sex was between us, and there ain't no way that the sex can be that good, and the two people havin' it don't have some kind of connection goin' on, something deeper than the physical. You felt it. I know you did 'cause I felt it, and it's scary 'cause it's too soon for both of us to be gettin' all deep and shit. Neither one of us is divorced and even if we were . . . like I say it's too soon. So that's why I stayed away, I had to get my mind right and not go jumpin' off the deep end, again, you know?"

It was my turn to sigh before answering.

"Yeah, I know exactly what you mean." I knew all right, but some part of me didn't want to accept it. My heart was telling me that Zane was the one I needed to be with. But in the end, I knew he was right.

"So what are we gonna do?" I asked, knowing the answer, but dreading it just the same.

"Well, I was thinkin' that we should chill, just for a little while until we sort things out and get our feelin's about other people straight."

"Yeah, okay," I said dully. "Let's do that, let's chill. But I just want to ask you one thing. Why couldn't we have decided to *chill* before we fucked?" I said without even flinching, and slammed down the receiver as hard as I could. This time, he didn't call back.

16

It's funny how timing in life never seems to be on my side. Here I was tripping about a guy that wasn't even mine. But back in the day when we were in school, he could've been. And I had let this same guy make wild, passionate, ultra-fine love to me, and then a week later we decide we don't need to see each other anymore. Timing. It just wouldn't cut me a break.

The first week without Zane was hard. Sometimes, I felt that I was just going through the motions, trying to live my life without him. I spent all of my free time with the kids, taking them to movies, to the bowling alley, and to the arcades. I even managed to make it to church a couple of Sundays in a row, but I was feeling so disconnected from the things that were going on there. I couldn't really articulate the changes I had gone through, or what the cause was. I tried praying, and reading my Bible, but the feelings just weren't there. I was in a valley, and needed to exercise a little faith, but for some reason, I couldn't even do that. I had been taught that you can't live a Christian life without faith, because without it, the very foundation of belief crumbles. How can you serve a God, who made Himself human, only to become God again, without faith? We have never seen Him, but we believe He exists by faith. But knowing this and living this can sometimes seem next to impossible.

I guess that's why some believers have what they call a crisis of faith. There comes a time when your spirit is torn between right and wrong, and the decision you make could deal a death blow to your belief. If that ain't a crisis I don't know what is. I had the feeling that my condition was critical, and I didn't have sense enough to call the doctor.

About the third week without Zane, it started to get easier. I had stopped half-sleeping at night, wishing that the phone would ring so that we could talk. In fact, one of the girls I worked with, Joletta Hughes, had introduced me to one of her friends, a man named Waldrick Gordon.

Joletta was the type of girl who could get men to do anything she wanted them to. She would have sex with a man in his car during her lunch hour, and most of the time, the guy would leave cards for her at the service desk. And when she would open up the cards in the break room, she would always pull money out of them. Mostly it would be one hundred dollar bills. And yes, I do mean the plural.

It wasn't that Joletta was exceptionally pretty or anything, although she was cute enough with long black hair that was cut into a shag, and her deep dimples. Being petite and having a nice figure didn't hurt her efforts at all, either. She was forever trying to give me advice on how to handle men.

"You know, you just gotta be nice to 'em and they'll give you anythang you want or need. You ain't gotta always screw 'em, neither," she told me, wrinkling her nose at me and making a face. "I know how you feel about that part. I'm goin' to introduce you to my one friend. He works so much he is too tired to screw! But he got money out the ass, and he is too, too generous with it," Joletta had told me before she introduced me to Waldrick.

Waldrick was one of the nicest, most considerate men I had ever met. He would always call before coming over, and he would always ask, "Do you need me to stop and pick up anything for you and the kids?" Most of the time, even if I said no, he would bring a surprise for the kids and me. We dated a few times but I never really felt a connection with Waldrick. Probably because he was the first guy I had dated after Zane, and I was constantly comparing the two of them. It wasn't Waldrick's fault, but he just couldn't replace Zane in my heart. And I couldn't bring myself to use him for his money like Joletta would have. That just wasn't me.

About a month after Zane and I had decided not to see each other, just as I was beginning to think I was better off without him, he started calling again.

At first, it was real quick.

"I don't want nothin'," he would say. "I just wanted to see how you was doin'."

I'd tell him I was fine, and we'd chitchat about nothing for a couple minutes and then we would hang up. That all changed when I started being friends with Waldrick. I wasn't always answering the phone when Zane would call, even though sometimes I would be sitting right there. I would let the answering machine pick up. I did that for a whole week one time.

"Where the hell you been?" Zane asked when he finally got me on the line.

"Oh, just out and about, you know, hangin' out with the kids among other things," I answered.

"Among what other things? You ain't got another nigga, do you?"

"Another one? I didn't even know I had the first one," I said, teasing him.

"Oh you didn't, hunh? What you think I'm suppose to be, Chewbacca or something?" he asked, referring to a character from the *Star Wars* movies.

"I didn't think you was supposed to be nothin'. We said we were chillin' out for a while, remember?"

The phone beeped, signaling that I had another call waiting before Zane could say another word.

"Hold on," I said. It was my sister Lynn on the other line, but I wasn't going to let Zane know. Let him do some wondering for a change.

"Hey," I said, after telling Lynn to hold on and clicking back over. "I got another call, I'm gonna have to speak with you some other time."

"Tell 'em you'll call 'em back, I was talkin' to you first," he said. I smiled.

" 'Bye, Zane." And I clicked back over to the other line.

17

It was Ian's Friday to spend with the boys, and Jadyn was going to take a trip out of town with Denise and Lee. That left me with a whole weekend with nothing to do. I didn't even have to work at all this weekend, so I was really going to be bored. There were a couple of books that I wanted to read, but when I picked one up and tried reading it, I discovered that I would get all the way to the bottom of the page and not know a thing about what I had just read, so I would start at the top of the page and try again. Same thing happened. My mind just wasn't on reading, so I finally quit trying. I was restless, so I called my cousin Phyl. She wasn't home, of course. No doubt out with one of her men again. Maybe I should be more like her.

I heard a car pull up in my driveway. I got up on my knees on the couch and peered out of the curtains. It was Zane's car. I let the curtain drop back to its original position. He had a lot of nerve coming over without calling first. What if I had company or something? It would serve him right if I didn't answer the door when he knocked. I knew he had seen me peek out the window and that he would probably be ticked if I ignored him when he knocked on the door, not that it would really matter right this moment. We were still in chill mode. I decided that I would not let him in, but would play a game with him. I quickly slid my feet into my sandals, opened my front door and went outside.

Before Zane could get out of the car, I had walked up to the window and tapped on it. I guess he hadn't heard me come out, because he jumped a little when he looked up and saw me standing by his car. He rolled down his window.

"Girl, don't you know you scared the shit out of me!"

"Oh, then I guess I'll stand out here and talk to you, 'cause I know it's funky in there!"

He rolled his eyes and said, "Very funny."

I went around to the passenger side and got in.

"Can I ask a question? Why are we sittin' out here? Am I not welcome inside your home anymore?" he asked, looking at me with puppy-dog eyes and blinking his eyelashes, feigning that his feelings were hurt.

"Well, you know you shouldn't have come without calling first," I told him.

Zane shifted in his seat and I could sense his mood changing. "Ain't that a bitch? Why I gotta do that?" he asked with a little bit of an edge to his voice. "I thought we had a long talk about this and we decided we wa'n't gon' see other people while we were givin' each other space."

I became slightly annoyed. Zane and I had not really discussed that part of our being apart.

"No, *you* decided that. I never told you I agreed to it. And this conversation is beginning to sound too much like an argument and I don't feel like it," I said, rolling my eyes at him and pulling up the door handle so I could get out of the car.

"Wait a minute, hold up. How is this arguin'?" Zane asked and lightly touched my arm. "I don't wanna argue with you."

"That's why I'm gettin' out and goin' in the house, before it turns into one!" I said stubbornly.

I got out of Zane's car and noticed that the gate to my backyard was open. I started walking toward the fence to close it. I didn't want any stray animals wandering into the backyard. And anyway, I hated to see the gate hanging open. I was halfway to the gate when I heard Zane start the car.

"It'll be a cold day in hell when I call yo' ass again!" he yelled, sticking his head out of the car window. "In fact, hell will freeze over! The'll be ten feet a snow in that muhfucka before my black ass drive out here again!"

At first I was hurt. This wasn't how it was supposed to go. He was supposed to come after me when I got out of the car, and apologize for coming over without calling. And then I was supposed to tell him that it was OK, and we were supposed to kiss, or something like that. Then I got mad. For some reason that I can't explain, I grabbed the tops of my shorts and panties and pushed them down, exposing my entire behind and turned my bare butt toward the car and yelled, "Kiss *my* black ass!," giving it a slap for emphasis.

Zane, who had begun backing the car down the drive, immediately slammed on the brakes, threw the car in park and jumped out of the car. When I saw the look on his face, I started trying to run the rest of the way to the gate and pull up my shorts at the same time. Zane and I made it to the gate at the same time. He tackled me, and I hadn't quite managed to pull up my shorts.

"Kiss yo' ass, hunh?" he said, kicking the gate closed.

Thick hedges framed the backyard and once the gate was closed, my neighbors couldn't see into my yard. Zane started tickling me and we wrestled in the damp muddy grass. I was laughing and so was he.

"Stop, Zane! Stop. Stop! I'm sorry, I'm sorry!" I said through the laughter, squirming and trying to free myself from Zane's grasp. But Zane had a firm grip on me and wasn't letting go.

"Nah, you ain't sorry."

Zane was tugging at my T-shirt and managed to push up my shirt and bra together. Suddenly I felt his mouth on my bare breast. He was licking and sucking one of my nipples, and because I hadn't been able to pull up my shorts, he had easy access, and had inserted a finger inside me, slowly moving it in and out. My laughter was changing to grunts and groans of pleasure. At some point during our wrestling and tickling match, Zane had managed to pull his pants down over his hips and he rolled over in the grass, pulling me on top of him. As he positioned me on top, he slid easily inside me, and holding my thighs with his strong hands, pulled me down and pushed himself up at the same instant, giving me all he had. As I rode on top of him, I felt a blade of grass tickling my bare behind, adding to the excitement. He pulled and pushed and I ground my hips into him, back and forth, back and forth, like riding a horse, enjoying the feeling of having all of him inside me. I was nearing my peak, and from the sounds he was making, I could tell Zane was, too. I felt my thighs begin to tremble, signaling my orgasm, and for the first time, when Zane released his hot wetness, I felt it splash deep inside me. . . .

We were covered with mud from head to toe. And although it had been sunny and in the upper eighties all day, it had rained hard for two days straight, so the ground was still damp. We stumbled into my kitchen from the backyard. I let my shorts fall to my ankles and kicked them off. I picked them up and headed for the washer that was just off the kitchen behind sliding doors.

"You better take off your muddy clothes, too, so I can wash them real quick," I said over my shoulder.

"Yes, ma'am," Zane replied jokingly, as he followed behind me, unbuttoning his shirt as he walked.

After I had started the washer, Zane and I stood naked and muddy in the utility room. I felt his strong hands cup both my breasts from behind as he bent slightly and began kissing the nape of my neck. His hands kneaded my breasts, and I turned slightly so that I could look at him. Zane was looking at me as if I were the most beautiful woman on earth. He bent down and kissed me, long and hard, lifting me into his arms at the same time. I wrapped my legs around his waist, and he carried me into the bathroom.

In the shower, we took turns washing each other and the sensation of Zane's soapy hands and the hot steamy water, got me excited again. And as I washed the mud off him, his desire was obvious. I took him into my hands and deliberately stroked him with my soapy hands.

"Ahhhhhhhhmmmmmmm, that feels good," he moaned.

Zane returned the favor by kneeling down and placing one of my thighs on his shoulder, as I gripped the towel rack and leaned against the shower wall; he started to pleasure me with his tongue, as only he could. But before I climaxed, he stood up and I groaned in frustration. His voice deep and husky, he whispered in my ear.

"Don't worry, baby, be patient, I'm gon' give you all you need and more. I got somethin' that will make you feel even better than this."

I put on my robe and Zane wrapped a towel around his waist as we walked back to the kitchen where he had emptied his pockets before handing me his muddy clothes. He picked up something that looked like a tiny envelope, and dipped his little finger in. When he withdrew his finger, there appeared to be something that looked a little like powdered sugar piled in a little pyramid on the very tip.

"What is that?" I asked naively.

"Just trust me," Zane said. "I would never give you anything that would hurt you. I just want to liven up the party a little bit."

I hesitated, still not sure I wanted to experiment with any drugs. I had never tried drugs at all, if you didn't include alcohol, and I hadn't even had much of that in my life. I wasn't completely ignorant about drugs; I had seen my cousin Dartanyan and a few of his friends smoke some weed and snort a little coke at parties before, it had just never interested me so I had never really paid that much attention to it.

Zane held the powder to my nostril and I inhaled. He dipped into the envelope again and held the contents to my other nostril as I inhaled again, and immediately began to sneeze. My nostrils felt as if they were on fire. Zane knew what to do about that, too. He took me over to the sink, and put a little water in his hand.

"Hold your head over the sink," he instructed and splashed water on my face, so that a little of it dampened my sinuses. He then snorted some coke himself, repeating the same process before he stepped back and watched me.

"How do you feel?" he asked.

I looked at him. "How am I supposed to feel? I feel the same, I don't feel any different."

"You will," he said as he led me over to one of my kitchen chairs and sat me down. He immediately knelt in front of me, and continued what he had started in the shower. The high started hitting me, and the music that was playing seemed to break down into the various instruments, and I could hear each one with new clarity. And then the sensations that Zane was giving me seemed to multiply in intensity; every time he touched me, it was a triple thrill. Zane stood and took me by the hand, changing places with me. He sat in the chair and pulled me onto his lap, holding himself rigid so that as I sat, I enveloped him in my warm, soft flesh. We rocked back and forth in the chair, my muscles gripping and releasing him like a fist inside me. It was a perfect fit, and both of us felt it to the max! Zane couldn't seem to get enough of me, and we tried every position in the book before we collapsed in a heap on the kitchen floor.

As I floated back to earth and found myself in Zane's arms, a part of me realized that I had crossed a threshold into the unknown. Something sinister was beckoning, and like someone sleepwalking, I blindly followed.

Part Two

THE DESCENT

18

I know how the prodigal son felt now. When he left his father's rich house he had wanted for nothing, no matter what disagreements or quarrels he may have had, but before long he found himself in dire straits, wallowing around with pigs, eating the scraps that they left.

There was one big difference between the prodigal son and me, though. After a while, he realized how low he had sunk, having spent all he had, and decided that he would do something about his sorry state. He decided that he would get up and go home to his father, and beg him for work as a servant in the house because he recognized that even the servants were living in better conditions than he was. But when he got home, his father was happy to see him and restored him to his former place.

I knew I was in a state more sorry than the prodigal son and I wanted out, too, but as I looked around for direction, there was no clear path home for me. And even if I could manage to find a path that led back home, I wasn't sure what I would find there. I didn't feel I had a home to go to, physically or spiritually. . . .

That first night that I ever snorted cocaine was the last. I never felt like doing it again. I wasn't the type of person who needed or wanted to get high in order to have fun. I became a pretty happy person after my divorce. My kids were good kids, they hardly ever gave me any trouble. I had left the warehouse after a few months, landing a very good job at a neighborhood medical center doing accounting and preparing patients' charts.

Zane and I were still seeing each other, though it seemed that the only reason we got together these days was to "jump each other's bones," as he put it. I was seeing other people and so was he.

Waldrick was a favorite of mine, because he spoiled me so much from the first moment we met. A gold watch was only the first of many gifts he graciously showered on me. But Waldrick was a workaholic and never took time to enjoy life. He never wanted to do much of anything except talk on the phone for a few minutes and make love every now and then.

Then there was Ike, the lover. He liked everything to be perfect, from the outfit he wore to the women he dated; he had certain standards that had to be met. I didn't know this when I first met him, but I would discover later that he could only love you according to his terms; if you failed to meet one of his standards or failed one of his tests, he would cut you off quicker than the electric company for not paying your bill. I probably wouldn't have even continued to date him if he hadn't been such a good kisser, a good listener, and funny as hell. He was generous, too, at first.

So between juggling dates with those three and a few others I'd met at work and at the store while grocery shopping, among other places, and working and spending time with the kids, my life was pretty happy and fulfilled. Until one morning when a call from Zane changed my life forever.

It was about eight o'clock on a Saturday morning.

"Hey, can you come over right now?" he asked as soon as I said "hello."

"What for?" I asked. "Is something wrong? Are you all right?" Zane's request alarmed me for a number of reasons, one of which was it was way too early for him to be up and about. He worked second shift at the post office and he usually slept until at least noon. The other was he didn't quite sound like himself, although I pushed that thought aside.

"Nothin's wrong. I just want to see you. I been thinking about us a lot lately, and I have somethin' I want to show you. Somethin' I want to share with you."

Now he really had me curious.

"What do you want to share with me? Sex? Did you wake up horny and you want me to come and fix that for you?" I teased.

"Well, that would be gravy, too, but nah it's more than that. It's a surprise."

For some reason, my antennas went up. I was feeling my sixth sense, which God had given us women for His own reasons, going off like crazy. But Zane was saying some of the things I had been wanting to hear for the longest time, so I pushed those warning signals down, enjoying all of this early morning attention.

"Tell me what it is. You know I don't like surprises," I coaxed.

"Just trust me. Have I ever done anything to hurt you?"

Mentally, I leafed back through the months that we had been seeing each other. I couldn't really think of a time that he had actually hurt me. Pissed me off a few times, but he hadn't really done anything to me.

"No, not really," I said.

"Then come on over. You'll like it, I promise."

I was quiet. For some reason, I was hesitating. Neither of us ever really paused for the cause when one of us called the other. We usually broke our necks trying to get to one another, because if nothing else, the sex was DA BOMB!!! But that wasn't enough today. Something wasn't right, I felt it.

"Are you comin'?" Zane persisted. "I'm all yours today and we can do whatever you like." It was his turn to do some coaxing.

I don't know what made me say yes but I did and we hung up the phone. I showered and threw on some jeans and a T-shirt.

I was almost positive that Zane had probably gone out and bought some kind of new sex toy or some new nasty movie that he was going to try to get me to watch with him. Or some mess like that. I perched on the edge of my bed, again hesitating.

In my mind, I began a quick recap of my relationship with Zane. How we had hooked up again after years apart, how we had so much fun that first weekend we'd spent together, how he had showed me off to all of his friends at the house parties we held at his house. How Zane laughed at his friends, who once sold cocaine and were now their own best customers, as the saying went. I remembered his best friend, Quin Green, who had started Zane out selling.

Quin was one of the scariest men I had ever met. He had to be around six five or six six. I mean, he was a giant, with huge hands and huge feet. And he was all muscle, too. Zane said that he worked out in his garage, bench-pressing cars and trucks.

He was ruthless in the way he treated his women and friends. Once, when Quin was playing poker with some of his boys, he thought one of them had cheated him, so he took a machete, cut off two of the guy's fingers, and told him that if the police came to his door, they would find little pieces of him all over the city. Zane always cautioned me to never get into a situation where I was alone with Quin.

"That loony muhfucka is my friend, not yours, and don't you never forget that. He ain't got love for no one. Shit, he would slice his own mama's throat if she crossed him. And the only reason me and him still cool, is I known that crazy bastard since elementary school, and for reasons I ain't sure of, I'm the only person that muhfucka trusts. But the feeling ain't mutual. I trust that crazy bastard 'bout as far as I can throw him. And since he weigh a good three hundred pounds, you know that ain't very far!"

I thought about the going-away party Zane had thrown for Quin when Zane and I had first started dating. I remembered Quin saying that it was going to be the shortest party he had ever been to, cause his bus was leaving at midnight and he was going to be the first one on it. But when I had left the party that night, Quin and his friends had still been in Zane's basement getting high.

19

I don't know what had made me remember that particular party at this moment. Maybe it had something to do with the strong feeling I had that I shouldn't go and meet Zane. But my heart overruled my sense and I grabbed my keys and headed out the door.

I tried to shake the uneasy feeling I had, but it wouldn't be shook. So I just ignored it and thought about how much fun Zane and I would have. The bad feeling followed me all the way to Zane's house. It just wouldn't leave me alone. Whenever I would try to press it down and bury it beneath some more pleasant thoughts, it would make itself known. It wouldn't always reveal itself as that bad feeling that I had when Zane first called. It would disguise itself as something else. I would be thinking about how much fun it would be to get together with Zane and think about something funny he had said or done in the past, and something would be hiding on the edge of my thoughts, niggling at me, until I would think: *Something's bothering me, but I don't know what it is . . . Don't go to Zane's. Turn around and go back. Oh yeah. Now I remember.* But then I would push the thought to the back of my mind again.

He had said that we could do whatever I wanted for the whole day, so I figured that after a rousing round of lovemaking, I would make him take me to lunch, after which we would do a little shopping for some things that I needed, and then I might even make him take me to a movie. I wanted to see Eddie Murphy's new movie, 'cause everyone was talking about how good it was.

When I got to his house, I used the key that he had recently given me to let myself in.

"Zane," I called out to let him know I was there.

"I'm down here in the basement, come on down here!" he yelled. When I reached the bottom step, I paused.

Zane was sitting on the carpet on the basement floor in front of the coffee table, dressed only in a robe. There was a big candle in the center of the table, and something else. I had never seen this thing before. It looked like a miniature glass fishbowl, without the big opening at the top that a real fishbowl has, and it had a little glass stem sticking out of one side.

"C'mere, ba'y," Zane said, standing up and holding his arms out to me. And in that instant, I remembered the dream I had when we were standing in a field of flowers. Zane had been standing with open arms and right when I reached him I had started to sink in the mud.

I went to him, and he held me in his arms in a long embrace before kissing me hello.

He sat back down on the floor in front of the table, and I started to join him.

"Wait a minute, ba'y, I want you to be ready, because when you hit this, you gon' be horny as hell and I'm gon' fuck your brains out!" He handed me the robe that I kept there for when I stayed the night at his house.

"You need to get naked," he said.

I was starting to get a little scared.

"Look, Zane, you know I'm not a drug person. I don't even smoke weed! And except for that one time you gave me a little bit of the powder, I have never even tried drugs."

Zane stood up and looked me in the eye.

"Ba'y, you know I would never do anything to hurt you, trust me," he said, massaging my neck and shoulders as he spoke. "This is somethin' different, everybody is doin' it because the sex is more intense. Great sex becomes spectacular! All the couples I know say it's the bomb, Samai," he coaxed as he undid my jeans and slid them down until they fell in a heap around my ankles. Soon I was naked except for my robe, and sitting on the floor next to Zane.

"Don't be scared, I won't hurt you, trust me," Zane repeated as he stood and put Kenny G on the CD player. Zane knew that I loved hearing the smooth jazz of Kenny G and he knew that it would relax me. It would be a long time before I would feel that way about hearing a Kenny G song again. Zane took his place on the floor beside me again.

I could see the little glass bowl even more clearly now. There were actually two stems sticking out of opposite ends of the bowl. Besides the glass stems, it had a tiny hole at the opposite end, toward the top. One of the glass stems had something stuffed into the outside edge. Zane picked up a little piece of a white substance and stuck it into the end of the stem.

"Now, ba'y, you put this stem in your mouth, and when I light the other end it's gon' make the bowl fill up with smoke. When I tell you to, you start sucking on the stem like you would a cigarette and hold the smoke in. Don't blow it out until I tell you to."

When Zane put the bowl up to my face, I giggled. I guess I was nervous. Zane gave me a look that said "Quit actin' silly," so I put on a straight face and placed the stem in my mouth. Everything happened real fast after that. It all went just like he said, and I was sitting there holding the smoke in, with Zane staring at me. I gave him a look like, "Yeah right, ain't nothing happening. I don't know what you're supposed to feel but . . ."

And then in mid-thought, a million bright lights flashed in my brain and a feeling of utter pleasure so intense overtook me without warning. I let the smoke out in a rush, panting, gasping, and breathing hard. In the background I could hear Zane asking me if I was all right, and my ears started to buzz. The feeling intensified even more, slowly working its way from my brain, blossoming and infusing pleasure all through my body, spreading like a white-hot sensor igniting every sensation.

I was instantly aroused, and when I turned my head, it felt like everything was moving in slow motion. I tried to focus on Zane but when I looked at him, he was smiling and trying to light up the bowl for himself. He drew in some smoke and held the bowl back to my lips. I took some more. I had never felt anything like this in my entire life. And then I heard bells ring.

Zane had opened my robe and was kissing and sucking my nipples, and although it felt good, it didn't feel the same. I couldn't focus on what he was doing, I could only focus on how good the drug had made me feel, and as the feeling started to fade the only thought in my mind was I wanted more. . . .

20

I didn't know exactly how to feel now that Zane and I had smoked up all the dope. One thing that I knew was that somehow I had to convince him to get more. As good and as intense as the pleasure side had been, now that it was over, the empty side was just as intense.

And empty is exactly what I was feeling. Empty and something else that I couldn't quite put my finger on.

Zane and I had gone up to his bedroom and we were lying in bed. Not talking, not having foreplay or making love or any of the things that the two of us would normally do in bed together. Not that Zane hadn't made an attempt to fondle me and get me in the mood, but it was as if I had become numb to his touch. Numb to everything around me except for the burning desire inside me to experience that high again that I had felt for the very first time. It seemed like it had all happened forever ago, although only a few hours had passed.

I could tell that Zane was feeling frustrated, or mad, or something. I didn't care really how he felt at the moment. I turned to him and again asked him to call Quin and see if he could get some more stuff. And that was one time too many.

"Will you please stop? Don't you know you are killin' me with this. I am so sorry, I didn't know that the drug would do you like this. You always seemed strong, never smokin' weed or wantin' a toot, or anything. I can't take you askin'—no beggin, for that shit like this. . . . Please, ba'y, please stop . . . I didn't know . . . ," he said and the tears got caught up in his throat before they squeezed by and started running down his cheeks.

And for that instant I could see myself. I was acting crazy, not myself at all. Zane was right, I had never wanted to do drugs, and I had to be acting really bizarre, because I had never seen Zane cry about anything.

I sat up and reached for Zane and he pulled me close and really cried as he held me. I didn't know if he was crying because of what he had done to me, or if he was feeling sorry for himself. It didn't seem as if I could reason anything anymore. All of a sudden I knew I had to get out of there, I had to get home. I pulled away from Zane and started to put my clothes on.

"Where you goin'? Don't leave like this," Zane said.

"I got to go, Zane, I can't stay here."

"I don't want you to leave like this. Stay here until the high wears off, please, ba'y," he pleaded, trying to sound firm but not being very convincing.

"No, Zane, I have to get home. I want to go home," I said, buttoning my pants and standing up.

I looked over at Zane and I noticed he still had tears in his eyes. I wished that I could turn back time for his sake as well as mine. But I had turned a corner, and there was no going back now. I kissed Zane on the cheek and left.

21

By the time I got home, I had halfway convinced myself that I was never going to do drugs again. I told myself that it was obvious I couldn't handle it and I didn't need to be doing anything crazy like that anyway. It scared me how I couldn't control the crave, how I had let it overpower my every thought like that. I was still scared, just thinking about it. I think what scared me most was in the back of my mind, even while I was trying to convince myself otherwise, I still wanted more.

Before I left his house, while Zane was crying that first time I tried rock cocaine, he had made me promise that I would never smoke with anyone else. He said he wished that I wouldn't smoke at all, but if I just had to try it again, or felt that I couldn't control the desire to have it, that I should call him. He told me that I wasn't ready for the street life and that I wouldn't be able to deal with it, that the wolves and snakes would eat me alive. And that shady people were coming out of the woodwork for the drug, and you never knew who you could trust. Zane said that he didn't want anything to happen to me.

That's what Zane had told me that first day. He had continued to educate me on the evils of street life every time we spoke after that.

One story that he felt I should know was about this couple who had been snorting coke for about ten years and decided they wanted to try freebasing, since a lot of their friends were trying it. Like Zane's friends had told him, the couple had heard that the high was supposedly way better than snorting, and it would intensify sexual feelings.

Zane said that Quin and some other dealers were at the house when the couple came by to get the hookup. Quin had even volunteered to rock it up for them so that they could try it right then and there before they left. The couple had agreed.

After Quin had cooked up the cocaine into a rock for them, he demonstrated how they should smoke it, first smoking some himself, and then holding the bowl for the couple. They loved the feeling so much that they started taking their clothes off at Quin's suggestion and began to freak each other right in front of Quin and his boys.

They didn't get far, because when the high wore off a few moments later, they didn't want sex. They wanted the hit. After the couple would get another hit, they would go back to freaking each other for a few seconds while the group watched. It wasn't long before the couple had gone through all of the cocaine they had bought, and bought some more. They kept buying until they had spent all their money.

Quin told them that there was a way the two of them could get him to give them more dope without money. Quin told them that if they agreed to perform sex on each other and whomever else he designated, he would make sure that they could get high as long as they wanted without paying him a dime.

The couple didn't even think twice about what Quin was asking them to do, they eagerly agreed. Then Quin told them that if they didn't perform as they were told he would not only keep the drugs, he would kick their asses like they had never been kicked before for wasting his time.

The couple was still agreeable, thinking there was nothing

they wouldn't do to each other or with one or two of the guys, too, if that's what Quin wanted; they were down for the orgy. So with Quin directing, the couple performed every and any sex act you could think of on each other and with Quin and his friends. The husband even watched as Quin and his friends ran a train on his wife, with every orifice filled with one of the men.

When Quin and his friends were totally sated, Quin had another idea. He brought out some more cocaine rocks and set them on the table. The couple had begun to get dressed when Quin told them not to bother. As they sat naked beside Quin, he gave them each a small piece of a rock to smoke in the pipe, when that was gone and Quin was sure that the crave was on maximum overdrive in the couple's head, he made one last suggestion.

He whispered to one of his friends who left the room. Then he told the couple, "There ain't but one more thang standin' between you and all the base you can handle." Quin's friend had come back and was holding a video camera and a leash with a big German shepherd attached to it.

As Quin's friend positioned himself with the camera. Quin told the couple, "Now, I got what y'all need. All you gotta do is serve up my dog Rocky, the same way you served me and my dudes. But if you leave anything out, your free high is canceled. Do I make myself clear?"

The couple gave each other a sick look, but neither of them objected, instead they went to the dog and began their task, as Quin's friend caught all the unspeakable things that they were doing to the dog and having the dog do to them on video.

After they had performed to Quin's satisfaction, he allowed them to get dressed, but to degrade them further, he gave them two small rocks that probably wouldn't last five minutes and kicked them out yelling after them, "You should be glad that I gave you that much 'cause the damn dog look better than that ugly ass troll bitch you call a wife. She wasn't really even worth *that* much!"

I knew that Zane was telling me horror stories to get me to forget any cravings that I might have for the drug. But it wasn't working, because I had already figured out a way that I could enjoy the drug without it taking me to the places that those other fools went to, spending their whole checks and getting their utilities disconnected and getting evicted and thrown out on the streets. I would be smarter than them all.

22

My plan was that when I got paid, I would go to Quin's house myself, without telling Zane. I wouldn't let him or anyone else know that I was planning on getting high again. The way I figured it, I would control the crave by controlling my money. I wouldn't bring my purse when I went, I would only take fifty dollars with me, Quin would "rock it up" for me and we would smoke it and I would go home.

I wasn't worried about Quin trying any of that crazy shit with me that he tried on that couple that Zane told me about. First of all, I would never let the crave take me there. If I got to craving that bad I would leave and sell my body on the street before I would let Quin and his boys have a sex show on me. Not that I would ever prostitute myself for the drug, either, but that's what I'd do before I'd be a freak show.

And in the second place, Quin knew that Zane would kill him if it ever got back to him that he had abused me like that. So I felt pretty safe going over to Quin's. What I didn't count on was Zane being there when I got there.

I saw his car in the driveway when I pulled up, so I drove down the street a little ways and parked. Damn! Why did his ass have to be over there? I replayed different scenarios in my head that I could present to Zane as a reason for my being over there. Nothing made sense, not even to me, so I knew Zane wouldn't buy any of it.

I knew that even though Zane and Quin had been friends since grade school, Zane didn't trust Quin. Even worse, Zane knew that I knew he felt that way, because he had told me this more than once, and he expected me to feel the same way about Quin, too. And in all honesty, I did.

I started up my car and drove away. Zane had probably saved me from a nightmare with Quin, and he would never know.

I wasn't ready to go home though, so I drove over to my cousin Dar's house, who lived right around the corner from Zane. I told myself that I was just going by to kill some time since I wasn't going home, but I knew that I was playing games with myself again.

Dar's real name was Dartanyan, and he was a street kid from the time he dropped from my aunt's womb. He was smooth at getting his way about things even when he was a little boy, tricking people, telling stories, or trading some no-good something that he made, making it seem like it was pure gold, to get some toy he wanted, or to get everyone to play the game he wanted, or even to get you to buy his favorite candy at the store with your own money!

He was just as slick and smooth as he got older, even more so. On the streets he rose from small-time hustler to deep pockets in no time flat. Everyone in the family knew that if you wanted to get the chronic, or anything else, Dar was the man.

But I pretended not to know that when I stopped by to see him that evening.

"Hey, what up, cuz?" he said when he opened the door and saw me standing there. He threw his arms around me and gave me a big hug.

"Aw, ain't nothin'!' I said back to him. "I just came by to see you since the person I went to see wasn't home. They just live around the corner from you," I explained, making sure to keep the person's gender vague in an attempt to curb my cousin's curiosity about things.

"Come on in, then, cuz. You know family ain't never gotta

have an excuse to drop by. I ain't doin' nothin', just chillin'. Dru and the kids is out of town vistin' her mother, so it's just me and you," he said, laughing as he ushered me into his living room.

Dar got me a beer and we chitchatted about nothing much. He entertained me with his adventures on the rough side, like the time he had to tighten up a would-be robber with his straight razor and his pistol.

"Yeah, cuz, this fool thought that he was gon' rob me with a damn claw hammer! That sonbitch drew that hammer back and I told him, 'You may hit me in my head with that hammer, ya no-gun-havin' muhfucka, but I bet I will either slice your throat with this razor or put a bullet between your eyes, or maybe even get yo' ass with both, before the lump on my head rise!'"

He had me cracking up. "So what happened, then? Did he try you?"

"The hell you think happened? Dumb chicken-ass muhfucka dropped the damn hammer and took off runnin'!"

We both fell out laughing.

I told him stories about my divorce and meeting Zane.

"Hey, ain't you still in church?" he asked me with raised eyebrows.

I felt a twinge of guilt when I replied, "Nah, not for a while. I been doing a little experimenting with some different things. You know, I went straight from Mom and Dad's house to Ian's house, and I was in church all the time we were married. And to tell you the truth, I was miserable! Not with church, but with Ian. You know he was a minister and he was all fake and stuff. And . . . I don't know, I'm just confused, you know?"

"Aw, itta be awright, cuz, don't think about that now," he said, patting me on my shoulder.

And for reasons I can't say, I just started talking to him about the drug and how I had tried it and how it made me feel.

"No shit?" my cousin said.

I was careful to leave out the part about who had turned me on to it. I made it seem like I was at a party or something and we just all tried it.

"Yeah, cuz, no shit. And you know I ain't never messed around with no drugs."

"Yeah, that's some pretty wild shit." Dar leaned back in his chair, looking me up and down, and I could tell he was trying to figure out where I was coming from. So I kept talking to try to change his focus. Everybody always said I was a good talker, said I could talk the smooth off silk.

"So anyway, I might as well tell you that I was going to get me some from . . . a friend . . . ," I stuttered a little because I almost slipped up and said Zane's friend. "But wasn't no one there, so I kept going." I held my breath waiting for my cousin's response. He could either get all big brother on me and lecture me about street life or we could party.

Dar stared at me for a beat before he spoke. "Aw, cuz, I got what you need."

I relaxed and stopped holding my breath, and my cousin was on his feet and walking into the next room. He threw the words over his shoulder. "Yeah, don't never go out by yourself looking for no drugs. You know you don't know nothin' 'bout no streets, and you liable to get yo'self killed out there," he said, echoing Zane's warnings to me.

He came back into the room with his bowl and other things that you needed to freebase. Some 151 rum, and a burner to melt the base into smoke. My cousin looked hard at me as he began setting things up. I could tell that he was still trying to figure out what, exactly, was up with me, gauging my reaction.

"Now, you sure you ain't hooked on this shit, right? I mean you ain't out here spending all your money and sellin' shit to get high, are you?" This freebasing thing was still so new, nobody could really see how deep it was going to get. Not even streetsmart young people like Dar.

I didn't want him to know how bad I was itching to try some

more, so instead of replying to his question right away, I stood up and did a pirouette, letting him take in how nicely I was dressed and how good my hair looked. I was glad that I had kept my hair appointment with my beautician.

"Do I look like I have a drug problem?" I asked with a big smile on my face, and I couldn't help thinking, *Not yet anyway.*

Dar just laughed and fixed up the bowl and held it for me. He lit it and I got a real rush almost immediately.

This time, I was better at holding the smoke in and let it out slowly instead of blowing it out in a rush. I heard the bells on my first hit.

Dar took a hit and then offered the bowl to me. I had that feeling of moving in slow motion again, but this time I waved the bowl away; the bells were still ringing and I was feeling so mellow I didn't need another blast right away.

"Damn, cuz, I wish I could feel what you feelin' right about now. You look like Scotty has beamed you all the way up!" he said, laughing.

I still couldn't talk, or didn't want to. I just wanted to chill with the buzz I had. I was feeling like I didn't have a worry in the world and not worrying about anything felt good for a change.

23

"What the hell were you doin' drivin' down Quin's street last night, hunh? Didn't I tell you not to fuck around with him by yourself? I told you that fool is crazy! And where the fuck you been? I been callin' your ass all damn night!"

Damn! Zane had seen me anyway, even though I had driven off as soon as I saw his car. He must have been in it when I pulled up.

"Look, don't quiz me!" I said. "I don't have to—"

"Quiz you? Quiz you, hunh?" Zane said cutting me off before I could finish my sentence.

"I'll be over there in fifteen minutes and you better have a damn good explanation, do you understand?"

I could tell Zane was mad. No—he was furious. I didn't feel like arguing. I hadn't left Dar's house until the crack of dawn.

"I hear you," I mumbled.

"No, I asked you, Do you understand me?"

My face flushed hot, he was talking to me like I was his child, and worse than that, I was feeling like a bad kid in need of chastisement.

I mumbled something into the receiver and hung up. I didn't have time to deal with Zane's drama, I had some drama of my own to consider. I was dead tired though, and right then, all I wanted to do was go to sleep.

There wasn't a scrap of food in the house and Ian would be bringing the kids home tomorrow. I had to get some rest so I could go to the grocery store and get some food for the kids. I would worry about thinking up something to tell Zane when he got here.

I don't know how long I slept. But I know I had the flower dream again, only this time when I got to the part where I wanted Zane to help me out of the mud, he reached for me with one hand and held the base bowl in the other. When our hands touched, Zane lost his footing and slipped, the next thing we knew he was in the mud even deeper than I was. . . .

I heard the doorbell ringing and woke up abruptly. I know I must have been sleeping good, because I had slobbered on the pillow. I reached up and wiped the wetness off my face with my hand as I rose from the bed to answer the door.

Zane was standing on the other side and when I opened the door, he walked right in and brushed by me without saying "hello." He sat down on the sofa and told me to come and sit down beside him.

"Samai, I don't want to scold you, and I don't want to argue, either. I just want you to tell me the truth. Please don't lie to me. What were you doin' on Quin's street last night?"

I glanced over at Zane and then down at my feet.

"Un-unh, look at me, I want to see your eyes when you gimme your answer," he said.

I couldn't look at him and I felt the tears well up in my eyes. Why couldn't I get a grip? What was wrong with me? Hot tears trickled from my eyes.

"You were goin' to ask him for the base, weren't you? Even after me warning you about that muhfucka. Are you that dense that you don't know danger when all the signs are lit up and flashing? Haven't I been tellin' you not to go out lookin' for that shit? What is your problem?"

I couldn't stand hearing about myself. I didn't want to face the truth. I wasn't ready. I got up and ran into the bathroom, locking the door.

"Leave me alone, Zane! Just leave me alone . . . please!" I said through the locked door.

Zane had come after me and was knocking on the bathroom door.

"Samai, Samai, come on out and let's talk. It doesn't have to be this way. Please ba'y, let's talk," I heard Zane saying through the door. I had my back to it and tears were running down my face. I didn't even bother to wipe them away. I slid down the bathroom door until I was sitting on the floor and covered my ears trying to block out Zane's voice.

"No! Just go home, Zane. Leave me alone," was all I kept saying. I guess Zane must have finally understood that I didn't want him there, 'cause after a while, all I heard was quiet.

24

I didn't see Zane for a while after that. I guess a month or so went by. I was good at lying to myself about things, and being addicted was just another one of those things. I fooled myself into thinking that I was fine, that I wasn't like those people in the streets chasing a high.

I never missed work chasing the drug, I was paying all my bills, and my kids had food to eat. I only got high on the weekends they weren't home, so they didn't know. Or so I thought. I was on top of things, I was controlling the craving, it wasn't controlling me.

I got up one morning to get dressed for work, and started to put on my favorite jeans. They went on much too easily, and when I put on the belt that I usually wore with them, I pulled it to the last notch and it still wasn't tight enough. I picked up a pair of scissors to make a new notch.

When I reached for the scissors that were inside my dresser drawer, I got a glimpse of myself in the mirror. I did a double take. Damn! Was that skinny person staring back at me really *me*? I moved the scissors in my hand to see if the reflection I was looking at would do the same. Of course it did. I dropped the scissors on top of the dresser and moved in closer to really take a look at myself.

I looked as if I were wearing clothes that were bought for someone else. I was lost in the jeans that only a month or so before had fit me perfectly. They were a perfect size ten, but they may as well have been size fourteen, the way they hung on me now.

How had—*when* had I lost all of this weight? I knew that doing the cocaine cut your appetite and that it made you feel like not eating anything, but I thought I was being careful about that. I thought that I had made myself eat something during my weekend binges. Looking at myself, I wondered how many times I had forgotten to eat. Who was I fooling?

People around me had commented that I was losing weight, but they attributed it to the fact that I was newly divorced. They said that no matter how much you thought you wanted to get divorced, something inside you, whether you admitted it to yourself or not, felt like you had failed at something, that it was something you had done wrong that caused the divorce. That resulted in a lightweight depression, and most of the time, it was the depression that made you drop the pounds. Hey, if that's what people wanted to think was causing me to lose weight, let them think it.

I went through a few outfits in my closet before I found one that fit OK. Then, I went downstairs to fix the kids some breakfast before I dropped them off at my cousin's daycare center that she ran out of her house.

Devon was the first one downstairs to the breakfast table as usual. Still sleepy, he shuffled over to me, gave me a Devon kiss and threw his arms around my neck when I bent down.

"Morning, Mom. I love you," he said, before taking a seat at the table.

It was funny how everything brought tears to my eyes lately. I blinked them back quickly because I didn't want Devon to see them. He wouldn't understand and would ask me a million questions that I couldn't answer.

"I love you, too, son," I told him, willing my voice to sound happy.

"What's for breakfast?" he asked.

"Well, do you want cereal, or bacon and eggs and toast?"

"Bacon an' eggs an' toast, Mom!" he said giving me a smile and perking up.

It wasn't long before the smell of bacon cooking brought E downstairs. He loved food, all kinds. He never complained about anything I made for any meal, as long as there was a lot of it.

"Morning, Ma," he greeted me, rubbing the sleep from his eyes.

"Morning, sleepyhead," I said from the stove without turning around.

Jadyn followed soon after, already dressed and ready for school, holding the cordless phone to her ear.

"Yeah, Viki," she was saying into the receiver, "I'm leavin' out now! My hair? Oh you know, same ol' same ol'. You leavin'? Yeah, meet me at the corner in two seconds. Two seconds, Viki! I ain't playin', don't have me out there waitin' like you usually do!" She giggled. "I'll tell you when I see you, my mom is all in my conversation!" She gave me a look and I flicked the dish towel at her.

Jadyn grabbed a piece of bread and slapped a couple of pieces of bacon on top before folding the bread over and biting into it as she opened the door. "See ya later, Ma!" she said and was gone.

I dropped the boys off at the sitter and headed for work. I didn't like being late and most of the time I would get there early. I never missed work and I was doing pretty good saving a little money. And with the child support that Ian was giving me every week, I had managed to have a little cushion against hard times.

The day was uneventful, and went by pretty quickly. Right before we were closing for the day, a woman in a minister's collar and her husband, who was dressed the same way, walked up to the sign-in window.

All the managers and supervisors had left for the day. Only a coworker and myself were there to sign in the last patients of the day and lock up.

My coworker was busy putting away charts so that we could

leave as soon as the doors were locked, so I went to the window to see what the woman wanted.

"Hi, can I help you?" I asked in my normal cheery professional tone.

"Yes, hi, honey. Me and my husband need to have these physicals done. See we are going to be foster parents and the state requires us to do this. Can you tell me what the price of this will be?" she said all in one breath.

I asked her the usual question. "Have you or your husband ever been here before, ma'am?"

She pushed the physical papers through the little hole in the window, and I looked them over as she spoke.

"No, honey, this is our first time here," she said pleasantly.

She appeared nice enough, though she was really, really overweight. She was very light-skinned and had her hair pulled back from her face in a tight ponytail. Her husband was the opposite of her, skinny and dark-skinned. He stood quietly behind his wife, not saying a word.

"Well, ma'am, the office call is thirty-five dollars and since you and your husband are both seeing the doctor, I can charge your husband a limited fee of fifteen dollars and that wouldn't include whatever charges would result from the physical. The fee for that would be determined by how extensive the physical is," I explained.

The woman's entire demeanor changed from pleasantly sweet to that of a shrew immediately.

"What? Now when I called up here earlier ta-day somebody told me that a physical was only seven dollars and me and my husband done drove way over here from the west side in all of that traffic! I'm not payin' all that money!"

I listened patiently as the woman ranted on and on.

"Ma'am, I'm sorry that someone misquoted you. The only physicals that are seven dollars are the sports physicals that we give to kids eighteen years old and under for sports at school and for Little League. What I can do, ma'am, is I can let you and your husband see the doctor today, and I can hold the physical papers here until my supervisor comes in tomorrow morning and you can speak with her and explain what happened and she might be able to help you with the charges, but I am not authorized to do that—"

The "minister" cut me off in mid-sentence.

"I'm not comin' all the way back up here! This is crazy! Why would someone quote me one thang and then when I get up here it's a whole 'nother thang! I can't believe this!" she went on and on and I listened to her without saying anything.

After a couple of minutes of her tirade, she looked innocently at me.

"I'm sorry, honey, I don't mean to take it out on you. I know it's not your fault. What is your name, baby?"

I had no problem giving her my name and apologized to her again. She asked for her papers back and left.

My coworker and I exchanged looks that said, "Where in the hell did she come from?" We laughed and proceeded to carry out our end-of-day procedures and to lock up the medical center.

When I got home that evening I went through the bills that I needed to pay that month. Thank the Lord that the judge had ordered Ian to keep health benefits on our children; Devon seemed to be accident prone. He was always breaking some bone while riding his bike or bouncing up and down on the bed. Most of the time though, he somehow managed to land on his head. Working at the medical center allowed me to get most of the children's medical needs taken care of for free, but I needed Ian's insurance to cover the extra medical expenses. Like the time Devon had hit his head and gotten a concussion, he had to be hospitalized overnight for observation.

The doctor had told me that if Devon hit his head one more time, they might have to put one of those protective helmets on his head. I hoped the doctor wasn't serious.

I got out the checkbook and started writing out payments on the various bills. I wrote out a total of $756 worth of checks. That included my rent, utility bills, and groceries. So much for the check from this payday. That was all of it and then some!

I took a bath and went to bed. As I closed my eyes, I was feeling pretty good. I hadn't spent any money on getting high for a few weeks so I was happy about that, too.

25

The day seemed like any other as I drove to my job; I got there a little early as usual. I was putting the patient sign-in sheet in the window, when my supervisor approached me. I should have known something was wrong by the way she refused to look me in the eye when she addressed me.

"Samai, Fran would like to see you in her office," Augusta said, not really facing me as she walked past.

I was not uneasy in the least. I thought that because I had been working so hard at my job, making suggestions to improve things for the patients, that maybe Fran was going to address the need for my long overdue raise. I felt I more than deserved one and hoped that Fran did too.

"Did she say what it is regarding?" I asked Augusta half-jokingly. My supervisor didn't even break a smile, which was unusual for her. She was ready to laugh at even unfunny jokes. She seemed to be busy doing nothing, picking up charts, stacking and unstacking the same ones and reaching up to carefully scratch her Jheri-curled head with one finger, so as not to get the Jheri curl juice on her hands. I shook my head and finished getting the window ready for patient sign-up and headed to Fran's office.

I knocked on her closed door and she told me to come in.

"Good morning, Fran," I greeted her, trying not to appear anxious or nervous.

"Good morning, Samai," she said. "Close the door and have a seat, please."

She didn't look at me, either. All of a sudden, I knew that whatever Fran wanted to discuss didn't have anything to do with putting more money into my pockets. She leaned over her desk, extending what appeared to be a letter toward me.

"Here, read this," she said and sat back in her chair.

I took the letter and began to read. The first thing I noticed was that it was written on church stationery. "Refuge Pentecostal Church" was printed beneath a black-and-white image of a church.

Dear Dr. Wallace,

I'm not one to cause trouble, but I just had to write this letter and let you know about one of your employees.

First, let me start off saying that both me and my husband are ministers. The Good Lord put it on our hearts to help some of the poor children whose parents are full of the devil and take it out on their own flesh and blood. God spoke to me and said that I should step in. He told me to stand in the gap and be a light in darkness and help as many of those little angels as me and my husband can. So we are going to become foster parents.

Well, doctor, in order for us to be used by God in this way, the foster agency told us we have to get physicals, to make sure that my husband and me are in shape and capable of caring for the little darlings that the Lord is going to send us. Well, that's when I called and spoke with Samai Collins and asked her how much it would cost for me and my husband to have our physicals there, and she told me seven dollars. So I told her I would be right over. She seemed so sweet . . . over the phone that is.

But when I got to your fine clinic, that girl changed into the Incredible Hulk. She told me in a very, very nasty voice that I had my facts wrong and that she hadn't spoken to anybody on the phone.

Miss Collins was rude and inflexible at every turn and absolutely did NOT help me or my husband with getting our physicals done.

Frankly, doctor, I was surprised that you would have someone like her working at your fine clinic. It left a very bad taste in my mouth. Lord knows the world is bad enough without people going out of their way to make good people like me and my husband feel bad. And you know, the Bible says: "Touch not mine anointed and do my prophets no harm." I think that would apply to me and my husband. I want you to know that neither my husband nor myself hold you at all responsible for this unfortunate experience with that young woman with the nasty attitude.

Sincerely,
Ministers Harriet and Eddystone Golden

I suddenly got a sick feeling in my stomach. This was the woman who had come in last week at the end of the day with her husband. I remembered that they both had on minister's collars. I couldn't even begin to imagine why she would go through the trouble of concocting such a vicious letter that was nothing but lies. Silly lies at that.

I finished the letter and smiled as I thought about the part about me acting like the "Incredible Hulk." Anyone who knew me would laugh at this woman's foolishness. I was always courteous and professional to everyone, and never had I behaved otherwise at my job. No way would anyone believe this crap. I looked up at Fran, still smiling.

"Oh, I remember this lady, she came in with her husband and wanted a physical, she said that someone had told her that it was seven dollars and—"

Fran cut me off, not allowing me to tell my version of the story.

"Samai, you know Dr. Wallace values his patients a great deal, and he would never put up with anyone working here and having this type of letter written about them."

My heart started thumping so hard against my chest, I was sure that Fran could hear it.

"What are you saying, Fran, don't you want to hear my side of the story?"

"The letter is written on church stationery. I doubt if anyone would bother to write lies on church stationery," Fran said with her thin lips in a tight line, her eyes finally meeting mine.

"Aren't you even going to talk to the girl who worked with me that evening? She can tell you that this woman is lying!" I said and I could hear the panic in my voice.

Fran just shook her head.

"That won't be necessary. We are going to have to let you go. Give me your badge. We will mail your check to you."

And just like that I was unemployed.

I sat there for a moment and stared at her in shock and disbelief. My mind was racing. Part of me wanted to reach over that desk and punch Fran dead in her smug white, pasty face! I stood up, unable to speak, and slowly laid down my badge on Fran's desk. I turned and walked out of her office certain that the only way Fran could tell how upset I was, was by how hard I slammed her door.

I walked past my ex-coworkers. Some of them asked me what was wrong. Others looked amused. I said nothing, I just grabbed my purse and walked out of the clinic.

I got into my car and drove away. I drove until I got to a nearby park and pulled into the lot. I had barely gotten the car into park before I burst into tears. What was I going to do? How was I going to feed and clothe three children, pay my rent and all my other bills without a job? That little bit of money that I had saved wouldn't go far once I paid my rent and utilities a few times. What was I going to do? I felt my world spinning out of control and I was helpless to do anything about it. I couldn't take this. Why was life so unfair? A million thoughts raced through my mind.

I thought about going up to that so-called minister's church on

Sunday and taking all three of my kids with me. I wanted her to see firsthand how her lies had cost me my job and who would be affected most by them.

I wanted her whole congregation to know that because she had lied in the name of Jesus I was out of a job. Just because she had chosen to write her lies on "church stationery." Like God would strike you dead or something if you wrote anything but the truth on a piece of church paper. I wanted to go, and would have. The only reason I didn't is that when I had asked Fran for a copy of the letter, she had refused, stating that it was the property of the company and she didn't have to give me anything. So I couldn't remember the address of the church. There had to be a million Refuge Pentecostal Churches in this city.

Anyway, even if I did find the right church, who was to say that the church would believe me over one of its own? I was sinking lower and lower into despair. I didn't know which way to turn. How was I going to tell my children that I no longer had a job?

I spotted a payphone not far from me, I pulled over to it and called Zane.

He was at work but when he heard how upset I was he promised to meet me at his house right away. I didn't even try to lie to myself this time. When I met Zane, I would make sure that he got the base for me.

26

As I was walking out of the clinic, my supervisor had handed me a note. I had laid it on the passenger side seat of my car when I had gotten in. I picked it up and read it now.

"Your son Devon's school called, he is ill and they want you to pick him up," the note said. I put the car in gear and went to get him.

Devon really didn't seem sick to me when he got into the car. I felt his forehead and he didn't feel warm at all. I had him open his mouth and say "ahhhh" so that I could see the back of his throat. That looked OK, too.

"What's hurting you, Devon?" I asked him, feeling his forehead again.

"I don't know, Mom, I just don't feel good," he said as he laid his head back on the car seat. "I just feel funny inside myself," Devon said, trying to convey his feelings to me in his cute little-boy way.

"OK. Mommy has to make a stop first," I told him. "And then we'll go home to see if we can find something to make you feel better." I tickled him, making him giggle.

When I got to Zane's house, I told Devon to stay in the car and to keep the door locked and that I would be right back.

"OK, Mom, but hurry up. I'm sick," he whined. I told him again that I would be right back. I would have taken him in with me, but I didn't want to take a chance that he would be his normal curious little-boy self and wander down to the basement where Zane and I would be doing our thing. I didn't want him to see me getting high. I planned to get a few hits, forget my problems for a minute and then leave. Zane knew what I wanted before I even told him. He had made a stop on his way home, and had everything ready when I got there.

It was really good stuff and after my first hit I went to another world, I didn't care about anything, not even my sick little boy who sat in the car waiting for his mommy to come and take him home.

A couple of hours later, Zane's brother came by. He yelled downstairs that someone had left a little boy in a car and that he was crying. Zane turned to me.

"You brought your son with you and you left him in the car all this time?"

He glared at me in disbelief. I looked at my watch. It hadn't seemed like hours had passed since I first walked in.

"Hey, Damon, can you go get him, man? That's Samai's little boy!" Zane yelled back upstairs.

"What? I don't believe this shit! You mean you assholes are so busy getting high, you left that little boy by himself?"

"He's all right, he's a big boy. He ain't scared of nothing," I said, trying to draw the last wisp of high out of the empty bowl.

I heard Devon come through the door asking for me, so I pulled myself away from the crave, and as I started up the steps, I saw Devon run back up the few steps he had come down. I had taken another hit before I started up the steps and I wondered just how much Devon had seen. He wasn't looking too happy when I reached the top of the stairs.

I reached for him and he snatched his arm away. That stung.

"Come on, son, let's go," I said to him.

"You left me, Ma!" he yelled at me, crying again. "Why did you leave me for a long time?" he asked, and then he stomped off and slammed the door without waiting for an answer.

I caught up with him in the car. He was staring out of the window on his side, refusing to look my way. I reached out to him, but withdrew my hand before I actually touched him. I started to speak, but what was there to say, really?

"Mommy is sorry, son," I said. "I will *never* do that to you again. I won't ever leave you alone again."

Devon didn't answer me and he didn't look at me; as the tears continued to stream down his face, he just kept his little face turned toward the window all the way home.

27

I was getting high more often and I was falling behind in my bills. The savings I had been so proud of a few months ago quickly dwindled down to zero between rent and utilities, buying food, and getting high.

It didn't seem like I had gone through $4,000 in such a short time. I kept telling myself that I was going to pay my rent ahead for six or seven months and split another $600 on the utilities to tide myself over until I could land another job, but each time I would take the money out of the bank to do it, I would end up running over to Zane's house to get him to rock up some powder for us to smoke. Zane couldn't fool himself or me any longer; he was just as hooked as I was.

He had stopped threatening me and telling me horror stories about life in the streets, and he was no longer telling me that I needed to pay bills instead of getting high. Now I didn't even have to threaten to go out in the streets and find some drugs if he didn't get them for me. I knew that when I brought him the money, he would be more than happy to go and get some so that we both could get high.

After a while, I gave up trying to pay the bills at all. One of my neighbors saw the electric company come out and turn the power off one day and came over to talk to me.

"Samai, how thangs goin', sweetheart?" Virgil asked as I opened the door and he stepped into my living room.

"What's up, Virgil? How is your little girl doing?" I asked, trying to make small talk.

"Look, Samai, I ain't goin' to beat around the bush. I know how it is. A single woman like yourself out here trying to do your best to feed and clothe your kids and keep a roof over y'all's heads and thangs," Virgil said. "I hope I don't scare you by saying that I been watching you. I don't mean like a stalker or anything. I meant, watching out for you, you know. I noticed that you don't really have a man over here or anythang , so I just been lookin' out for you that way, you know, to make sure you and the kids is OK and none of these crazy idiots out here that think it's fun to hurt women and kids and try to pick y'all out for target practice, you know?"

Virgil was standing by the door with his thumbs hooked in the belt loops of his jeans, and seemed to be having a hard time putting what he wanted to say into words.

"Anyways, I hope what I'm about to say don't offend you." Virgil hesitated, glanced down at his boots briefly, and cleared his throat before he continued. I hadn't said anything up to this point and I felt like I should say something to put him at ease since he appeared to be struggling with whatever it was he was trying to say.

He had been nice to me ever since I had moved into the neighborhood. Virgil was married and he and his wife had a little girl. I knew that he was a good family man, because he was always taking his little girl for walks around the neighborhood, and whenever he cut his grass, he would come over and cut mine, too, without me even asking him. And he never would take any money for it. I appreciated his kindness because it seemed genuine. I mean, he never tried to get me to go to bed with him, or even tried to flirt or anything. Virgil worked long hours as a firefighter and I knew he could've been catching up on some serious Zs instead of taking care of my lawn.

So I said, "It's OK, you haven't offended me, so far. Just say what's on your mind."

"Well, I don't really know how to tell you this, but let me just say that I don't have much money, my wife and I are strugglin' right now with payin' our bills since she lost her job. But if I could, I would offer you some money . . ." He paused for a moment. "What I'm tryin' to say is, I used to work for the power company, and I saw them cut your power off a little while ago, and I can show you how to turn it back on. I mean . . . I don't want you and the kids to be sittin' over here in the dark or anything . . . I mean . . . if you don't want to do it, I can do it for you and you can just watch me . . ."

I reached out and touched his arm. "Thank you," was all I said and followed him into the backyard.

He proceeded to show me how to remove the tag that the electric company had put on the meter and how to rehang it so that it looked as though it had not been tampered with. The meter itself pulled out completely and had two prongs that fit into a socket. "All you have to do," he explained, "is to take off these plastic boots from the prongs and plug it back in and you got power," Virgil finished, sliding the meter into the plug.

"Just in case you have problems with your gas bill . . ." He then went on to show me how the gas company would disconnect the power and how to turn it back on if that should happen.

"I know this may not be right, and you can't do it for very long. You have to pay your bill before it's time for them to come out and read it again, or the next time they'll put a stronger lock on it instead of just tagging it. And then we'll have to find a bolt cutter."

We both laughed before he said, "Poor people have to stick together and share hardships, right? The way I look at it, it's not really stealin' 'cause we eventually goin' to pay the bill. We just buyin' ourselves more time, right?"

"Right!" I agreed, and shook his hand. I held on to it a little longer than I should have and tears welled up in my eyes. Virgil pulled me to him and gave me a hug.

"Don't feel bad about this, sis, it'll be OK. You'll be OK," he said, and let me go before he quickly walked back across the street. That would be our last conversation.

Two weeks later, Virgil came home from work early and when he caught his wife screwing another man, a fellow firefighter at that, he snapped and got his gun. His wife had run next door to a neighbor's house, butt naked. Her lover had managed to get his pants on, and had walked barefoot to his car.

He had just got the engine running when Virgil came out of his house with the gun. He told the man in the car if he ever saw him around his wife again, he would kill him. The man looked at him and said, "Yeah right." Those were the last words he ever uttered, because my neighbor blew the man's brains out all over the car. I guess even nice guys have their limits.

Virgil got life in prison and they shipped him to another state. I never saw him again. But I never forgot him, either.

28

After missing a couple of payments, my landlord found out that I no longer had a job and gave me thirty days to get out of Dodge. I took the kids and went to my mom's for the weekend. I didn't tell her that I had lost my job and was being evicted, I just told her we wanted to spend some time with her.

After I put the kids to bed, I decided to drive around to Zane's to see what was up with him. He and a couple of his friends were getting high, just like I figured. My child support check had come a couple of days before, so I had a little bit of money. I was only going to spend about $100 on the drug, so I played it smart and only brought that amount with me and left the rest at my mom's.

One hundred dollars worth of cocaine seemed like a lot to me. It cooked up into two fat rocks, about the size of a fifty-cent piece if the coin had been round like a globe, instead of flat. I had been only putting a little crumb on the stem when I had first started smoking, now only six months later, I was filling the end with a big chunk. It hadn't taken me long to become a pro at smoking, holding the smoke inside my lungs a few beats, before blowing it out of my nostrils, not out of my mouth as I had when I was a novice. Blowing it out of your nose gave you maximum rush, I guess because your nose is closer to your brain than your mouth or some shit like that. Anyhow, with the rocks that Zane and his friends had cooked up, we had enough to last us for a few hours anyway.

A few hours somehow turned into a whole weekend. I don't know how the hours had melted into days. Zane's friends kept putting up money for more drugs, as long as Zane would let them keep coming back to his house to smoke. I guess they didn't feel like they could go home to their wives, they had already fucked up the rent money, now I guess they were onto food and utilities.

I didn't even think about the fact that I should call my mother and find out if the kids were OK and if she was all right keeping them. I wasn't *not* calling her on purpose. Calling her just never entered my mind.

By the time Sunday morning rolled around, I was feeling way down and hopeless. This was the first time I had spent an entire weekend smoking dope, and the first time I had gotten high when Ian didn't have the kids. I started going over the excuses that I could give to my mother for being away for an entire day and night without even calling. I knew that she would be worried. My mom was a natural worrier even when she didn't have a reason to do it. And when you gave her even an inkling of a reason to be anxious about anything, her worrying kicked into high gear. I knew that it must have been revving up to maximum overdrive right about now. I sat there replaying my story in my head before finally picking up the phone and calling her. She picked up the phone on the first ring.

"Mama—" I began. As soon as she heard it was me, she cut me off.

"Samai, child, where in the world you been? You got the kids and everybody else worried to death about you. We didn't know if you was layin' somewhere hurt or, even worse, somewhere dead. Why did you do this? Where are you at?"

I listened to all that she had to say and swallowed hard before presenting my lie.

"I'm sorry, Mama, when I got to Zane's house, he was going out of town and I know I should have called you, and I know it was selfish and stupid of me, but I didn't want you to tell me you didn't feel like keepin' the kids so I just went ahead and left with him. We just got back a little while ago."

My mother listened without saying anything, until I had told her my entire story.

"I shoulda known that sorry, no good so-and-so was involved some kinda way. It ain't no sense in you lettin' that man drag you down like he been doin'. Any man that really care about you is gon' try to help you be the best you can be, not the other way 'round," she said, and it was almost as if she could see right through the lies that I was telling.

"OK, Mama, I'll be there to get the kids in a little while," I said.

"Make sure you do, Samai DeShay, make sure you do, these kids are worried sick!"

"I'll be there, Ma, tell them for me," I said.

"All right, but you better hurr' up." And then she added, "I don't know why in the world you can't do right to save your life! Aubrae wouldn'ta ever pulled a stunt like this."

There it was again. I was always messing up. My mother would never let me forget that I didn't measure up to my sisters. Especially perfect Aubrae, who had married well, as had my sister Denise. Aubrae had only gotten pregnant *after* she'd gotten married. My younger sister Lynn wasn't yet married, but was working on her master's degree. They were her "good girls." I was the only one of the girls that had brought my shame to my mother's door.

I swallowed the pain from her words, because this time they were well deserved. I was definitely being the family fuckup right about now.

"OK, Mama. I'm sorry. I'll talk to you in a little while," I told her before hanging up. But that was before Zane's friends came back with another rock.

They had also brought a woman with them. She was short, but heavyset, and very dark skinned. Her hair had been shaved off and shaped like a man would, close to her scalp. She wore no makeup and her eyes looked like two pieces of black ice set into her face.

We all sat around the kitchen table; the woman had brought her own freebasing bowl with her, Zane's friends shared a bowl, and Zane and I shared one.

He no longer held the bowl for me, or allowed me to get the first hit. He always lit up first now, and always kept the bowl for as long as he could before passing it to me. I was getting more than a little irritated by his attitude toward me lately.

I took the bowl as he handed it to me and got a real good blast. This was some pure cocaine that hadn't been cut much. I could tell by the way my heart started racing almost immediately and how strong the rush was. Zane could keep the bowl for now. I was enjoying my bell-ringing buzz.

At about the same time that I had taken my last hit, the woman had taken a huge one. The amount of smoke that she was blowing from her mouth and nostrils, all at once, gave her the appearance of a mad bull snorting before he attacked. She had her whole side of the table looking smoky when she got done.

"Damn," Zane whispered in my ear. "She musta put a whole rock on that stem."

I didn't get a chance to comment. I didn't even know if I was going to, because my buzz was so strong. The woman turned and focused on me, her eyes locking on to mine with an intense stare. The voice that came out of her mouth didn't sound anything like hers when she spoke directly to me.

"What are you doing here?" she questioned. "You are not one of us!"

That was too much for me, it scared me so bad, I fled upstairs. It was the first time that I had left a room with cocaine still on the table to be smoked. I had left the room so fast that Zane came after me, the bowl still in his hand.

"You awright, ba'y?" he asked when he caught up with me.

I was visibly shaken when I asked him, "Did you hear what that woman said to me?"

Zane put the bowl back to his lips and lit the stem with a lighter. He took a long hit before finally answering me.

"Nah, ba'y, what did she say?" he asked, choking back the base smoke so as not to allow any of it to escape between words and lessen his rush.

Then it dawned on me that Zane had left the room with our stash still on the table. It was an unspoken rule that you never left your rocks on the table with baseheads in the room.

If you did, your stash was sure to have some pieces missing, or even be missing altogether when you got back. But when I mentioned this to Zane, he just opened up the fist that held the bowl. In it were our cocaine rocks.

"You didn't think I was that stupid now, did you? The way you left the room I didn't think you was comin' back. What did that tramp say to you? Do I need to throw her ass out?"

I knew Zane would never understand even if I could manage to explain to him what she said or how she said it. And that I felt as if it wasn't her speaking to me at all, but that some dark demon from the underworld had spoken through her. I knew that if I had told him that, he would probably think I was crazy, so I didn't even try.

29

It was midnight on Monday morning before I finally got to my mom's to pick up the kids. I used the key that she had given me to let myself in. I eased the door open and held my breath, praying that she wouldn't be sitting in her favorite chair that faced the front door. I breathed a heavy sigh of relief when I saw that the chair was empty. I crept into the room where the boys were sleeping. I didn't see Jadyn, so I guessed that she was with her aunt Denise. I roused the boys.

"E, Devon," I whispered their names as quietly as I could and gave them each a shake. Devon roused first. "Hi, Ma, where you been?" he asked, his voice still full of sleep. "I'll tell you when we get home," I told him. E didn't say anything. He wasn't too happy about having to get up out of his nice warm bed and being forced to go out into the chilly night air.

In the car, I let E and Devon sit in the front seat with me, stretching the seatbelt across both of them to secure them against any unforeseen danger. I wouldn't be able to do that much longer. It was hard to believe how much both my sons had grown in just one year. Devon, who had climbed in first, let his head rest against my side. I drove with one hand and let the other rest on E's thigh, to reassure him that I wanted him there.

All the way home, I cursed myself for being such a no-good parent. About how I was letting my kids down by being so weak.

I swore for the hundredth time that I wasn't going to get high anymore. That I wouldn't ever leave my kids wondering where I was. I vowed to go out tomorrow and get some kind of job somewhere. I didn't care where. I had to find some way to keep a roof over my kids' heads and food on the table. But more important than that, I had to find a way to keep busy so that I wouldn't have time to go out and get high with Zane, my cousin, or anyone else. I had to do it for the kids' sake as well as my own.

30

It seemed as if everyone that I was around was getting high. And if they weren't, they were thinking about trying it. Everyone was talking about the base. Most of us didn't think of ourselves as addicts. Addicts were the ones who had lost everything they owned, their jobs, their nice clothes, their jewelry, and were living on the streets. Even the ones that had relatives who allowed them to stay with them so that they wouldn't be homeless, ended up being thrown out on the street anyway because they were robbing their families blind to get high.

I was almost as bad as the rest of those who we pronounced addicts. And I was sure that others in my circle were there, too. I had lost my job, I smoked up the child support money that I was getting, and I was about to be thrown out on the street. But I hadn't sold any of my belongings, and I wasn't stealing from anyone else. I was almost, by our own definition, an addict and I didn't know how long it would be before I fit the bill completely.

I needed help, but help wasn't coming. I didn't even remember how I got started down this road in the first place. I just wished that I would see a detour sign soon, and that it would show me how to get back on the right path.

. . .

Sex between Zane and me had become almost nonexistent. Our intentions when we would get together would be to make mad passionate love like we used to, but all that ever happened was that one of us would suggest we get high.

The high was changing. There was a new drug in town and its name was crack. It was cheaper and easier to get high on than buying powder and cooking it up into a rock. Crack was already in rock form when you bought it. An amateur trying to rock up cocaine could waste it if they didn't know what they were doing. Crack made all that unnecessary.

Crack was even more addictive than freebase cocaine. It was cut with some other chemical that made the rush more intense, but it was also more fleeting. The rush of crack was over before you had a chance to enjoy the feeling of utter pleasure that it brought. Because it was so cheap, more people could afford it at first. And because the rush was so swift and over so quickly, it made you chase the high even more, which made you spend more money, especially those of us who got started freebasing.

We were always trying to make crack ring our bells like the base had, but like the men at the fair with the hammer, no matter how hard you hit, you could never quite ring the bell. So we were locked into a vicious cycle chasing a high that we would never be able to capture.

It was cousin Dar who introduced me to the crack high. The crave that came along with it was somehow more all-consuming than it had been with the base. I don't know what was worse, the depression, or the feeling of worthlessness that I'm sure every addict has in sober moments, no matter how few and far between those sober moments become. The feeling of utter isolation and hopelessness was unbearable. But even that was not enough to keep the urge to get high at bay.

With the coming of crack, there was no shortage of people to get high with—cousins, brothers, and friends. I no longer needed

Zane to get the drugs for me. I didn't even need his basement to smoke it in. My cousin Lena lived next door to a crack house, so I could go there and get whatever I needed, whenever I needed it, as long as I had the money. Lena wasn't getting high on crack, but she did like to smoke weed. She was cool about letting me smoke crack in her basement, as long as I brought along a little something for her, too.

No one used the base bowl to smoke crack. You smoked crack out of a glass stem, packed with a piece of a kitchen scouring pad that everyone called "chore." It was short for the actual brand name of the kitchen scouring pad. You just packed one end of the glass stem with it to hold your crack and keep it from melting away before it turned to the vapor that you inhaled from the other end of the stem. This new high was even harder to resist than the base.

31

I had to move out of my house so I finally gave in and let Jadyn move in with Lee and Denise. Jadyn had kept after me to allow the move and I had finally given in after we fought about it.

"Mom, I don't know why you don't let me move in with Aunt Denise. You know the schools are better in Gahanna where she lives. The counselors are even better there. They help you keep focused on your work, and help you choose classes that will help you reach your goals for what you want to be later on in life, and stuff like that," Jadyn had said.

"I know, Jadyn, but that would mean you wouldn't be here with your brothers and me anymore. That's a big step, letting you leave our home. That's also giving someone else authority over you. I'm not sure that's such a good idea. Besides, we'd miss seeing you around," I told her.

"Come on, Mom. It's not like I'd be leaving the country! I won't even be leaving the city, so it's not like you guys can't see me when you want. Anyway, you don't spend that much time with us anymore anyway. So I don't see how you would miss me all like that," Jadyn said, flopping down on the sofa.

I didn't much like her tone, or her last comment.

"What did you say? What do you mean, you don't see how I would miss you all like that? And you need to watch your tone, missy," I said a bit sternly.

"Oh come on, Mom! You always sending us somewhere on the weekends. You don't never spend time with me or my brothers anymore, so stop pretending you do! It's like we're invisible to you or something! The only reason you really don't want me to go is you won't have a built-in babysitter anymore!" Jadyn blurted out.

I rose from my seat and walked over to where Jadyn was seated. "Now would be a real good time to remember who you are speaking to. You need to stop right there!"

But Jadyn either couldn't or wouldn't obey me. It was as if she had been wound too tightly and just broke or something.

"No, Mom, you're the one that needs to stop! You been acting like you don't even have any kids lately. You just want to spend every second with Zane now! I know what you're doing! I'm not stupid! Even Devon knows! He told me and E about how you left him in the car that time while you were in the basement with Zane. How could you do that, Mom? Hunh? You don't care about us! All you want to do is hang around with Zane gettin' high!"

That's when I slapped her. Hard.

"Don't you ever speak to me that way, do you understand? As long as you live in this house—"

"I hate you! I wish I was dead! That's why I want to get away from this place and away from you!"

I slapped her again, and she ran into her room, slamming the door. I started after her, but then caught myself. I sat down on the sofa and buried my head in my hands. Jadyn knew about the drugs. They all did. I hadn't been fooling anyone but myself. Deep down inside, I knew that Jadyn had spoken the truth.

It was shortly after that argument that I decided to let her move in with my sister and her husband. I was thinking that a little time away from me and my problems might be a good thing. And when I got my act together, I would try to work on mending our relationship.

Since I still hadn't found a job and didn't have much money,

I asked my brother Earl if I could move in with him, his wife, and three kids.

Their home was a small three-bedroom two-story with a finished basement. Although it was crowded, my brother didn't turn me away. I told him that I had to move because I had gotten fired, and couldn't find another job yet. That satisfied him and he didn't ask any questions.

He had his own demons to battle.

His wife Joi had a good job with the local phone company, and Earl had his job at an automobile plant, and from that, along with a fledgling cleaning company he had started, the two of them made a living that was more than comfortable.

But Earl had been bitten by the gambling bug. It was an addiction that was just as powerful as any drug and would take you down just as quickly, only Earl didn't see it that way. He would explode into a fit of anger if anyone confronted him about his gambling.

Since I wasn't working, I couldn't contribute much to the household financially, but I contributed in other ways, like cleaning the house and preparing all the meals. I had even started helping Earl clean the buildings at night without pay to help pay for room and board.

Leaving to get high was even easier living with Earl, because after the kids went to school, I had eight hours to roam the streets, and hook up with others who were getting high. I needed to get high. After about a month of living with my brother, I had begun to feel that it was a mistake, moving in with him in the first place. I had to get out of there.

Everything that went wrong at his house, every spill that happened, any dish that was broken, anything left dirty, he blamed on me and my kids, even though he had kids, too, and spilling and making messes is what kids do.

He came home from work one day and one of the kids had left a cookie on the carpet and he stepped on it, smashing it into the rug, and then he yelled, "Samai! What did I tell you about lettin' your kids eat cookies in the living room? Now the damn carpet is ruined!"

I didn't even bother to ask him how he knew it was my kids that had been eating the cookies in the living room.

Another time I had fallen asleep in the basement and left the TV on; when Earl got home that night he went off, waking me up.

"How many times I gotta tell you not to leave the TV on? You're wastin' my electricity! I don't have money to throw away!" he ranted.

"I was tired, Earl. I guess I must have dozed off," I tried to explain.

"Look, ain't no excuse! When you feel yourself gittin' sleepy, just turn it off!" he commanded as he started back up the steps.

I got up one morning after one of Earl's tirades, feeling like I needed to see Zane. I needed to be held and kissed and told that I was still worth something, even if it was just good sex. I was determined that today Zane and I were going to make love like we used to. No getting high.

After the kids had been sent to school, I cleaned the house from top to bottom, even putting each of the closets in order. I put in a load of the laundry for all of us, before I went and took a nice long bath and dressed in my prettiest underwear, and a nice jean dress. I did my hair and makeup and borrowed a pair of my sister-in-law's hoop earrings and a matching belt.

I called Zane and told him that I was coming over. I told him that I didn't want to get high or anything, I just needed to talk. He said cool and to come on over.

Just as I was about to walk out the door, Earl came home unexpectedly.

"Where you goin'?"

"No place special, just to see some friends," I said, starting to walk past him. He grabbed me by my arm and slung me back into the living room.

"You're not goin' nowhere," he said.

I looked at him like he had lost his mind.

"How are you gonna tell me that I can't go anywhere? Who do you think you are? The last I checked, you were my brother, *not* my daddy. You don't tell me what—"

I saw his hand coming toward me, but it was so quick, I didn't have a chance to duck. His open palm caught me full on the face and caught part of my right ear. I found no pleasure in hearing the bells ring this time as I fell to the floor. He was on me in seconds, dragging me up by my dress collar and slamming me onto the couch before slapping me again. He gripped the collar of my dress.

"You're not goin' nowhere! Don't you know that shit will kill you! Do you think I don't know what you doin'? I see how you losin' weight and how skinny you are! I know what you're doin' sneakin' out of here every day instead of looking for work and I'm not gon' let you kill yourself! I love you, do you hear? I love you!" He was shouting at the top of his lungs.

I was actually scared. Love? That's not what I felt from him. Who had taught my brother that hitting someone, yelling at them, and throwing them around was showing them love? If this was love I didn't want any part of it.

Tears of hurt, shame, and pain coursed down my face. I watched as the expression on my brother's face changed and I could tell he was sorry for what he'd just done to me.

"Aw, sis, I'm sorry, I'm so sorry . . . ," he said, wrapping his arms around me. "I didn't mean to hurt you . . . I just hate seein' you like this . . . if I ever get my hands on whoever . . ."

My brother released me, not finishing his last thought. He stormed out of the front door, slamming it behind him.

I sat there crying, needing to get away more than ever. He had ruined my dress, and I felt more worthless than ever. I stumbled over to the phone and called Zane.

"Zane," was all I got out before I broke down and cried on the phone.

I still held the receiver to my ear and I could hear Zane's voice. It sounded like the old Zane.

"Calm down, ba'y. What's wrong?"

After a few moments I managed to tell Zane the whole story.

"That muhfucka is crazier'n bat shit!" he said. "You need to move on over here and leave all that bullshit alone."

I thought about his offer, and the only thing that held me back was, as bad as my brother was making us feel, I knew that it would be even worse at Zane's place. Not that Zane would be abusive toward me, or the kids, I just didn't want to risk the kids seeing me get high, I had already come too close to that once before with Devon. Zane also let anyone and everyone come get high in his basement now, as long as they brought some dope along for the house, and I didn't want my kids' safety to be compromised by a situation like that.

I told Zane, "Thanks for thinking about us, but the boys have already had to change schools once, I don't want to put them through that again."

"Well, it might be better for 'em to change schools, than to see their mama mistreated," he said with a snort.

Neither of us said anything after Zane's last remark. After an uncomfortable silence, Zane spoke again.

"Come on over here and let's get naked and fuck our brains out!" he quipped and, though he couldn't see me, I managed to smile just a little.

"You are so silly," I said.

"I'm serious as a heart attack. Get your ass on over here and I'll show you how serious I am."

"OK, I'll be there," I said, glancing at the clock. It was already one o'clock and the kids would be getting out of school at three-thirty. "But I won't be able to stay very long."

"OK, ba'y, see you when you get here."

Zane was a man of his word and he left me more than satisfied. Neither of us had any money, and amazingly, no one came over to get high, so we spent the afternoon making love like we used to. I was happy to find that Zane hadn't lost his touch. Since we hadn't gotten high, I was also happy that I made it back home before the kids did.

32

I finally landed a job at a warehouse, tagging merchandise and putting it on hangers. The pay wasn't nearly as good as the job I had had at the medical center, but it was better than nothing.

I had also run into my old landlord. His name was Todd Wilkison and I had known from the moment he set eyes on me that he liked me. He was nice enough looking, for a white man, although he was a little short for my taste. He had pretty blue eyes and brownish, blond hair. But the thing that turned me off more than anything was that he had no lips.

White people have notoriously thin lips as a rule, but his were nonexistent; where lips should have been, there was not one hint of fullness, only a thin strip of flesh. It reminded me a lot of those television puppets, *The Muppets*. If you have ever seen them, you get what I mean.

When I saw him, Todd made sure I knew that his reason for evicting me had been nothing personal. He would've gladly allowed me to stay rent-free until I got myself another job, but his wife was the jealous type, and he didn't see how he could explain why he would do something like that for me.

"Samai, did you find another job yet? 'Cause if you have got another job, I have a house for rent right around the corner from here. We can go over there and look at it right now if you like. Now it's not nearly as nice as the one you were renting before, but it's not bad, either, and if you like it, I'm sure we could work some-thing out."

"OK, Todd," I said. I was more than a little anxious to get out of my brother's house. "Let's go and take a look at it."

"All right," Todd said. "You can ride with me, I'll bring you back to your car afterwards."

I agreed and got into his car. I wasn't worried about him trying to make me do anything I didn't want to do. I might not be able to beat him, but he was so short, I could scratch him up so bad, he would have had a lot of explaining to do to his wife. Anyway, he didn't seem like the type to try something like that.

The house was the kind that is built on a slab instead of hav-ing a basement and a foundation. It only had two bedrooms, which wasn't really a problem at the time, since Jadyn was still liv-ing with my sister and her husband. It was something I could live with, and it *would* get us out of my brother's house.

"Todd, you were right about one thing, it's not nearly as nice as my old house," I started to say, and Todd didn't do a good job of hiding his disappointment at his premature assumption that I wasn't going to take the house. "But, I do need a place to stay. So how much are you renting it for?" I finished. And he broke into a smile.

"Well, Samai, here's the thing, I normally rent this for $300 a month—"

"Three hundred a month!" I said, cutting him off in mid-sentence. "I was only paying $350 for the other place and it had three bedrooms and a huge fenced-in backyard and—"

"Hold on a minute," it was Todd's turn to cut me off, "I said that's what I would normally rent it for, but I told you that you and I could work something out." He hesitated before continuing, "Samai, you know that I'm attracted to you, I think you're very pretty and extremely sexy," he said, inching closer to me, "I have wanted you for a very long time."

"Look, Todd, I don't know about this . . ."

"Just let me taste you . . . I just want to taste you. I promise I won't ask you for anything else," he said, his voice growing husky with desire.

I contemplated his proposition. "If I did let you do . . . that, how much would the rent be?"

Todd stepped to me and pressed his no lips against mine. He hadn't shaved and the stubble on his face, surprisingly coarse, irritated my face.

"Whatever you could afford," he offered. "I'll eat the rest." I couldn't help snickering. I don't think he realized what he had just said.

"I'm sure you will."

We both sat on the floor, and Todd was so anxious to put his lips on me, I could see his erection through his pants. In his case, it didn't look like what they said about white men was true. He appeared to have a pretty nice boner.

He tugged at my legs, so that I was forced to lie back, and slipped his hands into the waistband of my panties, sliding them down my thighs. I could feel his breath hot on my thighs as he kissed and stroked my inner legs. I felt his hand part my lower lips as he inserted a finger. It felt like he was pressing on my clit from the backside, forcing the tip to poke out. As soon as he did that, I felt his lips glide over it and an involuntary shudder went through my body.

He did things with his tongue that I never thought possible, all the while working his finger inside me, keeping my jewel fully exposed. He took it into his mouth, and rolled it between his teeth, licking and sucking all at once. Damn! I thought, leaning back and letting my body fully relax and enjoy the sensations of utter pleasure under his expert tongue-lashing. I guess this part about what they say about white men is true. They are some expert clit ticklers. . . .

33

I moved into the house about two weeks later paying $250 per month for the rent when I had it, and whatever I could afford when I didn't. Todd was as good as his word and was eating the rest, and me, on a regular basis.

I thought that he would want to go beyond the oral sex thing with me, but he never did, although he did start jacking off as he went down on me. If I was in a good mood, I would even give him a few jerks right before he climaxed. Once, right before he came over, I hid a small tape recorder under the bed and recorded him asking if he could lick me. I thought it would be smart to have a little insurance, so I saved it just in case he wanted to try to blackmail me into something I didn't want to do. If he did, I would flip the script on his ass.

I had worked my new job for about a month, and had gone the entire month without getting high. I stayed away from Zane's house, and only saw him a couple of times during that month. He would always come to my house and he knew not to bring any dope around my kids. I was so happy to have my own place again, I guess I didn't want to jeopardize it and end up being on the streets again.

I was doing fine until I hooked up with an old friend of mine. His name was Doobie Long.

Doobie was not his nickname; it was the name his mother had given him at birth. Doobie and I knew each other from the neighborhood we grew up in, on the west side of town. It was known to everyone as the "Hilltop." There weren't any hills that I knew of in our neighborhood, and it certainly wasn't built on a hill, so no one really knew how it got its name.

Doobie and I got close because once when we were younger, a dog got loose and had me cornered on the playground. He had risked getting bitten or worse, by chasing the dog off with his umbrella. I never forgot that. Doobie had given me my first French kiss when we were older, too. I never forgot that kiss, either.

I let my cousin Phyl talk me into going out to a club with her one Friday night, to have a drink or two to celebrate her birthday, and Doobie was there. We saw each other at about the same time and he walked over to me with a beer in his hand and asked me to dance.

He was still tall and skinny, and he still had that thousand-watt smile that lit up his whole face. We couldn't really hear each other talk, 'cause the music was so loud, but after that first dance, Doobie just kept coming back for more. I left early, because I was already tired from the long day at work, and doing all that dancing had put the nail in the coffin. I was dead tired.

As I was getting into my car, Doobie drove up in his truck and honked his horn. I guess it was just my time to keep running into old loves, puppy loves, and woulda coulda shoulda been loves.

"Hey, Samai!" he called, pulling his truck up alongside my car.

"Doobie! How did you know I was leaving?" I asked as he got out of his truck and walked over to me. I was still sitting in my car as he walked up.

"Now I know you gon' get out of that car and give me a good night hug," he said, and without waiting for my response, he grabbed the door handle and opened it for me. I got out and he gave me a bear hug, lifting me off my feet and swinging me around a couple of times.

"That music was so loud in there, I didn't really get a chance to talk to you like I wanted to. I made sure I was watching you so I could get with you before you left. I thought we oughta catch up on old times. So what's been up witcha?" he asked, still flashing his smile.

In my head I answered him, *Oh, nothing other than fucking up my life smoking dope, not going to church, and shit like that!* But out loud I said, "Well, I'm divorced and I have three kids that I'm pretty much raising on my own. How about you?"

"Hey, I'm divorced, too. You know me and Stevi ended up getting married. We got a daughter. Then you know me and Ruby had a son together, before I married Stevi."

"No, I didn't even know that you liked Ruby, much less slept with her! But I did hear that you and Stevi was married, though," I said, and I was truly amazed that he had a son with Ruby. She had screwed every man in the neighborhood, and everybody knew it.

"Yeah, I can't believe you got three kids, you don't look like you had any." He looked me over as he made the last remark. "You know them babies should have been ours together." He gave me a mischievous look.

"Don't even try that. You and me were just a puppy love type thing. You know that," I told him.

"Well, now that we both single, and neither one of us looks like no puppy, why don't we hook up and see what we can be now? Gimme your phone number and I'll call you."

"No," I said slyly. "You give me your number and I'll call you."

"Aw, why it gotta be like that? Why you gotta front me like that?" He acted like his feelings were hurt, but I knew that he was just playing.

"What? You can't take not being the one in control?" I teased. "Let me call you. I promise I will. Unless you're hesitating 'cause you ain't really single."

I looked him square in the eye on that one, as I issued the challenge.

"OK I'ma give you my number, but if you don't call I'ma get you next time I see you!"

I laughed as he took out a pen from his pocket and I handed him a piece of paper to write down his digits. "And you better not give me a pager number, either, 'cause if I call it and that's what it is, I'm not putting in my number, so we'll just never get together," I warned as he handed me the paper back.

"Aw, girl, I ain't trynna run no game on you, lighten up," he said.

I laughed again. "I'll call you this weekend."

"OK, and be ready to go out when you call me, too."

"We'll see. But listen, I gotta go," I said, getting into my car.

Doobie held the door for me and then slammed it shut.

"Awright, baby girl, but remember what I told you."

"You remember what I told you," I said, starting up the car and putting it in gear. As I drove away, I looked in my rearview mirror and noticed that Doobie was still standing there watching me drive off. That made me smile.

34

I hadn't seen Zane since the first month that I started back working, and I wasn't really missing him. I was trying to get away from the drug scene, so I was staying away and not taking his calls on purpose. We couldn't really help each other. And Zane didn't seem to really see anything wrong with getting high. He had lost his job behind chasing the high and not going to work, but he still wasn't ready to quit. I didn't understand how Zane had let things progress to the point that he'd lost that job. He had loved working at the post office.

I was also staying away from my cousins that I would get high with when Zane wasn't available. So I wasn't really hanging out. I was just working and taking my kids places and things. I still wasn't going to church, though. And the funny thing was, I didn't really miss it anymore, either, or feel guilty about not going. What I did miss a whole lot, though, was the relationship that I had with the Lord. I still talked to him, and gave him thanks in everything, but it wasn't the same.

Some people think that you are only supposed to thank the Lord for the good things that he brings into your life, but that's not how it is with me and Him. I thank Him for the bad as well as the good, 'cause I know that He was only allowing the bad things to happen to show me what I should be doing to make the good things happen, or to get me back on the right track. So I thank Him no matter what situation I find myself in. And trust and believe, that is not as easy as it sounds. But I make myself do it anyway.

For example, when I was living with my brother and feeling bad because of everything that was going on there, I was in the bathtub one day and all of a sudden I knew that things could have been a lot worse. So I raised my hands to God right there in the bathtub and I said, "Thank You, Lord, for a roof over me and my kids' heads and for the food that we have to eat and for the clothes on our backs, 'cause we could've been out on the street."

I ain't gonna lie, though. I did ask Him to get me out of my brother's house as soon as possible.

I called Doobie on Saturday night around seven o'clock. He wanted to come over right then and there. I told him to give me an hour to get dressed and he said OK.

At eight o'clock sharp he was knocking on my door. I let him in and he hugged me and gave me a kiss.

Inhaling deeply, he said, "Samai, you smell soo good! Let's get out of here before I do something to you that you ain't ready for."

I noticed that he was smiling.

I said, "How do you know what I'm not ready for? You might be the one who ain't ready."

"Ahhhhh shit now! I guess you told me," he said, making his voice a few octaves higher while making a fist and holding it close to his mouth as he spoke. "OK, let's go before you do something that *I* ain't ready for."

Doobie took me to the movies and we saw *School Daze*, Spike Lee's new movie. It was a musical, the first black musical that I had seen in recent times. It was funny, had some really good songs, but had a serious message, too.

It was all about college life on a black campus and how we had our own prejudices against each other and how we needed to wake up and see that what we have in common should bring us together more than our differences should keep us apart. I don't think we have gotten that message yet.

Doobie and I talked about the movie and how far we had come in recent years as a people. We both agreed that not a lot of progress had been made. He got real deep on the politics of the media at large sending us subliminal messages constantly about how stupid we are and how dangerous we are, even to each other.

"Take that phrase that the media is using every time you look around, 'black on black crime,'" Doobie said, taking my hand in his and swinging it gently back and forth as we walked down the path leading away from the movie theater. "Just the way the phrase is constructed suggests that we're the only people committing crimes against each other, when the fact is, all people commit crimes in the neighborhoods where they live. But you don't ever hear the phrase 'white on white crime' although you better believe white folks are killing each other, robbing each other, and cheating each other just as much as anyone else, if not more."

I had to admit he had a point. You don't hear "Mexican on Mexican crime," or any other group's crimes categorized the same way.

"You're right, Doobie, but I think some of that is our own fault. Black people who are in positions to object and do something about it, don't. Instead of questioning it or rejecting the phrase, we carry it like a banner against ourselves. Like it's some hip new phrase we can't wait to use, you know?"

"Whooweee, girl, come on and tell the truth, now!" Doobie teased, bending his knees in a fake bow, while flashing that beautiful smile. "You know, it's like Spike said in his movie: We need to check our alarm clocks and *wake up!*"

I liked the way that Doobie stimulated my thinking and how we could intellectualize with each other and debate our different points of view without getting heated up about it.

Doobie was easy to be with, and he must have felt the same about me, because we started seeing each other almost every free night we had.

The day that I will hold forever in my memory is when Doobie called at work and said that he needed me to leave right away and meet him at his house. I protested, but he wouldn't take no for an answer and told me to tell my boss I had a family emergency and had to leave.

"What's the emergency?" I asked, smiling to myself and thinking that since Doobie was a man, it probably would be he wanted to create a close encounter of the "intimate" kind.

He just laughed out loud and said, "I promise you if you don't come, you will *never* forgive yourself!"

That did it. I gave in and made my excuses at work and left. As I was driving to Doobie's house, for some reason, I began thinking about the time Zane had called me about a surprise that he had for me, and it turned into the worst times of my life. I shook my head as if the motion could throw off the memory. Doobie was nothing like Zane, and anyway, lightning could never strike in the same place twice.

Doobie rushed outside to meet me. He had a large suitcase in his hand and a big grin on his face. I stood and cocked my head to one side and put my hands on my hips. I know this nigga did not have me leave work just to drive his ass to the airport!

"Where the hell are you going?" I began. "And I just know that you did not pull me away from *my* job to play *taxi* for *you*."

"Calm down," he said walking up to me. "I think you need to rephrase your question. It's not 'Where the hell am *I* going?,' it's 'Where the hell are *we* going!'"

"What? Whatchu mean 'we'? You know I got kids and I can't just up and leave town at the drop of a hat. I need to get a babysitter—"

"Done. I got your sister Lynn's number from Earl. Her and Seymour are pickin' them up after school today."

I was stunned. Could this be possible? I guess Doobie could

sense my doubt because he held out his cell phone. "Here, you can call her yourself."

I dialed my sister's number and asked her if what Doobie had said was true.

"Yeah, girl! I don't know where you got him from but you better try your damndest to keep him around for a while. You go and have a good time and don't worry about the kids!"

"But—"

"'Bye!" Lynn hung up before I could say another word.

I looked at Doobie and he took the phone from me.

"Well, doubting Thomasina, what now?"

"I-I don't have any clothes—"

"What do you think I have in this big ass suitcase? I know all of your sizes and with your sister's help, I think we managed to get all the stuff you will need for the weekend."

I was grinning now. "OK! OK! Where are we going?"

It was Doobie's turn to cock his head to one side.

"Ah, mon, 'ave ya evah bin ta J'maycah?" Doobie gave his best impression of a native islander.

I let out a scream and leaped into Doobie's arms. I hugged him around the neck and he swung me around.

"Now we better get goin' before we miss the plane."

The trip was amazing. Doobie had taken care of every detail and all I had to do was get on the plane and go.

It was February and one of the coldest ones we had had in a while, so we both had on our heavy winter coats when we entered the airport. The weather was totally different when we got off the plane in Ocho Rios.

Everything was so beautiful, from the luscious palm trees, to the crystal blue waters, it took my breath away. Our room was on the twentieth floor of the Fantasia Hotel; it was huge and had a balcony with a view of the beach. It was obvious Doobie had been here before. He took me to this penthouse restaurant where we had a beautiful view of the village and all the shops and, of course, the deep clear blue of the ocean and the sandy beach. He ordered conch fritters and some other island dishes that tasted like nothing I had ever sampled before.

After dinner, we walked on the beach talking about everything under the sun, and it felt so right. It was the happiest I had been in forever.

We went back to our room and as Doobie closed the door, he gathered me into his arms and gave me the biggest, sweetest embrace. Then he held me at arm's length, gazing into my eyes.

"Samai, I wouldn't want to share this moment with anyone but you. I don't know what you're doing to me, but I just want to be where you are all the time. When I'm at work, the only thing that holds me there is that I know you're workin', too. But then I'm rushing to call you soon as I get home because I can't wait to hear your voice. When I'm with you, I never want to leave your side. If you have worked some kind of spell on me, please keep it going because I have never felt this way in my life, with anyone."

Before I could say anything, he covered my mouth with his and kissed me deeply. Maan, he could kiss!

He held the back of my head with one hand and plunged his tongue deeper, tickling my tongue with his. His other hand moved over my breasts. He didn't undo my shirt, but he was squeezing and kneading my breast through the material. He released my lips just long enough to bathe my throat with his hot kisses, blazing a trail from the base of my throat to the tops of my breasts before claiming my mouth again. He began undoing the buttons on my blouse and I didn't resist; by now I wanted him as much as he did me.

The things he said to me, and the way he was kissing me, had me in a spin. He reached behind me and undid my bra and slid it down over my arms along with my blouse and let it drop to the floor, never taking his lips from my mouth. Moments later, Doobie had me completely naked and panting.

He stood and stripped off his clothes before lifting me into his arms. He carried me back to the bedroom, carefully positioning me on the dresser, placing my thighs on either of his shoulders, before dropping down to enjoy a Samai appetizer. When he had feasted until both he and I were satisfied, he stood and lifted me into his arms as I wrapped my legs around his waist, making sure he could gain entry. Doobie slid himself inside me easily, and kissed me deeply at the same time.

He was even stronger than I had imagined as he gripped my thighs and pulled me back and forth; at the same time, he was pushing his hips up and back, gyrating and grinding himself into me. Never missing a beat, he pushed my back against the wall and I was gloriously impaled. I answered his movements with my own as we danced to the ancient rhythms that swept us higher and higher, exploding together on Mount Ecstasy's peak, before floating back to earth and surrendering to utter exhaustion. We lay on the bed and Doobie gathered me into his arms, pulled me to him, so that my head was resting on his chest, and then he wrapped me inside. I turned my head and kissed him before letting my head rest there.

"Damn girl, I knew you were something special, but I didn't know you could bring it like that!" he said, brushing back my bangs before planting a kiss on my forehead.

I just smiled and snuggled closer to him, throwing one of my legs over his.

Later on, while Doobie was snoring softly, I got up, slipped on my robe and tiptoed out to the balcony. There was a warm breeze blowing and the scenery was unbelievably stunning, the moon shining brightly against the backdrop of a deep midnight-blue sky, the dark waters of the ocean slapping the shore, sending little white-capped waves dancing away from the crystal sands of the palm-tree-lined beach. In the distance I could see white sails billowing on a boat that I imagined someone had taken out for a late-night tryst. I had to pinch myself just to make sure that I was really standing here. I closed my eyes, enveloping myself with my own arms, inhaling the clean fresh air. Suddenly, Doobie was behind me, his arms wrapped around me, nuzzling my neck.

"Come back to bed," he whispered hoarsely. "It's cold without you in it. I miss you." I turned and kissed him full on the lips.

"What was that for?" He smiled.

"Just because," I said, turning around to enjoy one last glimpse of the Caribbean night before climbing back into bed.

Life with Doobie just kept getting better and better after that: he sent flowers to my job, took me to exotic restaurants to dine, and made me feel like a queen. I smiled thinking about all the new things he was exposing me to.

Only one thing was putting a damper on our happiness. I hadn't found a way to tell him about my habit. I was worried for no reason, though.

On a Friday that Ian had the kids, Doobie showed up without calling. Although I had strict rules about that, and gave the person I was dating the same respect, I let Doobie slide. I didn't even call him on it.

"Hey, baby, I was thinking about you, so tough, I had to jump in my car and come over to see you. I didn't call 'cause I didn't want to give you the chance to tell me not to come."

He stepped into my living room and took me into his arms, giving me a long sensual kiss. When he began walking backward to the bedroom taking me with him, I didn't resist. He sat down on the bed pulling me onto his lap. We were naked and on each other before we knew it. I straddled him and rode him into the sunset. After we both climaxed, we sat for a few moments before Doobie started pulling away.

"Hey, baby, I got a surprise for you. I was gon' wait until another time, but this seems perfect," he said lifting himself from the edge of the bed, tossing me onto the mattress at the same time.

NEVER AS GOOD AS THE FIRST TIME | 177

"Hey! Don't be so rough." I rolled over, pulling the sheet across my nakedness, presenting my back to him.

"Sorry, baby," he said, bending down and planting a kiss on my cheek. "I'll be right back."

I heard his belt buckle jingle as he put on his pants. A few seconds later, I heard the front door open and close.

He must have left my surprise in the car. I turned over onto my back and smiled, stretching my arms over my head, before letting them fall back on the pillow. I wondered what he'd gotten me. It was so sweet of him to buy me a present. I wondered if it was roses, or maybe it was some more jewelry, maybe a bracelet or earrings. He liked buying me nice jewelry.

Doobie worked as legal counsel at the local child support enforcement agency, and I knew that he made good money, so there was no telling what the surprise might be. He had sure spent a enough of his money on trips, flowers, shopping sprees, and other things since we had been seeing each other, that's for sure.

I let my mind drift, thinking about which direction we were headed. Could Doobie be planning on asking me to marry him? YES! He was going out to the car to get the engagement ring! That had to be it! Samai Long. Mrs. Doobie Long. I smiled.

But my smile vanished as I remembered my addiction. It overshadowed my happy thoughts and chased away visions of me in a wedding gown. Dammit! I backed up my thoughts. First of all, before I could even think of being Doobie's wife, I would have to be totally honest with him about my drug habit. Although I hadn't done drugs in almost four months, the next crack binge could be only one bad situation away. I wasn't fooling myself. The beast within wasn't defeated, just on leave.

The only reason I hadn't given in lately was because between work, Doobie, and the kids, I had been pretty busy, and busy was one thing that could keep the beast at bay. I didn't have time to go around places where I knew people would be getting high. I still had dreams about getting high, and sometimes, it took everything within me not to call Zane or my cousin Dar to tell them I was coming over and to make sure they either had some crack or knew where to get it real fast.

Sometimes, I even imagined that I could smell the crack smoke.

No, I didn't know how long I would be able to resist the call of the monster inside me, and that scared me. That was another reason that I felt I would confide in Doobie as soon as possible. Probably not tonight, but soon. If he could accept my problem and not be judgmental, maybe he would be able to help me. Maybe he would even help me get into treatment or something, if I was lucky.

But what if he decided that he couldn't be seen with a crack addict? He might feel that associating with me might make him look bad if word got out. Shoot, it might even jeopardize his position with the child support agency.

Crack addict. I had never called myself that before. But ever since that drug had come on the scene, no one was freebasing pure cocaine anymore. And most people who had started out freebasing were crackheads now. That was an ugly word, but if I was going to be honest with Doobie, then I had to be honest with myself first. I decided that even if he decided he couldn't be with me because I was a smoker, I would have to tell him so that he wouldn't hear it from some other source.

I heard the front door open and close so I sat up in bed in anticipation, and couldn't help smiling. Doobie's voice came drifting into the bedroom before he did.

"Ready or not here we come. Now don't freak out on me, as wild as you are in bed, I'm sure you'll love it!"

But the smile froze on my face when Doobie rounded the corner. Then it slowly began to melt. He definitely wasn't holding flowers or a jewelry box in his hands.

What he was holding was a stem and a vial of crack. Damn! If I wasn't going to go out looking for drugs, the devil was going to make sure it came looking for me.

35

Getting high with Doobie was not like getting high with anyone else. Everyone else I knew shared the drug until it was gone. Yeah, when the drug got low, they might become a little possessive and a little less generous than they had been at first. But smoking with Doobie was the first time I had smoked with a true crack fiend.

He gave me one hit, and then excused himself to the bathroom, taking the crack with him and locking the door. At first, I thought he really was just going to use the bathroom, and was only taking the crack with him out of paranoia, afraid that I would steal some while he was away. But as the minutes grew longer, I realized that he planned on finishing his cache without me, locked behind my bathroom door.

The crave was on me and I wanted another hit of the drug. I contemplated my options. I could confront him through the locked door and tell him that he had no right to think he could get high in my bathroom without me. I could demand that he leave my house, risking that he would end up taking with him my slim chance of getting another blast. Or I could just wait for him to come out; after all, I hadn't contributed anything to the supply. In the end, my need for the high won out and I walked over and knocked on my bathroom door.

"Doobie?"

"Just a second, I'm coming out," he said, and I could tell from the sound of his voice that he had just had another hit from the crack pipe stem and was choking back the smoke as he answered me, trying not to let any of his high escape.

As I waited for him to open the door, I couldn't help but chuckle to myself. Only minutes before I had been considering how my being with Doobie might hurt his career, that he might be the one to rescue me from a life of drug addiction, and now here I was standing on the opposite side of my bathroom door, hoping that when he came out, he would have saved some of the poison for me.

When he finally emerged, he had that lost look in his eyes, and his eyes had grown as big as saucers. Although he didn't get down on the floor, I could tell that his eyes were searching the carpet between the bathroom door and the bedroom, looking for a nonexistent piece of crack that he fantasized about dropping.

It took me back to a time that seemed forever ago now. When I went to one of Zane's parties for the first time, and he had rushed upstairs to get me to watch the person he called "the carpet cleaner" on his hands and knees searching for base crumbs on the floor. The guy had had that same haunted look in his eyes that Doobie had now.

Doobie mumbled something as he brushed past me, and I knew that he had smoked all of the rock. He rushed back over to the nightstand that he had initially laid the crack on when he had come in from outside.

"OK, Samai, what did you do with the rock I left out here?" he said, patting down the nightstand as if that might make a crack rock appear.

I stared at him in disbelief.

"Nigga, is you crazy? You know good and damn well you took all your dope with you when you went into my bathroom and locked the door!"

Doobie wasn't having that. He spun around, glaring at me with a wild look in his eyes.

"My ass, bitch! I left some right here, 'cause I knew I would want another bump when I got through wit' what I had! Scandalous hussy, and after I let you get high for nothin'!"

I watched this stranger begin to rummage through the drawers on my nightstand, still searching for the same imaginary piece of crack.

"You what? You let me get high? Is that what you did? I thought you locked yourself in my bathroom with your shit."

Not finding anything on top of the nightstand, he threw it onto its side and peered underneath it. "I know one thing, you better not have smoked it, that's all I know!" he said as he moved over to my dresser and flung my belongings from the drawers and onto the floor, becoming more and more irrational in his search for the imaginary crack rock.

Suddenly, I felt threatened. Or what? What would this person do to me if he didn't find what I knew he never had? Quietly, I left the bedroom. I walked into the kitchen, overjoyed that a long time ago Zane had left me something that he thought I might need. I climbed onto a kitchen chair and stretched to reach the very top of the cabinets over the sink, feeling around for it, breathing a sigh of relief as my fingers closed around it. I walked back to the bedroom where Doobie was still emptying every drawer I had, tipping over furniture, totally destroying my bedroom.

"Doobie," I called to him calmly.

Whatever he was going to say when he whirled around to face me, holding pieces of my clothing in both his hands, froze on his lips as he found himself staring into the barrel of a .45 aimed squarely at his chest.

He got the rest of his clothes on more quickly than he had shed them. I held the gun steadily on him the entire time. I moved away from the bedroom door to give him space to pass me. It appeared that the .45 had sobered him up some, because if I'm not mistaken, he looked a little remorseful when he paused with his hand on the doorknob and looked back at me.

"I-I'll call you later," he had the nerve to mumble, but we both knew that even if he did, it would be a call that I would never answer.

I didn't lower the gun and relax until I heard Doobie's car pull off. Only then did I collapse onto the floor holding the gun in my lap.

I shuddered as different scenarios of what could have gone down played in my head. How had it come to this? How could someone I thought was a friend, who I had just shared my most intimate self with, turn into a complete stranger without a moment's notice? If he hadn't gone peacefully, would I have had the courage to shoot him? God, how could I have ever explained to my children and to the rest of my family how it had happened?

I needed to be with someone, no longer wanting to be home alone. I took a quick shower and threw on some clothes. Although I hadn't seen Zane in a while, he was the first person that I thought of to go to.

I pushed aside the thought that popped into my head that it probably wasn't cool to just drop in on him, no matter what had just happened. The need to see him was the only thing that mattered right now. I jumped into my car and headed toward his house.

As I pulled up to his house, I noticed that there were three parked cars in his driveway, bumper touching bumper. I recognized Zane's car and his brother Damon's, but the third car I didn't know.

This ain't cool, popped into my head again. *This ain't cool at all*. But I pushed the thought aside and rationalized that even if Zane did have a woman over, we were still friends if nothing else. Shit, he had always let plenty of people come over to get high with him, for all I knew that car could belong to one of them. He didn't have to have *female* company.

I got out and walked to the door while that last thought was still good. When I rang the doorbell, Zane answered.

I could tell by his expression that he was more than surprised to find me standing on his porch.

"Samai, what the fuck you doin' here?" he said as his surprise turned instantly into irritation.

"Hey, Zane, I hadn't seen you for a minute, so I just wanted to drop by and see what was up witcha," I said trying very hard not to fling myself into his arms and tell him about what had just happened.

"Hold up, hold up. Wasn't you the one who told me that I needed to call first before I made my presence known at your crib? What if I got company? Hunh, then what?"

From the tone of his voice, I could tell that his irritation was changing to being downright pissed at me. I couldn't believe that Zane was referring to that long-ago incident, right after the first time we had made love and he showed up at my place without calling. Suddenly, I knew without a doubt that I shouldn't be here, for more reasons than one.

I don't know why I had tried to convince myself that it would be otherwise.

"Sorry to have bothered you." My heart was about to burst with the fear and anxiety that was begging to be soothed, but I started to back off the porch. "Believe me, it won't happen again."

I turned and stepped off the porch, but for some reason I turned to look back at Zane, just in time to see a girl that looked a lot like Natalie Cole peering over his shoulder trying to get a look at me as Zane closed the door.

I couldn't explain why the sight of Zane with another woman hurt so much. We each knew that the other was seeing other people. I had just had sex with another man, but all of that knowledge did nothing to ease the pain of seeing him with that woman.

I drove around the corner to my cousin Dar's house, but no one was home. I still didn't want to be alone, so I drove around to my cousin Lena's house. I knew it wouldn't be a problem to get high. If she was home.

While I was smoking, I kept thinking about Zane and "Natalie Cole." I wanted to be with him so badly it hurt. I couldn't stand the thought of him making love to her the way he had me. I couldn't make my mind stop thinking about them and it was torture. Each time I took a hit, the desire to be there, to be with him was overwhelming.

I didn't know what was the matter with me. I couldn't get a grip on myself, yet I knew deep down inside, this wasn't me. I wasn't born to be sitting around smoking dope and not taking care of my children. Even as I kept lighting up, I knew this was not what I wanted to be doing. I needed to get myself out of this rut, this degrading demoralizing rut that I was in, but how? How could I get back to the way I was before this nightmare began?

Even in the state of mind I was in, I began to see what my dreams had meant. The ones where I was walking among the beautiful flowers and Zane joined me, and then we were both up to our necks in deep mud. The smell of something different in my dreams had been the smell of burning cocaine and then crack. The dream had been a warning or a premonition, I couldn't tell which. But I knew even then that I should have paid closer attention to it.

Now in my drug-induced haze, I could see clearly what I needed to do. Instead of looking for someone to help me, I had to be the one to help. I had to go and talk to Zane. I had to tell him about my dreams and get him to see that I would help him, help us escape this new slavery that had all but ruined our lives. I would get out and bring him with me somehow. Yes, that's what I would do, I told myself as I put another piece of crack on the stem and fired it up. Just as soon as this rock was gone, I would do it.

I forgot everything that I had told myself the last time I was high. I was in a pattern now, I would get up and go to work every day during the week. I would wash and clean and cook for the kids, get them off to school. But on the weekends, I would go and get high. Even on the weekends that Ian didn't have the boys. I would just ask one of my cousins or my sister-in-law, Joi, to keep them while I binged.

It was getting harder and harder again to keep my drug life separate from my day-to-day existence. The wall I had constructed to keep the two apart was developing some serious cracks, and I didn't know how long it would be before the entire thing came crushing down on me.

36

The kids were having a fund-raiser at school selling chocolate, and I had taken the order form to work with me and gotten them a lot of orders. You had to pay cash up front when you ordered, and so far I had collected $300 in my efforts to help the boys win one of the prizes for selling the most candy. I had told my boss that I was going to be about an hour late that morning because I had to turn in the money. It was too much to send to school with the boys.

Just as I was about to walk out of the door, Zane pulled up in the driveway. I hadn't seen him since the night I had gone over there unannounced a couple months ago and he had been with that other woman. I hated to admit it to myself, but my heart still skipped a beat, and I couldn't help smiling when Zane came around.

I opened the door and wrapped my arms around him as far as they would go and gave him a big hug when I saw him. He laughed.

"Oh, so you still glad to see me, hunh? I thought you hated my guts and wouldn't want to see me again after that last time," he said, hugging me back.

"Oh, you mean that time that you practically threw me off of your front porch 'cause you had company? Well, you know I can't stay mad at you, and anyway, it's not like I haven't been seeing other people, too."

"You have, hunh? Well, I guess neither one of us can be mad about that, now can we?"

He looked me in the eyes and said, "I missed you, girl. I tried not to, and I hate to admit it but I do."

"I miss you, too," I told him and really meant it. Even when I was with someone else, I was always wishing it was Zane, although I would never tell him that and most of the time I wouldn't even admit it to myself.

We kissed and it was like old times. I told him that I would have to go up to the boys' school, but that I would be right back.

"You can stay here, it will only take about ten minutes, 'cause their school is only a block away," I said, as I walked into the bathroom to finish my makeup and check my hair in the mirror one last time.

I grabbed my purse and keys and headed out the door. "Don't go nowhere," I told Zane as I closed the door.

He gave me a wink and a smile.

When I got to the office at the boys' school I made small talk with the secretary as I opened my purse to give her the money.

"You might as well mark the first prize with my sons' names 'cause I'm sure that they've raised the most money this year," I told her proudly.

"Ms. Collins, you are about the fiftieth parent to come in here and make that statement to me this week," the secretary said, smiling and shaking her head.

"I don't know which child is going to win the top prize, but one thing is for sure, the music department is going to have enough money to buy a lot more instruments for the children to play this year," she said, getting up and walking over to the counter where I was standing.

I didn't reply to the last comment she had made because by then I had opened my wallet and found that it was empty. The candy money and the few dollars that belonged to me were all gone. I placed the empty wallet on the counter and frantically searched through my purse, silently praying that the money had somehow fallen out of my wallet. Nothing. I checked in all the pockets in my pants, thinking that maybe I had been so happy to see Zane that I had forgotten stuffing the money in one of them. Nothing. The secretary looked like she was getting nervous.

"Is something the matter, Ms. Collins?" she asked, peering at me and the assortment of items that I had strewn across the counter. I began to stuff everything back into my purse.

"I-I must have left the money on my dresser at home," I told her, my face getting hot with embarrassment. "I'll be back," I said, hastily exiting the office before she could say anything else.

My heart sank. *Please God, please don't let it be true*, I prayed as I got behind the wheel of my car. Please tell me I'm wrong in what I'm thinking. I drove the block home as fast as I could. Zane's car was no longer parked in front of my house. My heart was racing and I was fighting back tears as I shoved the key in the lock and pushed open the door.

I knew Zane was gone, and as I looked around my living room, my legs got weak and I sank to the floor. Not only had Zane managed to steal the candy money and all the money I had, he had walked away with my boys' Nintendo game, our color TV and VCR as well. Everything I had managed to prevent going up in smoke was now gone.

I dropped my head in my hands and cried. What was I going to do now? Stealing from me was bad enough, but to steal from my children and the children at school. Once again my dream came back to haunt me. Now I understood why Zane had sunk even lower in the mud than I had.

37

I had to beg my boss for an advance on my next check to pay back the stolen candy money. I told the boys that someone had broken in and stolen our stuff. I hated seeing the sad looks on their faces as I told them that their game had been stolen, too.

"I better not find out who took it," E proclaimed. " 'Cause if I see 'em with it, they gon' get the beat down!"

Devon, who was fighting back tears, ran to their room and shut the door.

I wasn't feeling hurt any longer about Zane stealing from us, what I was feeling now was anger. I had made up my mind to confront him about it and tell him that I knew that my money and my belongings had gone up in the crack pipe. And that if he didn't find some way to replace it, I was going to the police.

I called Ian and told him that I had to work a double shift the next day, and asked him if he would keep the boys overnight and take them to school. After a brief argument with him about it, he finally agreed. I dropped them off, and headed for Zane's house.

His car was not in the driveway when I got there, but that didn't mean anything. When Zane wanted to pretend that he wasn't home, he would park in the garage and shut the garage door. I wasn't going to be fooled by that. I walked up to the door and used the key that I still had to his house and let myself in.

I didn't even stop to ponder whether it was right or wrong for me to do that; Zane had taken everything beyond reason when he had dared to go into my home and into my purse to steal from me. It made me bolder than I had ever been in my life.

Zane heard the door open and quickly ran upstairs from the basement, holding a baseball bat in his hands. He relaxed when he saw that it was me, but still held the bat in his hand.

"What the fuck do you think you doin' walkin' up in my house like you own it? Have you lost yo' fuckin' mind?" he asked, looking at me furiously.

"No, I'm the one that should be askin' you that!" I shouted back. "How the fuck you gon' steal from me and my kids? What kinda shit is that?"

Zane backed down and looked away. "I don't know what in hell you talkin' about."

"Oh, you know all right. You know! If you didn't steal nothin', then how come yo' ass didn't wait until I got back, hunh? How come you left? I wasn't gone more than five minutes, so don't give me no bullshit story about I kept you waitin' too long!" I challenged him.

"You crazier'n bat shit if you believe what you sayin' is true," Zane said, still not looking at me.

I was more convinced than ever that he had done it. If I had accused him of something he was truly innocent of, he would have been all up in my face loud-talking me and telling me to get out of his house. He was acting ashamed and embarrassed, though he tried to conceal that from me.

"What did you do with the money? Hunh? Did you sell all my shit for crack? Did you smoke all my money up yet? What? Did you pawn all my shit yet, or is it downstairs?" I started to walk toward the basement, but Zane tried to hold me back, grabbing my arm. I was so enraged by then that I managed to jerk my arm free and run down the basement steps.

There, sitting on the basement sofa, dressed in a short pink kimono, crack pipe in hand, was "Natalie Cole."

Zane had run down the steps after me. For reasons I can't explain, I wanted to kick Natalie's ass. I had never been so angry in my whole life. I lunged for her but Zane again grabbed me by the arm; this time he had a better grip and managed to yank me back. Natalie sprinted by me and ran up the steps.

"Yeah, you better run, you bitch!" I yelled up the steps after her. "If I get my hands on you I'll break your scrawny, scraggly neck! Don't you know that that dope you smokin' up was bought wit' my fuckin' money!! My shit—"

"Shut up, Samai!" Zane ordered. He had me by both my shoulders now, restraining me from going after the woman. I could feel myself getting hysterical, but I didn't care.

"Let me go, you crazy bastard!" I screamed at Zane, struggling and kicking at him.

He picked me up and threw me down on the sofa, laying on top of me and pinning me there.

"Let me go!" I screamed again. The zipper on my skirt, which zipped from waist to hem, had broken when he threw me down on the sofa, leaving my panties exposed.

"Get off me!" I had started to cry I was so furious.

"Not until you calm yourself down," Zane said.

"I hate you, I fuckin' hate your guts! You thievin', lyin', cheatin' dog! You would steal from my children? You lowlife bastard! I'll see you rot in jail!"

And in that moment, I really felt that I did and would. How could he steal from me and then go buy drugs with what he had taken from me? Then on top of all that, have the audacity to go get some woman to get high with at my expense. Never mind what I had gone through, to replace the money, the humiliation I had to endure asking for an advance. Never mind that he might have stolen the food right out of my kids' mouths. He wasn't thinking about any of that. He was just chillin' with this woman and never gave me a second thought.

Suddenly, I just wanted out of there, to get as far away from Zane as I could. I was so angry, I could feel my whole body trembling. I guess Zane felt it, too.

"Look, I'm gon' let you up, but don't try nothin' crazy. I ain't bullshittin' with you, Samai." Zane let me up and walked behind the bar to fix himself a drink.

I was crying so hard by that time, I could barely see straight.

I stumbled over to the phone and called my cousin Dar to come and get me.

"Dar," I said, when he answered the phone. "Come get me, please! This nigga is fuckin' over me!" I blurted out, my voice melting into giant sobs.

"What's wrong, baby?" my cousin asked, his voice a mix of anger and concern. "Where you at?"

"I'm around the corner from you, come and get me," I cried into the receiver. My cousin questioned me about the exact address. I gave it to him.

"I'll be right there," was all he said before hanging up.

I was still crying hysterically when the doorbell rang a few minutes later. I heard Zane's brother's voice upstairs, although I hadn't seen him when I walked in before. Then I heard someone coming down the steps.

I was standing in the middle of the basement floor crying and my cousin rushed over to me, taking off his coat and wrapping it around me to hide my torn and disheveled condition.

I saw that my brother Earl had come with my cousin, and from the calm steely look on his face, I knew that he was mad as hell. My cousin was trying his best to calm me down and get me upstairs.

"Don't cry, cuz," he whispered in my ear, "it's gon' be awright."

I heard my brother ask Zane in a calm quiet voice, "What the fuck is wrong wit' my sister, man?"

Anyone who didn't know my brother would mistake his tone as one of casual conversation, but I could hear the underlying fury in his tone.

As I passed him on the way out, I wanted to tell my brother to come with me and Dar. I was suddenly afraid of what was going to happen next.

Zane smiled in a way that only further infuriated Earl. Zane was pouring himself another drink from his wet bar when he answered, "You know how your sister is, man—" That was as far as he got. I saw my brother's fist plow into Zane's mouth, and then the soles of Zane's feet as he flew across the bar.

I could hear the calamity of the fight in progress as Dar led me across the living room with his arm over my shoulders. I was surprised to find Damon sitting on the living room sofa as we walked by. I couldn't help but wonder why he didn't go downstairs to see if his brother was in trouble and needed his help, or to at least find out what all the noise was about.

As Dar passed by the coffee table, he grabbed a new gallon bottle of bourbon that was sitting on top of it.

"Hey, you can't take that," Damon said. "That's mine!"

I couldn't believe he would challenge my cousin over the liquor, but not about what might be going on downstairs.

"You mean it *was* yours, it's mine now," Dar said, throwing Damon a warning look before walking out the door carrying it.

Dar put me and the liquor in my car. "Are you gon' be able to drive around the corner to the crib?" he asked.

"Yes, I-I think so," I answered him, tears still streaming from my eyes.

"Dar, please, just go get Earl and let's go please. Don't y'all do nothin' stupid, please!" I begged him.

Dar just looked at me. "You don't worry about this shit. You just go on. We gon' take care of this shit!" he said and only waved me off when I tried to say something further.

I pulled away and prayed to God that Dar would get my brother and follow me to his house.

The minutes seemed like hours as I waited for them to return. When they finally came through the door, my brother had a strained look on his face. I had never seen him look that way before, and my first thought was that he had killed Zane.

"Are you all right, Earl?" I asked him as he sat down on a chair opposite mine. He didn't say anything at first. I looked at Dar. "What happened?" I asked him.

"Dude got fucked up pretty bad. Cuz broke him off some. He bloodied him up real nice," Dar said with what sounded like admiration in his voice.

"Yeah, he's fucked, sis," my brother said. "He probably on his way to the hospital right now. He won't be fuckin' wit' nobody's emotions over this way again!" Earl pronounced, still not looking quite like himself. "I pistol-whipped his ass."

I stared at my brother, hoping that he hadn't beat Zane to death. What Zane had done to me was pretty low, but he didn't deserve to pay for it with his life.

38

I spent the next morning calling hospital emergency rooms. I wanted to make sure that Zane was still alive, or not hurt badly enough to be in a hospital. I knew I could never be with Zane again now. Not after what he had done to me, and especially not after what my brother had done to him. But I still had to know that he was OK. He wasn't registered as a patient at any of the hospitals in the area, so I assumed that he hadn't been hurt too badly.

Neither Earl nor Dar had asked me about what went on or what Zane had done to me that had got me all upset. I guess it was enough for them to see me standing there crying, with my skirt torn. I was glad that they didn't quiz me about it. I didn't want to stir Earl up again with stories about Zane stealing money from me and taking things from the house, including the boys' video game.

After a few days, I answered the phone and Zane was on the other end. I couldn't believe that he was calling me. The only reason I could think that he would be calling me now would be to set me or my brother up for some kind of payback. My first instinct was to hang up the phone after I heard his voice on the other end, but he read me pretty quick.

"Samai, don't hang up. I just wanna talk to you."

I didn't believe him, but I didn't hang up. I didn't say anything, so Zane continued, "Your brother is crazy. I thought he was gon' kill me."

And then there was nothing but quiet between us. Again I had the urge to just hang up. I was relieved that he was all right, but I still couldn't see why he would want to speak to me after everything that had happened. I definitely wasn't feeling anything toward him. Not anger, not hate, not love. I was just numb. I finally spoke first, breaking the silence.

"I really don't want to talk to you anymore, Zane. There is no need for you to call me ever again. There is really nothing left for us to say to one another."

I placed the receiver on the hook, ending the conversation before Zane could answer me back. I was sad and disgusted that we had come to an end like this. That we had allowed cocaine and crack to break us down and lead us into a labyrinth of lies, deceit, and treachery. Whose path lead everyone who set foot on it straight into a hellish nightmare.

The thing was, I realized that even if you did manage to find your way back to where you started, your life could never again really be the same.

Life after Zane was not much different. I was still getting high. Only now, the addiction was starting to spill over into other areas of my life. I could no longer hold it away from my "real life" in its own separate compartment. It would no longer allow itself to be confined there. I was bringing it home after work, and lighting it up in the bathroom while the boys played outside, sometimes locking the front door, ignoring the boys banging on it, until the rock was completely gone. Then I would let them in saying I had accidentally locked the door, and was in the bathroom.

Once when I had locked the door on my young sons, who were now six and eight years old, as they pounded on the door I heard one of their playmates who lived across the street from us yell out, "Yo' mama's on crack watch!"

I hurried downstairs and opened the door in time to stop E,

who had made it halfway across the street by then. I didn't want him fighting.

On weekends when they were gone, I would smoke from the time I left work until it was time for the boys to come back home. Once, I was so high, that I dropped the crack stem on the floor, breaking it into pieces. I remembered when that had happened to Zane and me while we were smoking and he had broken the antenna off an old radio and made a makeshift pipe out of it by wrapping one end with masking tape. I couldn't find any tape, so I just proceeded to try to use a broken radio antenna just like the glass pipe, but the crack melted too quickly and the heat transferred down the metal stem and was so hot that it burned my lips. It was a really bad burn, because when I got to work, the next day, everyone asked me what had happened. I told them that I had slipped and fallen down my stairs.

I had started going to work late and missing some days, failing to call in sick. After a couple of incidents like that, I was fired from my job again, only this time it was my fault. That sent me into a spin and after dropping the boys off at their dad's, I disappeared for a whole week, getting high with whoever had the crack for as long as my last check held out.

Todd had threatened to evict me from my house again after not getting the rent for three months straight. I produced the tape with him asking me for oral sex and told him to back off until I could find another place or I would call his wife.

"You know that's extortion and that I could have you arrested for that," he said halfheartedly. He seemed to be shocked that I had taped him.

"Yes, you probably could, Todd, but then your wife would find out what you don't want her to know anyway, wouldn't she?" I said ruthlessly.

The look that Todd got in his eyes almost made me sorry for

taping him. I almost regretted treating him the way I was, but sur-vival is more important than some man's hurt feelings. I threw my head back and gave him my most indifferent stare. I cared as much about him as he did about me. Hell, if he cared, he'd find a way to make things right so I wouldn't have to move.

Todd looked as if he had lost his best friend. "I'll give you more time," was all that he said, before turning and going out the door.

I knew that he was going to have a hell of a time explaining to his wife why he had given me a chance to fuck him over again, but that was his problem, not mine. I had to keep a roof over my kids' heads by any means necessary. I didn't even feel bad at all about what I had just done.

39

I knew that I couldn't get another job in the condition I was in since most jobs had begun making you take drug tests as a prerequisite to employment. I would never be able to pass one. So I was forced to go down and apply for welfare. I was feeling like the worst loser in the world. I could only imagine how my mother and sisters would react when they found out. They would never call me, but I knew that they would call each other. My welfare status would be the hot topic for them for quite some time. They would make themselves bigger by making me smaller, and then convince themselves that I was too far gone for them to be able to help me. Not that any of them had tried.

I shut my brain down and didn't allow myself to think about how low I had sunk. I shut down my feelings so that I wouldn't feel the embarrassment of asking for the institutionalized handouts. I didn't allow myself to feel anything. Because if I did, I would have to acknowledge that it was my own stupid, wrong choices that had brought me to this place. I just did what I had to do.

As I was coming back from the welfare department, my car stopped running. My cousin Dar's house was not far from where it cut out on me, so I decided to walk over there, since I didn't even have a quarter to use the payphone.

I was walking down the street wondering what I was going to do about my car, when I heard someone call out to me.

"Hey, stranger! Long time no see."

I looked in the direction of the female voice. It was coming from the porch of one of the four brick row houses. I remembered the face, but not her name. I knew it was a woman who had come to visit my old church a few times. I *would* have to run into her now, I thought, after all these years of not running into anyone I used to go to church with. To see someone now, while I was at a low point in my life, was unbelievable.

I had already looked her way, so pretending that I hadn't heard her was not going to work. So I said, "Hey, how ya doin? I haven't seen you in a while."

The woman started to come down off the porch and walk toward me. She gave me a big hug, like we were old friends.

"You know, my church has fellowshipped with yours a few times over the past few years, and we miss seeing you there. We always ask about you, but the only answer we get is that you don't go there anymore. Did you join another church?"

I looked at her and shook my head, not saying anything. All of a sudden I was thinking of the person I had been while I was in church, when this woman had known me. She would probably cross herself and run screaming if she knew what my life had become. For some reason, I felt like crying.

"What's wrong?" she asked me. She seemed to be genuinely concerned.

I still couldn't speak. Now I felt if I opened my mouth, I'd start boo-hooing for sure.

"Please, tell me. Who knows, it might be something I can help you with. And if I can't, I promise you that I will try to help you find someone who can."

I looked her over as she spoke. She had a pleasant demeanor about her, and she sounded sincere. She had the kind of countenance that made you want to trust her. But my motto was never trust anyone you've just met, and some people you could never give your trust to, no matter how long you have known them.

Thinking things over in my head, I really didn't have too much to lose. I had sunk pretty low since I had last seen this woman. I decided it would be safe enough to only tell her a little about my problems. Something that I wouldn't care if it got out about me.

"Well, I *am* having financial problems right now, and I have to find another apartment for me and my kids by the end of the month and—"

The woman started beaming. "Not to cut you off or anything, but my husband knows the man that owns these very apartments we are standing in front of! In fact, he's inside doing some repairs on one that the people just moved out of, getting it ready to be rented. And the good thing about it is, it's based on your income. I know this is not the best neighborhood or anything, but if you are pressed to get a place real quick, I know we can help you get this place."

I couldn't believe it. Based on your income! That would be perfect. Since I had just signed up for public assistance, I was sure that my rent would be very little. But not all low-income housing took welfare recipients. You had to have some kind of job to qualify. I was almost afraid to ask about this, but I knew I had to.

"I-I don't really have a job right now. In fact, I just came from signing up for public assistance," I admitted.

"Girl, that don't matter," she told me still beaming. "This landlord accepts that, too."

Unbelievable.

"Come on in and let's tell my husband that you want to move in here. It should be ready in about two weeks, or so. You'll have plenty of time to get things ready before then."

When I walked in the front door, my face fell. It was definitely a ghetto apartment. The woman saw the look on my face.

"Don't worry about how it looks right now. The people that just moved out really trashed the place. But my husband will fix it up real nice. It's going to have new cabinets and carpet and everything. Ain't it, honey?" she addressed her husband, who was up on a ladder doing some painting.

He seemed to recognize me, too, just as his wife had.

"Well, well, well, how you doin', young lady? We haven't seen you in ages," he said, coming down off the ladder to give me a hug, mimicking his wife. "It's sure good to see you. How you been doin'?"

"Not too good," I admitted. "I'm not really going to church anymore." A lump was in my throat and I could feel the tears begin to itch behind my eyeballs.

"Well, you will just have to come on over to our church and visit with us then, won't you?" he said with a smile. He had the same kind of gentle, sincere demeanor that his wife had, and I was instantly at ease with him as well.

"Honey, we was talking outside, and it turns out that this young woman is lookin' for a place to stay." She had thrown an arm around one of my shoulders.

"Well, this place ain't much to look at right now, but it will look a whole lot better when I get done. I'm goin' to fix these cabinets, and paint all these walls and thangs. You won't even be able to recognize the place when you come back in a couple weeks. And I will make sure that I tell Mr. Washington that I found him a tenant, so he don't need to put up a for rent sign!" he declared.

I didn't know what to say. These people didn't really know me, yet they were extending themselves to me. It was something entirely new; strangers wanting to help me without really knowing anything about me. I couldn't help wondering if they thought I was still a good old church girl, doing the right thing. Should I tell them how far I had fallen from grace? Would they still be so willing to help me if they knew about my addiction? I wanted to tell them, but I didn't want to put my being able to get the apartment in jeopardy.

Having an apartment that was government subsidized would really help me out right now. Especially since it usually meant that you could get help with your utilities, too. I wouldn't have to struggle so hard for a change. I decided that it wouldn't be too smart to spill my guts at this time, and probably it would never get to be the right time.

.The wife spoke again, taking a pencil and paper out of her purse.

"Here is the number where you can reach us. We will try to have everything ready for you to move in by the first of next month," she said scribbling down their name and number. Sherry and Robert Little. I quickly jotted down my name and number for them, too. I thanked them and told them that I had to be on my way, that I had to get home before my sons got out of school.

They hugged me again, and Sherry Little told me, "God Bless you, little sis, and remember He never leaves us nor forsakes us." I glanced at her and I could see she had tears in her eyes before I walked away.

Dar gave my car a jump and got it running again.

"What you need is a new battery, otherwise you gon' have to keep getting somebody to jump you once the car sits for a minute and the car cools down. Check with me later on in the week, I'll see if I can locate one for you," he told me, and I wasn't about to ask him how.

When I got home, I told the boys that we were moving again, and that they should start packing up their belongings. It seemed as if timing finally had cut me a break!

I heard a knock at the door and went to answer it. It was Zane.

He had a Nintendo game console in his hands. I wasn't sure if it was the exact one that he had stolen from us or not. Neither of us said anything, we just stood there staring at each other. After a few minutes, he just handed the game to me and walked away.

I wanted to say something, but as I played the options in my head, nothing sounded right. I probably could have thanked him, but I couldn't forget that he had been the one to steal the boys' game in the first place, not to mention my money and the candy money. I know, I should have been the bigger person, but sometimes you just can't stretch that far. So I just let him walk away.

40

The Littles called me about a week after Zane came over and dropped off the boys' game. They told me that the apartment was finished and that Mr. Washington, the landlord, wanted me to call him to set up a time for me to come sign the lease. Mrs. Little gave me the number. I thanked them sincerely and called Mr. Washington.

We set up a meeting for the next morning at ten o'clock. When Mr. Washington gave me his address, I recognized it as a mostly white neighborhood way out in the suburbs. When I got to his house, I couldn't help but admire it. It was a huge brick house that featured a wraparound front porch, black wrought-iron winding steps that led up to the balcony that stretched the width of the porch, and a long, perfectly paved driveway that was gated at the entry and led all the way to the front doors. The yard was equally as huge and nicely landscaped with lush green grass and neatly trimmed hedges. His house looked like a mansion compared to any house that I had ever lived in.

Mr. Washington looked nothing like I imagined. He was a very, very short black man—almost a dwarf or something—and if his voice sounded nasal on the phone, it was nothing compared to how he sounded in person. He looked so small when he answered the door, which had to be at least seven feet tall.

"Hello, Miz Collins," he said, extending his hand toward me.

Since he used the politically correct form of "ms." to address me, I could only assume that the Littles had told him I was divorced.

I took his hand and shook it. "Hi, Mr. Washington, it's nice to meet you," I said, and I was glad that I had worn a nice skirt and blouse. He seemed to be sizing me up.

"Come on in, please," he said, stepping aside to let me pass him.

"Just go straight back to the first door on your left, that's my office," he directed.

He came in behind me and walked over to a huge wooden desk. When he took a seat in the chair, his feet dangled above the floor like a small boy's.

"Have a seat, Miz Collins."

He was shuffling through some papers that were laid out on the desk, before finding my lease. "OK, now your portion of the rent is eleven dollars a month, you pay gas and electric, I pay the water. I don't play around with the rent. I know that it doesn't seem like much to you, but I expect you to pay it each month, I will and *have* evicted people for nonpayment of their portion."

As Mr. Washington spoke, he took on the air that he was better than everybody else. I couldn't stand black people who acted that way. But on the other hand, eleven dollars a month for rent? I couldn't believe that I had gotten so lucky. It would definitely make the government check I would be getting stretch further, until I could clean myself up long enough for my pee not to test positive for drugs, and find another job. I definitely wasn't trying to keep getting government checks forever, like some people did.

I wasn't passing judgment on anyone. I knew that once you got into that cycle, it was sometimes hard to break free, with the government monitoring every extra penny you managed to make, as if what they were giving you allowed you to live comfortably, which it didn't. It only allowed you to squeak by.

If they would allow you to work and give you the stipend for a few months, then eventually you would get to a place that you would no longer need the assistance, while making a place for yourself in the workforce. I didn't think the government wanted anyone to get to be self-reliant—if you did, then a lot of them would be out of work, too, not having you as a statistic to manage.

"Miz Collins . . ." Mr. Washington brought my thoughts back to the matter at hand.

"Yes, Mr. Washington, I'm sorry, you were saying?"

He peered at me over his glasses a few beats before continuing. "I was saying that if you agree to all the terms I have outlined here, I need you to initial each paragraph, here, and then sign here . . . ," he said, pointing to each area mentioned with his stubby little fingers.

I read over each paragraph before putting my initials beside it and signing the bottom, just as my mother had instructed me to do years before.

"You don't have any way of knowing if what they said and what they wrote are the same things unless you read for yourself. Plenty of people have been tricked into signin' things and agreein' to things they never had no intentions of, just because they wouldn't take the time to read for themselves!" my mother had admonished, and I never forgot her words of wisdom.

After I had signed the one-year lease, I shook hands with Mr. Washington again, before he handed me the keys and showed me the door.

"Now, if you have any problems, don't hesitate to call, Miz Collins. You'll find my number at the bottom of your copy of the lease," he said in parting.

I thanked him and went on my way.

I decided to go and give the apartment another look, now that I had the keys. Everything did look much better, just as the Littles had promised. As I glanced around the room at the new paint and the new cabinets, I suddenly realized how far I had fallen. New paint could not hide the fact that it was still a ghetto apartment, far shabbier than any place I had lived before. A roach crawled across the wood floor as if to investigate the intruder who had come on the scene, a silent confirmation of my last thought. I had never had to share my home with these disgusting creatures before; I prayed that they would be gracious enough to keep themselves well away from us. I didn't even step on it, for fear that I would have to carry its bug guts around on my shoe.

Remembering that Mr. Washington hadn't said where he wanted the payments made, I went next door to ask my new neighbor if I could use the phone. I probably could have called him from home later, but it gave me an excuse to see who I had for neighbors.

A cute, pleasant-looking, dark-skinned woman, who was slightly overweight, answered the door. "Yes, may I help you?" she asked and smiled, displaying a dazzling, even-toothed smile. I immediately relaxed.

"Hi," I began, giving her a smile of my own. "I'm Samai Collins, and I'm moving in next door. I was wondering if I could use your phone?"

She opened the door wider and invited me in. "My name is Gina Whitethorn. You sure can. Just excuse the mess, I haven't had a chance to clean up yet."

"Oh please, don't apologize," I said sincerely. "I hate housework myself and try to put it off as long as possible every day."

We both laughed as she led me into the kitchen.

"Ugh, I know what you mean. Here's the phone," she said, pointing to a cordless phone that was mounted to the kitchen wall. Her apartment was not as nice as mine; she had some cabinets that were off the hinges and needed repair, among other things. I wondered why Mr. Washington hadn't told Mr. Little to make the necessary repairs while he was fixing up my apartment.

As Gina walked away, her hip brushed a drawer and the front fell off. I had to make myself stand steady and not cringe as a whole tribe of roaches started spilling out of the drawer, scurrying down the side, like a brown roach waterfall. Not wanting to embarrass her, I quickly picked up the phone and started to dial, not looking in Gina's direction. I swallowed hard to keep my gorge from rising.

After the call, we went into the living room, and chatted a few minutes.

"So, when are you moving in?"

"Well, probably this weekend, if I can get one of my brothers to help me."

Her eyes lit up when I mentioned that I had some brothers.

"Brothers? Are they single?" she asked, raising one of her eyebrows.

I laughed. "Well, one of them is, but I'm not sure you're ready for my brother. He can be a trip sometimes when it comes to women. Anyway, he lives in Florida, and I don't think you want to try to have a long-distance love affair."

Gina wasn't intimidated. "Well, I'll be the judge of that, if and *when* the occasion arises. He might not be ready for me! But we will discuss that more after you're all moved in. If you need me to help with anything, just let me know. Me and my son Lamont will be glad to help you. I can't wait until you get moved in. I'll have to fill you in on our 'lovely' neighborhood, and where the thugs live and who the real gangstas are."

"How old is your son?" I asked her, thinking about E and Devon and trying to ignore the fact that "gangstas" would be living close by. "I have two sons, six and eight, and they will love having a boy their age living right next door."

"Lamont is eight, and he is my only one, thank God. I'm not havin' any more," she said rolling her eyes.

"Well, I actually have three kids. My daughter is almost fifteen, and is stayin' with my sister, right now. . . ."

"You have a daughter that old? You don't look like you do!" she said dramatically. Up until that point, I had never thought about how Jadyn's age would make me seem older.

"Well, I'm probably not much older than you are, but I have to be going, the boys will be gettin' home from school pretty soon, but we will definitely talk again."

"You got that right, girl, I can see we are going to get along just fine!" Gina said.

"Yep, I think so, too," I said, standing up and walking to the door. "Meanwhile, I will try to decide whether or not to introduce you to my brother."

"Yeah, you do that," she said, smiling again.

The boys seemed OK about moving again after living in our third home in a little more than two years. I was glad that their grades hadn't suffered too much, they were still making Bs and Cs, with only an occasional D. I knew that they could do better, but after moving around so much, and changing schools more often than the school cook changes lunch menus, I didn't want to push them too hard. Once we were settled down in one place long enough for them to get back into a regular routine, we could work on bringing up their grades.

I told them that our new neighbor had a son their age. "When I was leaving the apartment the other day, I saw some other boys on our street who looked about the same age, too." That made them smile.

"Mom, can we have them spend the night, once we meet 'em and stuff, and if we like 'em, can we, Mom? And can we have a pizza party, too?" Devon asked, jumping around in circles.

"Well, we'll see, we'll see." I told him noncommittally. I didn't want to get his hopes too high before we knew for sure if the boys even lived on the street. Even if it turned out that the boys did live on the street, I still would have to meet their parents and see what kind of folks they were.

The Friday before we moved in, the boys and I went over to our new apartment to clean. No matter how well the Littles may have done in getting the apartment ready, I still never felt right about moving in without cleaning things myself, with some good old bleach. I didn't think anything could sanitize a place better than what my grandma had used.

Gina had come over when she heard us next door, and brought her son, Lamont, with her. They all liked each other right away, just as Gina and I had. The boys ended up playing more than they were cleaning, so we sent them outside while we finished up. Gina filled me in on the neighborhood as we cleaned.

"Two dykes live right across the street from us in that brick house. One of 'em has twin boys. They are around ten or eleven years old and she doesn't let them out of the yard much. They don't bother anybody, the dykes don't, but they aren't very friendly, either. I still speak whenever I see 'em. Y'all gon' hear a lot of shooting out here. But don't be scared, there haven't been any accidental shootings, anyone who was shot so far, was shot on purpose. Lucky for us, these gangstas hit who they aim at. Not so lucky for the ones they're after though."

Gina smiled when she said the part about the shootings, but I didn't take any comfort in the gangstas being good shots. I guessed living in the neighborhood had made Gina kind of callous.

"I know Mr. Washington didn't tell you this, but this apartment, the one you're movin' into, used to be a crack house," Gina said as she bent over her bucket of soapy water and bleach, dipping her rag in and sloshing it around a little bit before wringing it with both hands. She straightened back up as she continued. "Rumor has it that Mrs. Glynn down the street got sick of all the fightin' and all the people in and out of here all times of the day and night, so she called the police and told 'em that this was a drug house and they better do something about it. I don't know why, but they listened to her, and word is they watched the place for about a month or so, and then swooped down on it and arrested everyone in here. I don't know why none of them messed with Mrs. Glynn after that, but they didn't."

A crack house! How ironic, here I was trying to get away from drugs and had moved into a house that used to have the drug sold from it. I glanced at Gina, and I guess that she could tell from my expression that I had had enough stories about the hellhole I was moving into for one night, because she suddenly got very busy wiping out the refrigerator and didn't say another word for a while.

That Saturday was Ian's regular weekend with the boys. They were so excited about the new place, that they didn't want to leave. For the moment they didn't even notice that it was nowhere near as nice as our old place. They were too excited about all the new friends they had to play with. Ian convinced E and Devon to come anyway by telling them they were going to see a football game at the local college. That did it. My boys loved football, especially E. He still had that little hard blue football, although he didn't carry it around anymore. He did take it out every now and then and toss it around, even though I had gotten him a real football a while ago. So it didn't take much to convince him, and Devon would do pretty much what his older brother did at this point. So they went with their dad.

After they had left, I did a couple of hours of unpacking and setting things in order until I got tired. I looked around at all the empty boxes and realized that I had barely managed to make a dent. As I stood on my feet, my back let me know that it wasn't too happy with all the bending and lifting that I had been doing by sending a sharp pain up the middle and across my shoulders. I reached back and placed one hand on my lower back and stretched, I was surprised to find that I was pretty sore. I must be getting old, I thought; moving had never made me sore before.

I decided to take one of my famous two-hour-long steaming hot bubble baths to relax and ease out some of the soreness. I had planned to catch up on some reading while I soaked, but I hadn't unpacked any of the books yet, and I couldn't find the box they were in. Instead I slid into the soothing hot foam up to my neck, eased my head back until it was resting against the folded towel I had placed against the back of the tub to use as a cushion. Then I closed my eyes to just enjoy the peace and quiet.

Just as my muscles were letting go and I was getting settled, I felt something crawling across my face. I sat up and instinctively brushed whatever it was away. A big fat brown roach plopped into the water with me. It must have crawled down the wall and into my hair before finding a path straight across my face. I jumped out immediately, feeling sick that the disgusting thing had been on my face! I watched it as it swam around and around in my bubble bath trying to find a way out.

For some reason, watching it swim hopelessly around in circles like that took my mind back to a day in the seventh grade and a girl named Stacey. She was the one that a lot of the kids picked on because her family was poorer than most and she came to school smelling like pee and looking unclean and uncombed most of the time. I never teased her, I wasn't too far from being picked on like her myself. I mean, I was always clean when I came to school, but my clothes were mostly hand-me-downs from my older sister, so I sort of knew how she felt.

This particular day, the last bell had rung and everyone was rushing to get their lockers open and to get out of the building for the day. Stacey, who usually hung back in a corner trying not to be seen, for some reason went right up to her locker to get her things, not caring about the crowd of kids in the hallway for once. I guess she was taking a stand, in her own way, deciding not to let the other kids intimidate her any longer. She quickly worked the combination on her locker and jerked it open. I could tell her courage was starting to leave her stranded though, as she seemed to be having second thoughts.

She tried to hurry even more, shoving in books she wouldn't need to study that night and reaching in to get others that she would need.

As she reached for her coat, Doug Mason, whose locker was

next to Stacey's, made a big show of pinching his nostrils together and fanning his face while he loudly proclaimed, "Peeeeeeey-eeeeeeeeew! Somebody staaankkkkkkks!," causing people around him to turn and look his way. He was making exaggerated movements as if not to touch anything close to the girl.

Her courage had completely left her by then because she hung her head and jerked her coat from the hook. The hard motion made something shoot out of one of her pockets and fall on the floor with a loud *clack*! Whatever it was, it spun around and around in fast circles on the tile floor and the girl was frozen in place, too stunned to move.

Everyone inched closer to the spinning object to try to figure out what it was. It had begun to slow down by then, and slowly it became something that we could recognize. It was a ham hock bone that had been sucked clean of every scrap of meat and gristle, and was as clean as a whistle. I guess that was why it could spin around like a top the way it had. But that wasn't the worst part. Sitting on top of the still spinning bone, looking like it had enjoyed the ride as much as any child on a merry-go-round, was a big fat roach. How it had managed to stay on top of that bone like it did, with all that spinning, was amazing to me. Everyone looked from the roach on the bone to the cringing girl almost in unison, everything deathly quiet. Then Dougie Mason started cracking up, laughing very loudly. And when he did, the rest of the crowd roared with laughter, as the girl finally found her feet and took off running down the hallway. . . .

Just as quickly as I had been taken to the past, I suddenly was back staring at the spinning roach in my tub, still absently wondering what had become of that girl. I noticed that the creature had not been able to get out of the sudsy water and I took satisfaction that it had drowned itself. I pulled the plug and watched with fiendish pleasure as its nasty little corpse got sucked down the drain. As it sank into its watery grave, I vowed to call Mr. Washington first thing Monday morning and demand that he exterminate the place, and if he refused, I would call the health department!

41

Mr. Washington had responded to my call right away. "I will not live with roaches, Mr. Washington," I had told him bluntly. "I can't even enjoy my bath without them jumping in with me!"

"Calm down, Miz Collins," he said with what passed for mild concern. "I don't expect you to. I will send someone out on Wednesday. Now you will have to make arrangements to be gone for ten hours, because the exterminator will set off bombs. You have to remove all opened food, and anything else that can become contaminated. Once you are allowed back in, any dishes, silverware, et cetera will have to be thoroughly cleansed," he instructed.

I was more than happy to abide by everything he was telling me. "No problem, Mr. Washington."

"We will do all of the units at once, so that the problem is taken care of. I will inform the other tenants," he said before hanging up. He didn't even give me a chance to thank him.

That Wednesday, the boys and I went to stay the night at my sister Lynn's. I took the boys to school from there. We would not be allowed back in the apartment until after six that evening. I planned on picking them up after school and taking them to get pizza and then to the library. I figured it would be about six by the time we did all that.

Gina and I pulled up to the apartment at about the same time.

"Well," I said to her as we walked up the steps that led to our apartment building together, "are you ready to do some serious cleaning?"

She grinned at me. "As ready as I'll ever be, and if it means no more roaches. Let's get to it."

Neither of us was prepared for what we saw when we opened the door. The place was covered with dead roaches. Everywhere you looked, everywhere you stepped, everywhere you touched, were dead brown creatures of every size. Gina and I stepped back out of our apartments at the same time. She looked just as sick as I felt. We both spoke at the same time.

"Rubber gloves and scarves!" we both said at the same time.

"I'll drive," I said.

We drove to the corner drugstore and got what we needed, gearing up before we had to go back inside to tackle the disgusting job of cleaning up the dead roaches.

"I'll tell you what, you help me and I'll help you," I said to Gina as we got out of the car.

"It's a bet!" Gina said.

It took us four hours just to sweep up the piles of dead insects from both of our apartments, and another three to get everything washed down. We had already taken the towels, sheets, and pillowcases off the beds and out of the linen closets and taken them with us to launder, so they were ready to go back on the beds once everything was all cleaned up.

"Girl," Gina began, once the boys were all in bed and she and I had collapsed on my sofa, "did you ever in your worst nightmare dream that we were living with that many damn roaches?"

I thought back to the first day I had met Gina, when I had asked to used the phone and was treated to the roach waterfall pouring out of her broken kitchen drawer. But I saw no need to mention that to her.

"Child, please! I don't think I'll be able to eat anything for at least ten years!" I said, and I knew that it would take about that long for me to forget the piles of brown death.

"I feel the same way you do, and I hope I keep feelin' this way for a while. That way, maybe I can lose some of the poundage that I have been tryin' to get rid of for years!" she said, grabbing a handful of her midsection with both hands. I looked at her and we both burst into laughter.

"Well, if that's the case, maybe we should have taken pictures and sold them to people who want to lose weight," I said, still laughing.

"Yeah, we could've made the pictures into magnets for people to stick on their refrigerators!"

We both stopped laughing at Gina's last idea.

"Ewwwwwwwwwwwwwwwwwww!" we said at the same time before cracking up laughing again.

42

Getting high was getting to be a thing of the past. Or so I hoped. Again.

I was at the grocery store when I saw Zane. He was not looking his normal, neat self. His curly hair, usually perfectly groomed, was long and shaggy and looked like it needed a good combing. He wasn't dirty, but his pants weren't tightly creased the way they usually were. And his shirt looked like he had taken it straight from the dryer and put it on without bothering to iron it. It wasn't really wrinkled, but it didn't have the crisp look that an ironed shirt would. The Zane I knew would have never set foot outside looking like that. He hadn't really seen me, and I didn't feel like letting him know that I had seen him. I hurried to the checkout line, paid for my groceries, and left.

I was sitting in the living room watching nothing in particular, mostly just having the TV on to keep me company, when someone knocked on my door.

I was surprised to see my brother Rob, my brother Earl, and my mother standing at the door. I was really surprised to see Rob because he had moved to Florida shortly after graduating from college. He had formed a production company that was doing really well out there and kept him extremely busy. He usually only came to town for holidays, Mom's birthday, or if there was trouble. It wasn't Mom's birthday, nor was it a holiday, so I wondered what problem could be big enough to warrant a visit from my oldest brother. I smiled at first, because none of my family ever came over anymore just to kick it with me, but as I invited them in my joy quickly died down when I saw the looks on their faces. They weren't looking too happy to be there.

"Hey," I said still trying to sound cheery. "What are y'all doin' here?"

Mom didn't say anything. Rob did all the talking.

"Yeah, Samai, Mama gave you her mortgage payment to mail off for her a few weeks ago, do you remember that?"

I smiled. "Yeah, I took it over to the post office and got a postal money order like she asked me to." I looked at my mother, but she looked away, still not saying anything.

Earl was looking down at his shoes, and Rob was staring at me with a cold hard look in his eyes. A thought slowly began to form in my mind.

"What's going on here? What is the matter with y'all?" I asked, looking from one to the other, my eyes finally resting on my mother.

"What's going on is, Mama got a letter from the mortgage company. You know that she was already two months behind on her mortgage payment when she gave you that $749 to send off to get her caught up. The letter said they never got it," Rob said, giving me a stern look. "It turns out that some woman cashed that money order around the corner from the post office at the bank. We want you to come inside the bank with us, so that the teller can get a look at you and see if she thinks that you're the person who cashed that money order."

My heart dropped down to my shoes. I had done some things that I wasn't too proud of since I had been doing drugs, but stealing from my mother was *not* one of them. I felt the tears start to well up in my eyes. I looked at my mother for some sign that she didn't really believe that I had stolen from her. There was none.

As I gazed at her, I thought about a time when I was a real small child, not even in kindergarten yet. I had come into the kitchen where my mother was making dinner and was watching her. The longer I stared at her, the more I began to wonder who this woman was. What made her my mother? Suddenly it almost seemed that my mother had become a stranger to me. I ran over to her and grabbed her around the waist and all of her smell and warmth flooded me and I smiled as I thought, "This is Mama!" Just to touch her had been enough to make a stranger my mama again. When I looked her way again, she blurted out, "I don't know what to think, Samai, you were the last one with the money and they didn't get it!" She didn't say it in a mean way, but her words cut into my heart just the same. She was once again becoming a stranger right before my eyes, only this time I couldn't think of a way to turn her back into my mother.

As I stood there, looking from one of my relatives to the other, I couldn't help but wonder how could they be so willing to offer me up to those who had accused me. Where were the protective instincts that a family was supposed to have that said if one member did do something so outrageous, we would deal with her or him within the ranks of the family and stick together to get the money back?

What if I were guilty? Why were they so eager to turn me over to strangers? It appeared that they had all decided that I was guilty before they had gotten there. Not one of them thought that I was innocent, so they all were willing to turn their backs on me. I knew that if I were standing on the other side and one of them were in my place, I would never have agreed to this kind of treatment. I felt something in my heart turn freezing cold, and stony. Everything I did now was as if I were on autopilot. I grabbed my coat.

"Let's go," was all I could say.

On the trip over to the bank, Rob kept saying, "If you did it, you need to confess now before we get there. . . ." Or something like that. I couldn't really make out what he was saying, because the hurt and coldness had spread throughout my body and all I could feel was numb and disconnected.

I was the first one out of the car, and walked right into the bank. I stood at the door and waited for my mother and brothers.

Rob went up to a gentleman dressed in a nice suit and spoke with him and a police officer. If I had been guilty, I would have had two federal offenses, I thought: stealing from a bank and stealing from a post office, since it was a postal money order that had been cashed. If the teller said that I was the one who had cashed the money order, I would be in a lot of trouble. I'd be facing a trial that could get me federal time. I guess the family didn't care about that, either. For a split second, I pictured the officer slapping the cuffs on my wrists and locking them tight before he led me away, while my family just watched, shaking their heads. They would be willing to let me go to prison over less than a thousand dollars.

The man in the suit looked at me just as I had looked at the roach in my bathtub. He walked up to me and said go with him, as my family stood watching in the background. He led me up to a young, flustered-looking black woman, who couldn't have been much over twenty. She looked very nervous and had the look of something else that I didn't quite recognize in her eyes. It may have been fear.

She looked at me carefully, staring at me for long minutes before she shook her head, tears starting to flow from her eyes. "I don't think that was her. I just don't remember!" she said before bursting into tears and being led away. I felt sorry for her and hoped that her lapse of judgment would not cost her her job.

I turned and walked out of the bank and stood outside to wait for my family. Once we were back inside the car, all of them started to speak at once.

"I knew that it couldn't have been Samai," my brother Earl began. "The teller's description didn't fit Samai at all. The teller said that the woman who cashed the money order was very attractive," he said.

I wasn't quite sure if he didn't realize or didn't care that he had just said that I wasn't attractive. It didn't matter. Each of them was trying now to somehow justify what they had done to me. Not one of them had been for me before we went into the bank. Why had they let it get to this? Why hadn't they told those people that I would never do something like this? Why hadn't one of them said, *We don't believe that you would do this but . . .*

The ice inside my heart had started to melt. It was running down my face in cold streams.

43

I had always felt not quite a part of my big family, that I didn't really belong. I was the only one who had become pregnant as a teen and didn't have a college degree. I had a marriage that had ended in divorce. I couldn't keep a job. Worst of all, I'd become a drug addict and ended up on public assistance. My mother had always been proud of the fact that despite hard times, she'd never had to depend on the government to care for our family or herself, not even after Dad had died. I was the complete opposite of everything my mother expected from her children and I was mounting up a wealth of reasons for my mother and my family not to love me. And after that episode with my mother's mortgage payment (postal money orders are insured, so she got the money back), I felt even more disconnected. Like an outsider.

I felt so alone after that. As if I had been abandoned and nobody really cared about me.

I didn't have a reason anymore to try to stay off the drugs. Whenever I got high, it made the pain in my heart fade for a while. So I tried to stay high as often as I could. It became like when I'd first moved into the slab house, when I was getting high whenever I could, even when the boys were outside playing.

Gina and I had become very close and shared a lot of secrets, but I never told her about the drugs. Although I knew that she suspected I might be doing them, she never confronted me about it. There were a lot of times when she had shared food with my sons because I had spent all of our money and even the food stamps to buy drugs. But Gina remained my friend and never complained about anything.

Beyond my family's betrayal, none of them ever confronted me about my addiction. I began to wonder if they talked about it as coldly as they had spoken of me stealing my mother's mortgage payment. They showed no real concern for me. If I had stolen the money, why didn't anybody question what may have driven me to do it?

I was spiraling downward again. I stayed away for weeks at a time getting high, leaving my sons with different relatives while I was binging.

I had even started seeing Zane again.

I was shocked at his appearance, once I had seen him up close. One of his front teeth was missing. He said that was due to a fight that he had. He didn't tell me that it was over drugs, but I could only imagine that it was. The crave had not even spared his stunning good looks, it had reached in with its claws and raked over those as well.

Zane never talked about the beating that Earl had given him. I cut him short when he had tried to tell me about it. I saw firsthand the effect that it had on him though. Once, after we had begun getting high together again, we had been driving down a street that was well known for the profusion of crack that was in the area, looking to make a buy. Zane and I had been having a normal conversation, when all of a sudden his already fair skin took on a ghostly shade of white, and his hands were trembling as they held on to the car's steering wheel. My brother Earl's car had just passed us on an intersecting street. There was no way he could have seen us, he never even looked our way, and he would not have known the car we were in anyway; it was borrowed from one of Zane's female friends. Zane never said anything about what had scared him so bad, he didn't have to. We both knew. I thought briefly about the pitiable state that crack had brought us to.

I was getting sick of myself. Lying on my stomach in the middle of the bed, I couldn't imagine getting out of it. Lucky for me and for them, the boys were gone to their dad's and Jadyn was still at my sister's. I didn't even know her anymore. We rarely talked and when we did, she seemed so cold and distant. Almost as if she wished she didn't have to talk to me at all. I thought about picking her up today and taking her to lunch so that we could talk.

Lunch? Who was I kidding? The days that I could treat my kids to a meal at a restaurant were long gone. Hell, I would be lucky if I could scrape up the few dollars it would take to make my eleven dollar rent that was due on Monday. Me and Zane had smoked up the government check I had gotten last night. We had even spent an hour or so looking everywhere for enough change to make a twenty-five-dollar buy. We looked between all the cushions in the chair and couch and on the floor beneath them and out in his car. We even went into the closet and looked through pants and coat pockets. Most of the time we wouldn't find enough, but we lucked out this time, between the two of us we scrounged up thirty-five bucks. Zane left after we smoked that up.

Now I didn't even know where I was going to get food for the boys to eat when they came home on Sunday. My pickup day for my food stamp card wasn't until the fifth day of the month, that wasn't until Wednesday. Then I still had to drive down to the re-demption center, stand in a long line where the wait was at least two hours long, to trade the card for the books of food stamp coupons, before I could even go grocery shopping.

Coming down off the high, I didn't like the person that I had become yet I felt helpless to do anything about it. I rolled over onto my back and let one arm dangle over the edge of the bed, and draped the other across my eyes. I didn't like feeling helpless, either. I basically had become a stranger to myself.

What had happened to all my dreams? Who was this person who had unzipped my skin when I wasn't looking and stepped in to take over my life? Why had God allowed me to come to this place? I had been happy going to church and serving Him. I loved singing in the choir and our morning worship services, so I couldn't understand how I had ended up so far away from everything that I loved. I kept comparing myself to the prodigal son and once again envying him. At least he knew where home was and how to get there. And at least his father still loved him. My father was dead, and from the way things looked, I had become someone that even my mother didn't feel like loving.

I wanted a change, but how? Even if I couldn't get back to where I started, how could I at least start down the long road to find myself again? I needed help, but there was no one who I could turn to. No one who cared.

I care.

I sat up in bed. I knew I wasn't losing my mind on top of everything else. It seemed as if someone had spoken to me and it sounded like they said . . .

I care.

My eyes darted around the room and I jumped up out of bed. Walking quickly over to the closet, I jerked the door open. There was no one there, of course, and there was no other person in the room with me, either. And suddenly I realized that it was the Lord dealing with my spirit, trying to reach me, to tell me that He was still there for me.

But for some reason that I couldn't figure out, I got mad.

"If You care so much, how come You took away what little I had?" I said out loud. "Why did You let me meet up with a drug dealer, hunh? Why did You? Why did You let me get strung out on this shit! I didn't go looking for it. I wasn't out running the streets!

Why did You let this happen to me?" I stood in the middle of the floor questioning God. I waited for Him to answer, but all I heard was silence.

"Why Me? WHY ME?"

Why not you?

I didn't have an answer for that one. It was true that I wasn't any better than anyone else, so why should someone else suffer in my place?

After a while, I lay back down on the bed and covered my eyes with my arm again, wishing desperately that I could hear that strong, quiet voice speak to me again. Because for a second, even when I was standing there screaming at God, I had felt what it would be like to know real peace again.

44

After the day that I'd heard God's voice again, I decided to try once more to get myself straightened out, to get out of the self-destruct mode I was in. I decided to cut everyone off except my kids. We didn't have any money, but I was going to start doing things with them again like we used to do. Even if we couldn't do things like going to the movies or the arcade, we could go to the park and to the library. And while I was at the library with them, I would start doing the one thing that I had loved since I was a little bitty thing. I would read.

Reading always took me out of myself and to anyplace that the story was set in. I lived inside the book as I read. I was right there traveling through time and space, with each character, feeling whatever they were feeling, seeing whatever they were seeing, and sharing everything that happened to them, and about them. Give me a good book, I could read for hours.

On our first trip to the library, I checked out ten books. Six books that were for me, and two each for E and Devon. I was so busy counting our books and rounding up E and Devon to go check out that I didn't even notice the tall guy standing in front of me. I walked right into him.

"Hey!" he said.

"Oh, excuse, me," I said, without looking up. I moved to go around the person when I felt someone grab my elbow. *I know this fool ain't got the nerve to grab on my arm after I excused myself for bumping into him.* I spun around and jerked my arm away. But the words that I was about to hurl at my assailant froze on my lips. I looked up into gentle brown eyes at the same time they looked down into mine.

Bennie! I hadn't seen him since he had gotten into the police academy. "Hi, Bennie," I said, and the way he looked at me made me self-conscious about my appearance. I was about thirty pounds lighter, and I knew that the clothes I wore were nowhere near as nice as those that I had worn before. I was dressed in a worn sweatshirt and dirty white tennis shoes, and didn't have on a drop of makeup. My hair, which was in braids that were months old and should have been taken down long ago, was pulled back into a ratty ponytail. Damn, why did he have to see me looking like this after all this time?

Bennie stepped closer to me. "Can I get a hug?" he asked opening his arms wide for me. I hesitated for a second before allowing him to envelop me in his strong embrace.

"Where you been girl? I been wondering where you ran off to. You stopped coming to church and just kind of fell off the face of the earth, you know?"

I pulled away from him.

"Yeah, church . . . I know. Bet nobody ever thought I'd leave, did they?"

"Well, a lot of folks, including me, have wondered what happened to you. Not trying to be nosy or anything, just out of concern for a faithful member dropping off like you did."

I got an attitude right away. If the members had been that concerned, why hadn't any of them stopped by or called to see about me?

"Sure, I bet they were concerned. I didn't get any calls from a single person. Ain't nobody been by my house to see me, neither, so I can see how much they cared."

"Look, Samai, have you forgotten that you moved away? You

never told anyone how to contact you. You weren't even working at the same place. No one knew how to reach you."

"No, you look, Bennie. I had stopped going to church long before I moved. I still had the same address for months, so don't try to make excuses for them! I don't want to hear it. The truth of the matter is no one cared enough to try to help me. End of story." And then I got a lump in my throat because I felt that what I had just said was true. No one cared about me. But I swallowed hard, because I wasn't going to let Bennie or anyone else know how much that hurt.

"I'm not making excuses for anyone, Samai, but you have to . . ." I looked up at Bennie and I don't know why but he didn't finish his sentence.

"Okay, Samai, you're right, maybe the church should've . . . maybe we all should've done more to try to find out what was going on with you. I'm sorry we didn't but that's in the past. And all of that doesn't change the fact that I've thought about you and worried about you, too. Are you all right? Do you need anything?"

I looked down at the floor. I was so ashamed. Seeing the look in Bennie's eyes when he asked me that question let me know that he could see how far I had fallen from grace. Same old Bennie, though, still trying to help me out.

"No-no, I'm doin' OK. I just was gettin' some books for me and the boys and . . ."

Bennie took me gently by my shoulders and put a finger under my chin, forcing me to have to look up at him.

"Samai, whatever you're going through, whatever is happening in your life, don't ever forget that whoever else has let you down in life, whoever has failed you, it's not God. He is still there for you. He still loves you, no matter what you may have done. That will never change. Do you understand that? Don't let the enemy blind you to that fact, or the fact that there are people out here who genuinely care about you and want to help you. But how can we help you if you won't let anyone know what you need?"

For a moment, I wanted to break down and cry and tell Bennie all that had gone on since I had last seen him. I wanted him to hold me while I shared all my pain and anguish with him. I wanted to, but I didn't. Instead I just cleared my throat and told him,

"Well, it was good running into you again, Bennie, but I gotta go."

Bennie let go of my shoulders and looked into my eyes as if searching for something.

"All right Samai, but if you ever need me for anything I want you to know that you can call me. I don't care what time of the day or night it is," he told me, and then reached into his pants pocket as if to get something to write with.

"Hold on a second," he said, and he walked over to the counter to write down his phone number for me. When he came back and handed me the folded-up paper, he gave me another hug.

"You make sure you use this, you hear?" Bennie gave me a grin and another hug. "And you and your family will always be in my prayers."

"OK," I said, and I watched Bennie turn and walk away. Again I suppressed the urge to run into his arms and bare my soul.

Once I was inside the car with the boys, I unfolded the paper Bennie had given me with his number on it. I gasped as I saw that his number wasn't the only thing the paper held. Bennie had also folded a crisp new $100 bill inside.

The next day, after the boys were on the bus and on the way to school, I cleaned house. I got rid of all the hidden crack stems under my mattress, on the very highest shelf of the bathroom cabinets, and every other hiding place that I had. I took them out into the alley behind the apartment, and threw them in the trash container that I knew I would never reach down into and try to dig them out.

Just as I walked back into the kitchen, the phone started

ringing. When I answered it, I was surprised to find my sister Denise's friend, Carmen, on the other end.

"Hey, Samai," she said when she heard my voice. "Are you busy?"

I frowned a little when I recognized Carmen's voice. It wasn't that I disliked her, she was a really nice and sweet girl. I just hated the way that my sister treated her more like a *real* sister than she did me.

Denise and Carmen shared everything. They were almost the same age, had gotten married around the same time, even having their first babies within a year or two of each other. They shared the same ideas about what made you successful—surrounding themselves with expensive things, from cars, to houses to jewelry and fine clothes. I wouldn't say that I was jealous of her relationship with my sister; I just didn't understand why my sister didn't feel that the bond between blood sisters was stronger than any other. When I had asked Denise about it once, she had said simply, "I don't think there is a difference." She held her hands out and extended them palms up. "You have sisters in one hand and friends in the other."

She lived by that model every day. She had no idea how much that hurt, and she never would. What she also didn't see was that in her world, sisters and friends weren't equal, she always held her friends in higher esteem. It was her friends that she called to babysit, it was her friends that she called first whenever tragedy struck, and her friends that she shared good news. I don't think she ever realized that in shutting out her sisters, she shut out any real relationships with her nephews and nieces. Her friends and their children took our place.

So other than those feelings that I had to deal with, I had no real animosity toward Carmen.

"No, I'm not busy. Not right this minute," I said, thinking, I did want to finish cleaning the drug residue from my house and settle down and do a little reading before the boys got home.

"Well, I'm not gon' keep you long. I just wanted to invite you to this retreat that Denise and me are going on. It's on next Thursday, Friday, and Saturday." A retreat is a church function similar to a shut-in, only you are not in church for a whole night and day. Instead you reserve rooms in a hotel and have workshops to help your spiritual growth, and help you solve problems that may be common to Christian women. And in between the workshops, you have breakfast, lunch, and dinner. And, of course, nightly worship services. You can even have free time to go shopping or just be alone. It's just a time to get away and renew yourself, your beliefs, and friendships. If you have any friends.

"I don't have any money for stuff like that," I began, feeling a little bit defensive.

"No, I want to pay for everything for you, if you'll let me. I really want you to come," she said, only hesitating a little.

I thought about what she had just said. I really didn't like people giving me "gifts." It made me feel even more like a failure. Like I would never be able to do these things for myself. And also I wondered how many people she would tell that she had footed the bill for my room and food and stuff.

Then for some reason, I don't know why, my heart softened. I didn't really see Carmen as the type of person who would do something nice and then ruin it by telling everyone who cared to listen, and even some who didn't, what a great thing she had done. That really wasn't her. Yet I couldn't bring myself to commit.

"It's nice of you to offer, Carmen, and I really do appreciate you thinking about me—"

Carmen cut me off before I could finish, "Don't give me your answer now," she said. "Just think about it for a little bit. You can let me know by this weekend, OK?"

I half-smiled to myself. That was Carmen, using gentle pressure to get you to do something. "OK, Carmen, I'll think about it. I'll letchu know by Sunday."

"OK, I'll talk to you then," she said, and hung up before I could say anything else.

Later on, while I was doing the dishes, I thought about Carmen's offer. I was thinking about all the times that I had told myself I wanted to start over and leave the drug thing behind me. I also thought about how I had heard God's voice telling me that He still cared about me. Maybe He was using Carmen to show me that. It's one thing to think about wanting to stop doing drugs, and a completely other thing to actually do something about it.

Maybe if I went to the retreat, it might be the first step to the road back home. But even if it wasn't, how could I be any worse off than I was now?

45

I rode with Carmen, Denise, and one of their friends in a rental car down to the retreat. I was quiet for most of the ride, and Carmen had my favorite gospel group's newest CD playing. There was something special about the group called Commissioned. Their lyrics and style were real. They spoke of trying to live in this world and remain true to the Lord, even if you got caught up in some things that weren't exactly Godly.

Like the song that was playing now. "The Ordinary Just Won't Do." I asked Carmen to hand me the CD cover.

I leaned back and read the lyrics along with the mellow voices that sang a message to my soul. And as I listened, I thought back to another time, not so very long ago, when another singer had sung my truth. It could not compare to the truth I was hearing now.

> So many weaknesses and faults I've got to learn to
> Share the innermost and secret thoughts.
> The ordinary person just won't do

As I listened, something in my heart began to soften, and tears stung my eyes. The others in the car were so caught up in their conversations, they didn't notice.

I need a love that's pure and true
I can only find it in You, Jesus . . .

As they sang the last lines again and again, I could feel it in my heart. I would never be able to get my life together until I got my soul together first. Right then and there I decided that whatever it took, that was just what I was going to do.

When we finally got to the retreat, the service had already begun, so we wore what we had on and joined the worship service. Having decided that I was going to give my heart back to the Lord, I was most excited to get inside.

We sat near the front, and the woman of God was preaching a very moving message about how God didn't care how far away you went from Him, He would always welcome you back. No sin was too great or too small for Him to forgive, because He loved us, and had died for us.

I had closed my eyes and had my head bowed. I was thinking about the relationship that I had once had with the Lord. And then all the things that I had done since I had left church. And the tears began. I felt a heavy weight pressing on me so hard thinking about how I had hurt the people that I loved, how I had let my children down, that I couldn't stand. I fell to my knees and cried out to the Lord. The sobs that wrenched my heart wracked my whole body.

"Jesus help me," I wailed, not caring what anyone thought; I just wanted someone to help me. I thought that some of the sisters would come and lay hands on me and pray for me, and that God would hear them and deliver me from my addiction. Instead, what I heard through my tears was the voice of the minister who had preached such a good message of forgiveness.

"Oh God," she said softly into the microphone, "that's why we have to stay clean before the Lord, so we don't end up like that." And all of a sudden, I felt cold, like every eye was on me.

But I stayed on my knees, not moving, still hoping that the minister or someone would come and pray for me. The minister continued to talk, but she didn't ask anyone to come and pray for me. And no one did. I wondered why at least my sister and even Carmen didn't come to pray with me. After a few more minutes on my knees, I stood, wiping away my tears with the palms of my hands, feeling like there was no help for me anywhere. I saw Carmen and Denise over in a corner praying for some other woman. As I slowly walked back to my seat and sat down, I felt my heart turn to ice once again.

46

After I got home from the retreat, I felt all my resolve not to get high start to vanish. I couldn't understand why God hadn't come to help me when I needed Him most. Instead He had let His minister leave me stranded and insult me by calling me unclean. I was more confused than ever. Still, I somehow managed not to give in to the urge.

Devon and E came rushing into the house one day very excited about something they had to tell me.

"Ma! Ma! Guess what?" they both said together.

"Hey, slow down. One at a time," I said, smiling at their excitement.

"Let me tell 'er," Devon said and E let him.

"Mom, we wanna play football. The Firefighters are comin' to our neighborhood and Mr. Berry said that we can play. Can we, Ma? Can we?" Devon asked, his eyes pleading with me to tell him it was OK.

I looked at both my sons. Devon at seven was nothing but skin and bones. I had heard some stories about little kids getting hurt playing football. I had even heard that a couple of kids had gotten killed. I looked over at E. He had always been stockier than Devon, but at nine years old, he still looked too little to me to be playing football. Although he held his emotions in as usual, his eyes reflected the same longing look that Devon's had.

"Please, Ma?" he added his pleas to Devon's.

"Wait now," I said, trying to buy myself some more time before giving them an answer. "Where are we gon' get the money to pay for uniforms for both of you? You know I'm not workin' right now. And how are you going to get back and forth to practice? The car's not runnin', either."

"We can walk to practice," E said, ignoring my first question. "Practice is right over there behind Hamilton Elementary School. And Mr. Berry said that he will take the team to games in his van," he explained.

"But you still gotta have uniforms and football shoes and stuff," I said again. "How are you goin' to get money for that?" I hated to see the look of disappointment on their faces, but I didn't have the money for all that extra stuff.

"But, Mom, Mr. Berry said . . . ," Devon began.

"I don't care what Mr. Berry said. Mr. Berry doesn't live in this house, or help me pay these bills! If I don't have the money, I don't have the money!" I said, raising my voice, and I could see their spirits sinking as they looked down at the floor.

"We don't never have no money for nothin' we wanna do no more," E said. "Come on, Devon." He slung his arm over his brother's shoulder and they walked out the front door, closing it behind them.

Tears stung my eyes. What E had said was the truth. We weren't doing anything fun anymore. I had been selfishly spending all the money we had on getting high. Maybe I could go around to some thrift stores and find what they needed.

I knew their dad wasn't going to help much; he had started to change when he remarried a couple of months ago, spending less and less time and money on the boys. His new wife had a daughter, and he seemed to be focusing all of his extra time and energy on her and her mother.

Maybe I was just afraid that they would get hurt and that was causing me to find all these excuses for them not to play. I was being overprotective, and that could never be good for a woman trying to raise boys into men on her own.

I went to the door and called them back in. They dragged themselves in slowly, their heads hung down in defeat.

"Look, I am not promising y'all nothin', but I will talk to this Mr. Berry and I will come with y'all to the first practice. If it doesn't look too dangerous, *and* if we can get you a couple of uniforms and shoes from somewhere—"

They didn't wait for me to finish. They both jumped up knocking me over onto the sofa.

"Thanks, Ma!" they said, laughing and giggling as they wrestled each other trying to give me hugs and kisses. They ran back outside to tell their friends that they would probably be playing football with them. I watched as they gave each other high fives and started hitting each other like boys do when they are happy about something.

47

Between Mr. Berry, the boys' coach, and me, we managed to scrounge up the gear the boys needed to play for the Firefighters. I found myself at most of their games and was surprised to find myself become their biggest cheerleader.

I would yell and scream encouragement from the sidelines as loud as I could, not caring if the other parents approved or not. Not even caring if I was the only one cheering her kids on. E and Devon would sometimes look over at me and pretend to be embarrassed by my carrying on, but I knew deep down inside they were happy that I was there to watch them, and happy that I was cheering them on, too.

At one of the games, after they had been playing for a while, Devon, who would put all he had into each and every play that he was put in for, had managed to jump high enough to block the rival team's punt.

As the players from both teams scrambled to try to recover the ball, Devon, who, having been tackled, was lying on the ground, saw that the football was only inches away from him. He extended his fingers out as far as he could trying to reach the ball, just as a few defensive players from the other team decided to jump on top of it, crushing Devon's hand in the process. Once the refs cleared the pack of boys off Devon, he sprang to his feet holding his hand and hopping up and down.

I jumped the fence and sprinted toward my son, ignoring the rule that anyone other than coaches, players, or refs on the field could cause the team to lose. As I got closer to him, to my surprise he was not shouting about being in pain, but instead was yelling: "My season is over, my season is over!"

He was greatly disappointed. But as I drew close enough to examine his hand, I discovered that his index finger was bent at a ninety-degree angle across the remaining two fingers. I felt faint but managed to stay on my feet and get my sons in the car for the drive over to the hospital.

Once we were inside the emergency room, the adrenaline that had been pumping and had kept Devon from feeling the pain of his broken finger had worn off and the pain hit him full blast. His lips turned white and dry looking as he held on to his hand, somehow managing not to let the tears in his eyes fall down his cheeks.

"It hurts, Ma," he said, as the nurses sat him in a wheelchair and wheeled him into one of the back rooms.

"Can you get him something for the pain?" I asked one of the nurses.

"Yes, ma'am, we'll give him a couple of Tylenol with codeine," she answered, rushing off. She returned shortly with the two tablets and fed them to my son. "There," she said after Devon had managed to swallow. "You should start feeling better in no time flat! Let me know if you need anything else," she said, as she closed the door.

Before long, two technicians came in to take Devon down to X-ray his hand. His index finger had a compound fracture, the bone protruding through the skin, and the doctor decided that the bone would have to be set with a pin and that Devon would have to have surgery to mend it properly. He set it temporarily with a splint and had us set up an appointment for the surgery. I wanted to step outside when the doctor set the bones back in place, but Devon wasn't having that.

"No, Mom, stay with me and hold my other hand," he insisted.

So with my legs turning to jelly and my stomach doing flips, I stood there listening to the bones crunch as the doctor moved them back to their proper position. I thought I would collapse on the floor any second, but I didn't. It's amazing the things a mother can and will endure for the sake of her children.

I found myself alone again on a weekend when Ian had the boys. I had immersed myself in a book from the library, something about Italy and godfathers and things. I was trying the best I could to keep my mind off getting high. Reading always worked for me, as long as none of my cousins or people I got high with came by the house. I could never say no, if that happened.

I guess I had fallen asleep reading, because I woke up to a knock at my door. Not thinking, I went and opened the door without asking who was on the other side.

I was shocked and amazed to see Doobie standing on the other side of the door. My first instinct was to slam the door in his face. I hadn't seen him since that episode where he was tearing up my bedroom looking for the imaginary piece of crack. I wondered how he had found out where I lived.

"What are you doing here? How did you know where I lived?"

"Sludge told me."

Sludge was Doobie's older brother. Sludge and my brother Earl had been friends since junior high school, and still kicked it sometimes.

"Don't blame Earl or Sludge for telling me where you live, neither one of them knew about the disagreement we had. And it just came up in the conversation—"

I started to close the door. I didn't like Doobie referring to that scene he had made at my house as a "disagreement."

"Wait, Samai," he began, seeing the door closing in his face.

"Wait for what?" I snapped. "For you to fuckin' lose your damn mind again, tearing up my house and threatening me and shit? I don't think so! And if you don't get off my porch in the second after I close this door, the police will be comin' for your remains!" I said, and slammed the door as hard as I could before locking it.

48

I was restless after Doobie had been gone for a while. As much as I wanted to smoke, I wasn't trying to let him in, even if he had a whole ounce of crack. But his presence had set my mind thinking about getting high. I wanted a blast. I wanted to have another bell ringer and have my mind go blank and not care about anything. I had never gone out alone to buy crack on the street, but I didn't want to call Zane, or my cousin, or anyone. I didn't want anyone to know that, despite the fact I had vowed to quit, I was about to get high yet again. I wasn't ready to admit to anyone, not even myself, that I couldn't quit smoking crack.

After an hour or two more of arguing with myself about the drug, I finally gave up, took $60 of the $125 that I had out of my purse, put on my shoes and jacket and went out to find some drugs on my own. I thought about knocking on Gina's door for a second, and asking her to hold my other $65 so that I wouldn't spend it all on crack. I actually went to her apartment and raised my hand to knock. But then a thought caused my hand to stop in midair before it could strike the wood on Gina's door. What in the hell would I tell her? Anything I came up with would be an admission that I had some kind of drug problem or something, that I couldn't trust myself with my own money. I took my hand down and not bothering to step across the banister that separated our two apartments walked down Gina's front steps to the sidewalk below.

As I walked down the street toward one of the boys that I knew was holding crack—I had seen him enough times selling in broad daylight to know—I felt bad lying to myself. I knew the real reason that I hadn't knocked on Gina's door was because I knew I wouldn't have gone out looking for dope if she had opened the door. She would have invited me in, immediately reading that something was not right with me and she would have fixed me a glass of wine, or handed me a beer, and we would have started talking. Even if I had never gotten around to telling her what was really wrong with me, she would have kept me talking until I no longer felt like getting high.

Yeah, that was the real reason I had changed my mind about getting Gina up. I wanted to get high, and I didn't want anyone trying to stop me. Not even myself.

As I got closer to the crack boy, I was wondering what I would say to him. I had never bought any drugs on my own off the street. I didn't want to seem stupid, that would be just asking him to rip me off and give me something that was too small for my money, or even worse, something that wasn't even real. I had seen some people get ripped off that way, buying a rock that seemed generous, and a steal for the money, even tasting it didn't help. If you took a little piece of the crack and rubbed it on your lips or gums, it was supposed to make them "freeze" or go numb, like pure cocaine would. But the crack boys had learned that putting the stuff that mothers put on their babies' gums when they start to cut their first teeth—the stuff that you could get from any drugstore for a few pennies—could make anything that looked like a piece of crack freeze your mouth. Some users were so anxious to get high they were tricked into buying little broken-off pieces of a candle, not finding out that they had been duped until they got back to their place and tried to light up and didn't get so much as a puff of smoke out of the crack pipe.

I didn't feel like getting my little bit of money ripped off like that, so I slowed down, trying to think of the right thing to say, wracking my mind to try to come up with any of the phrases that Zane had used to make a buy. I stepped off the curb and almost walked into a car that was turning the corner. A loud blast on the horn and a name flung from the driver's lips brought me up short and probably saved me from being seriously injured or worse.

The car had pulled a little ahead of me on the opposite side of the street and stopped. I wasn't really scared, though I probably should have been. There were too many houses I could run up to if the guy tried to grab me or force me into his car.

As I drew closer, the guy in the car started rolling down his window. I sized up the houses on either side of me, to see which one was most likely to open the door to a screaming stranger on the porch. One of the houses had a big truck in the driveway and the porch light was on. I figured that a man had to live in that house, more likely than not, and just as I was about to make a bee-line for the front door I heard someone call my name.

"Samai! Samai, it's me, Zane!" he yelled, sticking his head out of the window, so that I could see that it was really him.

"Zane, what are you . . . ," I started and then stopped. There was no reason to finish the question. Of course he was out here for the same reason I was. Everyone knew that around this area, there was a crack boy on every corner selling, and the cops didn't even really care that much.

The only time they really cared was if somebody got shot or killed behind a drug transaction, then they would have to pretend that they were doing something about all the drugs and thugs and true gangstas in our neighborhood who were getting rich off other people's misery. As soon as the neighborhood stopped talking about it, things went back to normal with the crack boys on every corner again.

So I knew what brought Zane to my side of town.

"I just left your house," he said. "I was looking for you and wanted to see what you was gettin' into tonight."

I stared at him for a few beats before answering.

"I'm gettin' into the same thang you gettin' into," I said. "I'm gon' see what Captain Kirk and them are doin' up in the Starship Enterprise!"

49

Together, Zane and I had about $150, and that was enough to buy three fifty-cent rocks. We decided to buy two right away, and save the other fifty to go out and get some more after we smoked that up. It was really all the same, but geekers liked to play games with themselves about how to make the dope last.

We decided to go back to my place to get high, instead of going all the way to the other side of town to Zane's house.

It had been a while since I had smoked. I had been too caught up with the boys' football games, making sure I was at each one. I can't explain what made me give in to the urge this time.

The urge was always with me. It was my constant companion. I could push it away, or ignore it for a while, but it never went away. It would appear in my dreams and make itself seem so real, that I would wake up smelling the distinctive sickly sweet aroma, and longing for it like a long-lost love that had suddenly disappeared without warning.

One dream I had stood out among all the others: I was driving down a long road in a nice new car. The road was peaceful and I was alone enjoying the scenery when a figure dressed in dark clothing appeared in the seat beside me. He didn't scare me, in fact I kept driving as if I hadn't even noticed his appearance. But when I glanced in the rearview mirror, I could see that the backseat was filled with crack pipes of all sizes and shapes, filled with thick white crack smoke. They were piled from ceiling to floor, blocking my view, and the figure beside me was laughing wildly. . . .

"Ba'y, what are you doin'?" Zane's voice broke into my thoughts. His voice was strained from the effort of trying not to let the hit from the pipe escape his lungs and trying to get my attention at the same time.

I looked over at him and saw that he had the pipe extended for me to take my turn. The stem was full of the milky-looking smoke as I placed my lips to the end and inhaled deeply. Zane had another piece of crack ready and plopped it on the hot end. It sizzled loudly before it melted, evaporating and mixing more thick white smoke with the smoke that was already in the stem.

Zane put his lips to the stem again, not even bothering to exhale the previous hit from his lungs, he inhaled so long, that he began sinking slowly back onto the bed, crack pipe still in his hands. It scared me. I thought he was OD'ing or something.

"Zane!" I called out, taking the stem from his hand. He exhaled loudly and blew all the smoke from his lungs, filling the air around him with a white misty cloud.

"I'm OK," he managed to say and looked at me, his eyes not focused and looking far away, and I knew that he was hearing the bells ring. Then he smiled, and confirmed what I had thought.

"Whew, bell ringer!" he said happily. I watched him for a few more seconds to make sure he was OK before I took another hit. I decided to take it easy and put only a small amount on the end of the stem. It wasn't long before I was feeling just like Zane.

Neither of us wanted another hit right away, so Zane started talking.

"What happened to us, ba'y? Why couldn't we hold thangs together and make the shit work?" he asked with a sad look on his face.

I didn't have an answer for him. I could have said because of this stupid shit that you started and dragged me into. But I realized that it was my fault, too. I could have said no.

For some reason, Zane's question irritated me a lot. So what I said was, "I don't know, and right now I don't care. I don't want to blow my high, discussing this depressing shit right now, so can we talk about something other than that?" I glanced over at him when I finished my sentence, and he flinched; I knew that I had hurt his feelings, but I really didn't care at the moment. I just wanted to enjoy my high without getting all deep and shit.

"Hey, I was just thinkin' out loud is all," Zane said. "Wa'n't tryin' to get no shit started." He took the pipe from my hand and loaded up the end with the drug before taking another mega bop.

As I watched Zane, my heart softened a little. I felt bad about what I had said to him. I knew that he was trying to forget all the mistakes he had made. Trying to forget how he had lost everything he had to the thing that he was holding up to his lips right then. And all at once, I could see how weak Zane really was. How weak we all were. Trading our lives and our souls like cowards hiding behind a cloud of smoke that really didn't provide a hiding place at all. How could something so diaphanous and fleeting hold us in such an iron grip and bleed the life out of us so completely? Rob us of our dreams and goals.

No it wasn't robbing us, we handed everything over freely. Not only our lives, but the lives of our children and all others who loved us. It had us by the throats and wouldn't let us up until we had nothing left. No money, no pride, no food, no shelter, no job, no friends, not even a soul.

Zane's last blast was wearing off.

"What you thinkin' 'bout so deep?" he asked, preparing himself another hit.

Ordinarily I would have told him that he had had three hits to my two and was preparing hit number four, but I didn't even care right at the moment. I was sick and tired of this shit. Sick and tired of not being who I was meant to be. I knew that I wasn't born for this. My destiny wasn't to end up some drug-addicted bum on the street, my kids ashamed to acknowledge that I was their mother.

I wanted to get up and walk away. I wanted to tell Zane to take the drugs and leave, to go away, to disappear and never come back.

I wanted to, but the next time Zane extended the pipe toward me I took it.

Zane and I smoked for hours, not really talking much, and suddenly we found ourselves with the last hit. It would be our very last for the night anyway. Zane had gone back to drug boy over an hour before and spent our last fifty on a rock. All that was left now was a hit that we were to share.

I knew that I still had the sixty-five dollars left in my purse, but tonight, I was determined that I wasn't going to spend it. E's class was going on a field trip on Monday and he needed ten dollars of the money for lunch and admission to the zoo. And I wasn't going to disappoint him. I was through trading my kids' happiness in on a high. I could at least muster up enough courage and strength for that.

We took our final blasts and enjoyed it as long as we could. It wasn't much of a blast, since we had been using big pieces to begin with. It wasn't long before we started feeling empty and our eyes took on the look of a hungry child that hadn't been fed in a while. I knew that if Zane stayed around much longer, I would lose my resolve and give him the rest of the money that I had, so I spoke up.

"Well, I'm kind of sleepy, I guess you should go, since neither one of us has any more money."

Zane looked at me. "I'm too tired to drive, ba'y, do you mind if I crash here tonight?"

I stared at Zane blankly for a moment, trying to determine if he had some other motive besides sleep in mind. I wasn't feeling anything at all like having sex with him. I didn't have any rubbers, for one thing, and since AIDS had come on the scene, I was being really careful about who was getting the panties. I stretched out on the bed turning my back to him.

"You can sleep here if you want to, but that's all," I said firmly.

"Don't nobody want nothin' else," he said, suddenly sounding offended.

"Look, you can take your ass on down the road if you gon' get an attitude," I said.

"Ain't nobody got no attitude woman," he said easily slipping out of his pants and shirt and getting in the bed next to me. I didn't say anything when he snuggled up to me and grabbed me around my waist. It had been a while since anyone had shared my bed. I relaxed and went to sleep.

I woke to the feeling of Zane's lips and tongue laving one of my nipples. I pushed his head away and sat up in the bed. I discovered that I was completely nude.

"What the—?" I said, suddenly wide awake. Something wasn't right. I looked at Zane and saw that he was fully dressed. Why did he have clothes on and why was I naked? What was going on? I glanced around the room. Zane had turned on the dim lamp that sat on my nightstand beside the bed. He had the crack pipe and what looked like a big chunk of crack beside it. I looked Zane directly in the eye.

"Where did you get the money for that crack? I thought you said that you were broke?" He looked away from me. I didn't like that already.

"Aw, I didn't buy this shit, I hid this when I first got back that last time, so I could surprise you—" he started, but I cut him off.

"Bull shit! Why would you get dressed?" I leaned over the bed and down at his feet. "You even got on your shoes! You think I'm some kinda idiot or something?"

Zane didn't say anything and he still wouldn't look at me.

"Why won't you answer me? Where did you get that shit from?"

"Look, don't worry about it. I got it covered. Dude let me git it on credit, so will you chill?"

I let my eyes search Zane's face for a minute. I couldn't tell if he was lying or not. I looked at my purse. It was still resting on a shelf over the bed where I had left it. I thought about checking it, but before I reached for it, Zane put the stem up to my lips.

"This is some good, shit. It's even better than the first shit we had," he said. I hesitated only a moment before taking the pipe between my lips and inhaling the crack smoke deep into my lungs.

As I held it in, waiting to feel the warm glow start to spread across my brain like white lightning, the feeling overtook my mind. It hit in a warm mellow rush. Zane was right, it was better than the last batch we had smoked. It gave you a head rush that was much closer to the base. I turned my head to look at Zane, and once again felt like I was moving in slow motion. Zane noticed, too.

"You got it, didn't you?" he exclaimed excitedly.

I knew that he was referring to the moment the high hit you and swept you up above the bells and propelled you into utter pleasure beyond reason. It was the feeling you got the first time you hit the crack pipe, the feeling you chased but never quite caught each time you got high.

I nodded my head trying to smile, enjoying the intense pleasure. I wanted to stay there, up above the clouds floating somewhere on another plane where nothing and no one else existed. There was nothing except me and intense pleasure.

I watched as Zane tried to catch up with me, but although he came close, I could tell he hadn't quite reached euphoria.

Too soon, I started coming back to reality. I wasn't ready to do that, so I reached for the stem to set it up for another blast. But I suddenly realized the crack pipe was gone. Zane was no longer seated on the bed; he was standing by the bedroom door with his coat on.

I was puzzled, not quite comprehending what Zane was doing.

"Where are you going?" I asked, trying to get up off of the bed.

Zane zipped his coat before answering. "Home," he said simply.

"What do you mean 'home.' I thought you wanted to spend the night here?" I said, rising from the bed and wrapping the sheet around me at the same time.

"Look, I changed my mind, OK? Now don't start trippin'. Just lay your ass back down and go back to sleep."

"Go back to sleep? Go back to sleep!" I laughed out loud.

"How in the hell do you think I'm going to be able to just go back to sleep? If you were going to leave, why didn't you just leave and not tease me with that bullshit little hit you laid on me just now? What kinda shit is that?"

"You didn't think it was bullshit a second ago when yo' ass was flyin' high!"

"So you just gon' take the shit and leave me feeling like this?"

"Like what?" Zane said, acting like he didn't know that one hit that took you there would never be enough, and that the crave would be on maximum overdrive at the thought of not getting another blast.

"You know like fuckin' what! Don't act like you don't," I said, my voice rising.

Zane ignored me and started through the door. I was suddenly angry.

"Go ahead, take your shit and leave!" I ran back to the bed and reached for my purse. "I'll go and get me some more. I got money, you scandalous bitch!" I yelled at him.

Zane looked back over his shoulder and snickered. It was an evil sound.

"Think again . . . you mean you *had* some money."

Suddenly it sank in. That was why Zane had been fully dressed when he had reached over and removed my bra and panties and suckled at my breast. He had gone in my purse and stolen my money. Again.

I launched myself at him.

"You fuckin' snake! How could you do this to me . . . why are you doing this to me?" I said trying to hurt him, wanting to rake him with my nails. But I was no match for Zane's size and strength, he grabbed both my wrists in one of his hands and flung me to the floor.

"Why? Why, you stankin' little skank? You stank ho! Because I want you to take a good look at yourself for once and see what you are. You always lookin' down on me and everybody else, like you better than us or somethin'! Like yours is the only shit that don't stank! What makes you think that, bitch? You ain't got a job, you lost *two* muhfuckin' houses! What? You think you better 'cause you ain't have to go back and live witcha mom yet? You livin' in this shit hole neighborhood, piss poor and gettin' high off the county! Take a look at yourself now, you geekin' for the drug just like the rest of us. How do you feel? Hunh? How you feel now? You ain't no better'n no-fuckin'-body else, you understand! You ain't no better'n me!" Zane looked at me with such utter hatred and contempt that I almost cringed. And then he turned and walked slowly, almost casually, down the steps and out the front door, slamming the door behind him. I lay on the floor crying for the longest time.

I was crying because I knew Zane had told the truth. I *had* thought that I was somehow better than most crack addicts, although the reasons I used to convince myself of that eluded me at the moment. I was crying because, despite my best efforts, the money that I had tried to save from the drug was still gone. How was I going to get the money for E's field trip now? And on top of everything, the crave was still on maximum overdrive. I needed to have another hit. I let the sheet fall away from me as I crawled around on my knees searching for a piece of crack that we may have dropped on the floor while we were getting high, and laughed at myself, even as I continued to crawl around, raking my hand across the floor.

Crack addicts very rarely dropped anything on the floor, and if they did, they knew right away and always picked it up. No one was going to let a piece of high go to waste like that. Then it hit me. This used to be a crack house. Maybe one of its former occupants had stashed some dope somewhere and forgotten about it. That was even less likely to have happened than Zane and me dropping some on the floor and not noticing it. But I couldn't make myself stop. I crawled naked on my hands and knees over to the nearest wall and ran my fingers along the baseboards where the floorboards and the wall met. . . .

Part Three

OUT OF THE PIT

50

I awoke to bright sunlight streaming through the bedroom windows. At some point, I had gotten up off the floor and into the bed. Nothing seemed quite right. The sun looked too bright, the room too shabby, and I was feeling strangely disconnected. Like I was a paper doll that someone had cut out of the world and didn't quite know where to put me. I lay on the bed, staring up at the ceiling, thinking about everything that had happened the night before. How Zane had let his true feelings about me slip out. How he had stolen from me yet again. How he had left me craving the drug and not caring what happened after he left me alone.

Why should he care about me? I didn't even care about myself. I was letting life carry me through the days, and weeks, and months, with no real direction, not creating a life for myself, but letting life create me. Letting it define who I was and what I would be.

I had to do something, or one day I would wake up and be an old woman. Or even worse a homeless old crack addict.

I moved my hand and felt the pain shoot across my fingertips from the cuts the razor blades had inflicted the night before. I examined them closely in the bright sunlight. It wasn't as bad as it had seemed last night, and I wondered absently if that applied to my life as well.

I got up and put on a T-shirt and panties and went downstairs. I wasn't really hungry, and even if I was, there wasn't anything to eat in the house anyway. I had to figure out a way to borrow some money from somewhere by tomorrow. Besides not having any food, I needed to get the money for E's field trip.

I still felt disconnected from the world, as if I were on autopilot or something as I walked into the living room and sat on the couch. After searching for the remote and finally locating it beneath the sofa, I hit the power button and turned on the set. I knew that I needed a change. I had to get some help from somewhere somehow. But I didn't have the first clue where to go or who to ask.

I sat in front of the TV looking at the usual early Sunday morning gospel shows, and then I hit the channel button to flip the station. Not that I had too many options. Cable TV had gone up in the crack pipe just as had most of all the other luxuries we'd enjoyed pre-crack.

My finger was still on the button, but for some reason it stuck and the channels were no longer flipping. Suddenly, I found myself staring at Tim Dawson's face, the used car dealer turned preacher. I pressed on the channel button, but it still wasn't working. I started to stand up and go over and manually change it, but for some reason I sat back down.

I didn't much like him. For one thing, I had tried to get a car from him once and he hadn't seemed like too much of a Christian at the time, trying to get me into a raggedy car for a huge monthly payment that I couldn't afford. Much less the sky-high interest rate he was taxing me.

His words broke into my thoughts. He was saying that Leon Isaac Kennedy was coming to his church to preach a revival beginning that night.

Leon Isaac Kennedy! I had heard of him. Not only had I seen some of his movies before he gave up acting to become a preacher, I had a major crush on him. I had also heard that once he had become a preacher, he had opened up a big church in California and that a lot of celebrities had come to his church to hear him preach because he was such a powerful speaker, full of the Holy Spirit.

I had even heard that the famous singer, Smokey Robinson, who was once a cocaine addict who had been hooked on freebasing, had gone to him when he was on the verge of losing everything, and that Leon had prayed for him. They say that Smokey had been instantly delivered from his addiction. And now the Reverend Leon was in our city!

An idea was forming in my head. Maybe the Lord had brought him all the way from California just for me! Maybe this was my chance to break free from my addiction. I flicked off the TV and put a tape into the cassette player. It was a tape of my favorite gospel group, Commissioned.

> *And with each passin' day, the heartache and pain seem to remain.*
> *But with the Word in front of you,*
> *He's tellin' me and you what He wants us to do! If My people called by My*
> *Name would humble themselves and finally get together there would be a*
> *change!*

Wow! Once again it seemed like the music was singing my life, just as Luther Vandross had done a few years back. But this time, I felt something stirring inside my spirit.

As I listened to them sing about quitters never winning, I decided to put God to the test.

I reached up and fingered my braids that once again were in dire need of a rebraiding. There was no way that I was going to go out in public with my head looking through like this. I also hadn't been to church in so long, that I didn't have anything decent to wear.

I thought about all the clothes that my sister Denise had in her closet. She had enough to start her own shop if she wanted to. She was also very selfish when it came to letting me borrow her clothes. My sister would happily and freely loan any of her clothes to one of her girlfriends, but if I asked, she almost always said no.

So I told God that if I called Denise and she let me borrow something to wear and did my hair for me, I would go to this service tomorrow night.

I couldn't help feeling smug about calling my sister, I already knew what her answers would be. I knew her well enough. First, she would act like my calling her was an imposition, then she would find some excuse to get off the phone, or just simply hang up on me. Maybe I wouldn't call her after all. I didn't feel like dealing with her stinking attitude, like she was better than me.

Commissioned's voices broke into my thoughts again.

"If you wanna see my face and you wanna change your situation, if you wanna hear from me you gotta get it together—so I can bless you! Get it together! So I can bless you!" They repeated the chorus over and over again. "Get under my shadow—Get under my wings! You'll find that I wanna bless you. . . ."

The words of the song bolstered my resolve to test God and I dialed Denise's number. She picked up the phone on the first ring.

"Yeah," she said.

"Denise," I began calmly. "What are you doin'?"

"Nothin', me and Lee are just watching a movie. Why?"

Here it comes, I thought. I decided to delay the inevitable a little while.

"Where's Jadyn?"

"She went back to church with Nickie," she said, referring to one of Jadyn's friends from school.

"Why didn't you and Lee go back?"

"Lee wasn't feeling too good, and didn't want to go, so I decided to stay with him," she said. "So what did you want?" Something in her tone was different, she didn't quite sound like her usual detached, uncaring self. Not that she was gushing with feelings of love or anything, but something was different. *Well, here goes.*

"Oh—well, I was just watchin' TV and I heard that Leon Isaac Kennedy was going to be here this week at Tim Dawson's church. . . ." I hesitated, suddenly unsure of what to say next.

"Oh, yeah? So you thinking about going or something?"

"Yeah, I was thinkin' about goin'," I said, still not sure of how I was going to ask her about loaning me something to wear.

"What's stopping you?"

"Well, I really don't want to go by myself . . ."

"I'll go with you," she said, totally out of character for her. It caught me off guard for a second because I definitely wasn't expecting that one.

"I ain't got nothin' to wear and my braids are through!" I said in a rush.

"You can wear something of mine and if you take your braids down, I'll do your hair for you. . . ."

My mouth fell open. I was speechless. I knew that nobody but God could have made it this easy and simple.

"OK, I'll call you tomorrow."

"OK, see you tomorrow," Denise said.

"Oh yeah, Denise," I said, a thought suddenly forming in my head. "Could I borrow twenty-five dollars until next week?" I asked and I could have bitten off my tongue. A lot of people were figuring out that twenty-five dollars was the amount that most crack addicts asked for when they were broke. That was the lowest dose that crack was sold in at the time. Denise didn't answer right away, as if wondering what else I was going to ask for.

"Yeah, Samai," she finally said, and we hung up the phone.

I sat there totally amazed by the power of God.

I spent the whole next morning and afternoon taking my braids down and listening to Commissioned singing on my tape player. Each song seemed to confirm that this was the day that things were going to change for me. I had an unfamiliar feeling in my chest. It was creeping into my heart. I couldn't be sure, because I hadn't felt like this in a long time, but it felt a little like . . . hope.

51

Denise called when she got off work and said that she was coming to get me.

"Did you take those raggedy braids down?" That was Denise, never biting her tongue for anything or anybody.

"Yes, I took those raggedy braids down," I answered, mimicking her voice.

"Lee said that he will watch the kids for you. He said he hasn't spent any time with his nephews and he wants to take them to the park or something while we're gone."

"OK," I replied, and I was kind of surprised because no one had volunteered to come get the kids or anything for a long while. "I thought I would just bring them with me. . . ."

"Girl now if you was two boys ages seven and nine, what would you rather do? Sit in church with your mama or go have some fun with your uncle in the bright sunshine in the park with the trees, playing tag football and—"

"OK, OK, I get the picture, you're right, now hurry up, you still gotta do my hair and it's already five and we need to leave out by no later than six forty-five to get a seat, 'cause I bet it's going to be crowded!"

"OK, I said I'm on my way, and have the boys ready 'cause Lee is going to meet me there."

I said all right and we hung up the phone.

When Denise got there, she told me that Mom had decided to go with us, so we would need to hurry up so that we could pick her up and still make it on time.

When Mama got in the car, it was immediately filled with the smell of raw garlic.

"Pyew, Mama," Denise said. Like I said, she had never been one to bite her tongue. "Have you been eating raw garlic again?"

"Why, can you smell it?" Mama asked, looking like she was about to get out the car and go back into the house. Somewhere Mama had heard that eating raw garlic would lower your risk of a heart attack and cure other ills.

"Mama, don't pay no attention to Denise, so what if we can smell a little garlic? That church is big and ain't nobody gonna be paying no attention to a little garlic!" I said, giving Denise an evil look. But she pretended she didn't see me and kept right on talking, rolling her eyes and stuff.

"I just don't understand why you had to bite off some raw garlic tonight when you knew you was going to church. Did you think some vampires was going to be up in there or somethin'?" Denise said, making a stupid face.

"Oh hush, child," Mama said waving her hand at Denise like she was going to hit her. "Keep it up and I'ma go on back in the house and won't go!"

"Unh-uhn, not after you made me drive all the way over here," Denise teased.

"Aw, shut up, Denise, and leave Mama alone," I demanded and changed the subject. "Where's Lynn at?" I asked about our middle sister. "Why didn't she want to come?"

"I told her about it," Mama answered. "Her and Seymour musta been plannin' on going someplace else 'cause she didn't say anything about coming."

"Oh, OK," I said, rolling down the window on my side

slightly, trying not to let Mama see me doing it. That garlic *was* strong.

The parking lot was so full that we had to circle it a few times before we found a space. I felt a wave of panic. What would I find inside? Would everyone know that I had been smoking crack. What if the preacher called me out in front of everyone? Maybe this was a bad idea.

"You gonna sit there and daydream all night or are we goin' in?" Denise demanded loudly, glancing back at me and rolling her eyes again before she opened her door and got out.

I said, "Whatever, Denise!" as I opened my door and stepped out onto the pavement.

It was just as packed inside the church as it had been in the parking lot. As the ushers tried to find three seats together, I noticed two of the deaconesses from my old church. Oh, no! Not those two! Why did it have to be them? They were the biggest gossips in the whole world. They were constantly trying to be the first to get the scoop on what was going on in everyone's lives. Being careful to focus on the bad and totally ignoring anything positive, of course, as any good gossip should. On a scale of one to ten on the gossip scale, they had to be at least one hundred! Oh well, maybe I wouldn't have to go up front to be delivered from my addiction. God sometimes just healed you or delivered you right where you sat. Then those two busybodies wouldn't be able to make me their latest feast. I could see them now preparing roast Samai, raking me over hot coals. Nothing would give them more pleasure, I was sure, than to be able to go back and tell how they had seen me after all these years, and that they had discovered that I was a drug addict. Anyway they didn't seem to recognize me, if they had even seen me. Maybe they had forgotten who I was.

The ushers finally managed to find three seats together and Minister Dawson was introducing the Reverend Leon Isaac Kennedy as we sat down. The lights were bright and there had to be at least two thousand people there. I wondered absently if they were coming to hear the message or to see the former movie star. I guess in the end it didn't matter what your motive was for being there, so long as you got to hear what *thus saith the Lord.*

Oddly enough, the message was about drug addicts and the prodigal son, comparing the two by saying both had wandered far away from home, away from who they were supposed to be.

"Just like the prodigal son, God our Father is waiting to clean us up and restore us to our rightful place in the kingdom of heaven, our home. God doesn't care about how far away you have gone, or what you have done while you are out there! He doesn't care if, like the prodigal, you have lain down with pigs and are eating their sloppy leftovers! Did you hear what I said? God is not interested in whether or not you have chosen to lay down in the sloppy pigsty of adultery! God doesn't mind that you are wallowing around in the muck and mire of DRUG ADDICTION, the low places out there in the world! NO, HE DOESN'T! All God wants, do you hear me, church? All our Heavenly Father wants is for *you* to come back home and He will welcome YOU with open arms! Not only that, but HE WILL forgive YOU ALL! NOT SOME BUT ALLLLLLLLLL of your sins and transgressions and YOU WILL be made like new!"

I hung my head and the tears started rolling down my face and dripping into my lap, not because I felt sorry for myself and the horrible state that I found myself in, but because I realized that God loved me so much. *Still.* He loved me in my drug addicted poor pitiful condition so much that He had brought this man here and He was speaking to me through his mouth. I felt the warm glow of the Holy Spirit overshadow me with such sweetness and love that I could hardly stand it.

And then the preacher started saying, "There is someone here tonight that God has been dealing with in the Spirit. He has been troubling your spirit and He has brought you to this place because He wants to deliver you from your addiction. I want you to trust in the Lord tonight. Come on, step out on faith. If that person is you, I want you to walk out in the aisle tonight. The Lord will deliver you. Your deliverance is now, don't let the enemy rob you of your opportunity to be set free. . . ."

I felt the unction of the Holy Spirit, and I wanted to get out of my seat and run down the aisle. But I kept thinking about the two busybodies and how they would run and tell everyone.

Don't be ashamed, Samai. Trust in Me. Keep your eyes on Me.

The Lord was dealing with my heart. Maybe my sister or my mother would go down with me. I lifted my head and glanced over at them. Both of them had their heads bowed and their eyes closed and both of them were crying. Were their tears for me?

"Yes, Lord, have Your way, Lord," my mother was praying.

I guess some things in life, no matter how you may wish it to be otherwise, some things you just have to do alone.

I made up my mind. I wanted to be delivered more than I cared about what those gossips would say. So what if they told someone, (or more likely *everyone*) I got in the prayer line for drug addicts? If it meant that I would no longer be a slave under Pharaoh Crack's rule, then so be it!

I got up out of my seat before I could change my mind and stood in line. Everyone in line was right down front lined up single file across the aisle directly in front of the stage where the minister was preaching.

He came down off the stage, and brought his microphone with him. I watched as he went down the aisle whispering in each one's ear and they in turn whispered something back to him. He made his way down the aisle until he got to me. All of a sudden, it felt as if every bright light in the place shone on me, illuminating me like the brightest ornament on a Christmas tree, so much so that I imagined I could feel the burning heat that emanated from each bulb. For a split second, right before he leaned down and whispered in my ear as he had all the others before me. For a split second, I wanted to say "Never mind!," run back to my seat, and take my shameful addiction with me. I fought the urge, because I knew in my heart that God hadn't brought me to this point for nothing. I knew that this time, He really was here for me and He wasn't going to leave me in need and without help.

The minister leaned toward me. This was it. There would be no running away now. He leaned toward me and whispered, "What is your addiction, my sister?"

Suddenly, I was overwhelmed with the shame of speaking aloud about the addiction. I contemplated lying to the minister about why I had gotten into the prayer line. Even though I knew that it had me by the throat trying to choke the life out of me and rob me of my purpose, I was again filled with doubt. In the end, I decided that I had come this far, why let the devil cheat me out of my deliverance?

I leaned forward and placed my mouth as close to the minister's ear as I dared and to my surprise, only one word would escape my lips.

"Crack," I whispered as softly as I could. Then the preacher did something that he had not done to anyone else in the line. He spoke into the microphone.

"What did you say?" he asked, as he extended his microphone until it was right next to my lips. *Oh Lord, here it is.* Out of all the people standing in this line, why had he chosen to put me on Front Street? I hesitated for a moment, my throat feeling suddenly parched and itchy, then decided to go for broke. What did I have to lose but my pride?

"I'm addicted to crack," I whispered again, knowing that this time the mike had magnified my whisper until it boomed my shame throughout the sanctuary.

"She said she is addicted to crack!" the preacher announced loudly into the mike and in my mind's eye I could see the two gossips smile and give each other looks.

"She is the one that God has been dealing with tonight! This is an addiction straight from hell! God is going to deliver her with

His Mighty Hand!" he said as he strode from one end of the aisle to another. He walked back over to me and said, "Lift your hands to God and thank Him for His Goodness," as he laid his hands on my forehead and prayed.

"Oh Father, Your child stands before You needing the help that only You can give. *Instantly* deliver her, Father!"

When he said those words I felt myself being carried away in the spirit as I fell flat on my back. All of a sudden a bright white light overpowered me and filled me with warmth and love and I felt the peace of God.

Samai, your life will never be the same. . . .

I don't know how long I lay there, but I knew that the Lord was speaking to me, telling me of His plan for me. I had always thought that when the preacher called people up, laid hands on them and they would fall out on the floor, that the preacher was pushing them down, that it was just a big show. I knew now that what I had thought was a lie. The simple truth is no one can stand in the presence of a Holy God.

After what seemed like a long time, but was actually only a few minutes, I opened my eyes and sat up. To my surprise, the floor was full of people lying flat on their backs with their eyes closed. Some had their arms outstretched toward heaven, tears streaming down their faces. Others were standing with their arms lifted above their heads, praising God in what sounded to me like a foreign language, but I knew from past experience it was a special prayer language that was a gift from the Holy Spirit.

As I gathered my legs beneath me and began to stand, I was momentarily startled as strong hands gripped my arms and helped me to my feet. I turned to thank them, but before I could speak, a woman who was standing beside the man who had helped me, wrapped her arms around me and gave me the most gentle hug. And as she embraced me, she whispered a prayer.

"Father, I thank You for sending this sister into my path, I stand in the gap for her, O Heavenly Father. Yes, she may have made some mistakes, O God, but I thank You because You have forgiven her and You love her, O Lord. I thank You for her deliverance, Father. I thank You because from this night forward, she walks in Your power, in Your mercy, but most of all Father, she will know that You love her, no matter what."

As the woman prayed, once again I felt the tears streaming down my cheeks that came from my heart. But this time they were tears of joy.

52

I always knew deep down inside that the Lord had never left me, that wherever I was, He was right there, too. Not being a controlling God, He never stopped me from doing what I thought I wanted to, never attempted to *make* me do the right thing. He was just there, giving me a gentle and sometimes not so gentle reminder of His presence. I know now that he wanted me to choose Him.

But he still wasn't going to force that choice on me.

After that night in church, things were far from perfect. I mean, nobody came up and gave me a good paying job so that I could get off welfare.

Zane was still around ringing my phone, though I never would answer if his number showed up on my caller ID box, and I would hang up on him immediately if he blocked his number so that it wouldn't show on the caller ID screen, or called from a number I didn't recognize.

I still lived in the same cracked-out neighborhood, in the same old used-to-be a crack house apartment. And I still had dreams about getting high.

I felt different inside. Even though I still had those crack dreams, I had something else, too. I had a new determination deep down inside and it was growing stronger with each passing day. It was a determination to fight back, to stop letting crack rule and ruin my life. I could be the mother that my children needed me to be. I could be the woman that I knew I was born into this earth to be. Not the addicted, weak mess of a woman that I had been. I could create a life for myself, instead of just allowing life to create me. I knew that God had a better life planned for me, a purpose for my life and if it was the last thing I did, I was going to find out what that purpose was.

53

I was having one of the best sleeps I had had in a long while. The you-know-you're-going-to-have-trouble-pulling-yourself-out-of-the-covers-in-the-morning-it-feels-so-good kind of sleep. So I wasn't happy when the ringing telephone interrupted it.

I put the pillow over my head to drown out the sound, hoping that I would be able to ignore it completely and sink back into my wonderful subconscious state, but that wasn't happening. I threw the pillow back and stared bleary eyed at the red digital readout on the clock, trying to bring the numbers into focus. I should have known: one o'clock in the stankin' morning!

I grabbed the receiver off the still ringing phone and growled into it.

"Who in the world is this callin' me this early in the daggone morning?"

"Samai! Samai, you gotta listen to me!"

It was Zane.

The anger rose hotter than ever, making my heart and my temples pound. This fool had some balls of iron, to think he could call me like this. I hadn't answered his calls or seen him since that night he had stolen the money for E's trip out of my purse. All the money I had, really, and left me in a mess on my bedroom floor. The anger turned to rage as I thought about what he had done and how he had the nerve to dial my number this time of the morning.

"You lowlife, thieving, scum of the earth! What in heaven's name would *evah* make you think you could pick up the phone and dial my number again in this life or the next? Your sorry ass ain't done nothin' but cause me pain and misery since I met you! I wish to God I had never laid eyes on you! I wish you *would* ask me anything! I wish you *would*, you stankin' piece of garbage!"

Zane was trying to speak on the other end but the words kept pouring out of me like floodwater over a dam.

"Why you callin' me, you snake? Hunh? Why you callin' me? You want to see if I want to go inhale some more poison into my lungs? Hunh? What? You outta money and you geekin' for another high, so you thought you would call me—"

"Close your mouth and listen to me if you wanna keep breathin'!"

Zane bellowed into the receiver. His words momentarily stunned me into silence. Keep breathing?

"Listen, Quin is in town and he done lost his fuckin' mind. He talkin' some bullshit about you owe him some money and he gon' get what's his one way or the other."

My throat went dry and I could barely speak. Quin was someone who I only wanted to think about as being on the fringe of my world. If not for Zane, the chances of me even coming in contact with a psycho like Quin were slim and none.

I remembered the insane things that Zane had told me that Quin did just for laughs, I didn't even want to imagine what he could do to someone who made him angry. And now, here Zane was saying that Quin might be after *me*? I swallowed hard to keep the panic I was feeling in check so that Zane wouldn't know how his words were affecting me.

"What? What do you mean Quin thinks I owe him some money? How could he think that when I haven't even seen or heard from him since that night in your basement when he was going to catch a bus outta town—"

"I don't know! I don't know," Zane said, sounding nervous, and

I thought I detected a little fear in his voice, too. "You know how crazy that nigga can get. You remember that chick that was at my place that night you lost your mind and called your brother over and me and him had that fight?"

I came close to correcting him and telling him that he meant the night my brother whipped his ass. But I just grunted.

"Yeah, I remember, but what does that have to do with Quin thinking I owe him something?"

"Well, Quin had seen her at the house one night and he wasn't a bit shy about makin' it known that he wanted to hook up with her. Shit, once she found out that Quin was holdin' it wasn't no secret that she wanted to get next to him neither. That bitch latched on to Quin and they been hangin' out like they all in love and shit ever since. I know for a fact that skank is the worse crackhead in this city, even though she covers it up by still managin' to keep her shit together. You know, convince people she don't be geekin' and shit. But anybody that know her knows she will do anything to get that next bop when her ass get to smokin'!"

I could see that Zane was more than a little jealous and ticked that a woman had actually chosen to be with another man over him, no matter what her reason was.

"I bet it blew your mind that she chose Quin over you, didn't it?" I couldn't help saying. "You always did want to be the one all women wanted to be with, even when you were supposed to be with me."

It made me sick that I had let Zane's good looks blind me to the truth about him for so long. Now I was wondering what in the world I had seen in him, other than that. Why in the world had I blindly followed him wherever he led?

"Look, you the one that was on *that* shit, I never said that I liked that bitch, much less, loved her. Anyway, why you on that shit now when I'm trynna tell yo' ass that this skank done created a monster that ain't none of us gon' be able to tame?"

"I really ain't caring about none of this mess you're talking about. Because from what I'm hearing, that woman has got you mixed up in some low down, dirty mess, and since you're no stranger to that type drama, contrary to what you might believe, that would be *your* problem *not* mine. First of all, since you and Quin are so tight, he should know that we ain't been together in I don't know when. And second, he ought to know that whatever I may have become since foolin' around with you, crazy *ain't* one of them. And crazy is what anybody would have to be to cross a lunatic like Quin. I ain't never been in his world like that. So if he got any sense, he will be hunting down the ones who have been."

Zane blew out his breath and sounded even more nervous than he had before when he said, "It ain't my fault that dizzy broad decided to steal from Quin and then blame it on us."

I was stunned. "Blame it on *us*? There *is* no us! How could you let that bi—" I cut off the word, suddenly feeling strange about using it. ". . . that woman involve me in this scheme, when she doesn't even know me? You and her are probably the ones who . . ."

And just like that it clicked. That Zane was behind this whole thing. From the beginning. He had planned everything, getting Natalie Cole to get next to Quin and his dope so that he could have all the free highs he wanted. But something had gone wrong. Something had caused him to concoct this story, to try to put the blame on Natalie and set me up to take the fall with her. Dirty bastard! Was there no end to how low Zane would sink to have what he wanted?

I knew there was no use in asking him anything, but I couldn't stop myself.

"How could you? How could you do this to me and my kids! You put me and my kids' lives in jeopardy, for what? So you could *try* to play that gangster role and get high off of somebody else's stash and then when the mess hit the fan, you *lie* about it so you wouldn't have to face the consequences like the slimy snake you are! Yeah, that's what you did, didn't you? Didn't *you*? Just the fact that you would try to put your dirt off on two women shows what a lowlife you truly are!"

Zane was quiet. "Shit! What you trynna say? I-I wouldn't do nothin' to hurt you or your kids." So unconvincing.

"You wouldn't, hunh? Is your mind really that cloudy that you don't remember how you stole my kids' video game, our T.V, VCR, the candy money that E and Devon had collected, the money for E's field trip, the money for our food! You did this Zane, don't try to lie now. You set Quin on me, and you didn't give a damn about my life or that my kids would be in danger, too!"

"Look, I didn't know the bitch had stole from Quin. She had loot, she had dope, and she wanted to get high with me! She didn't tell me she stole the shit till it was all gone. She gone start gettin' all hysterical and shit and I asked her what the fuck's the matter. And that's when her dumb ass told me what was up."

I was quiet. Fear was squeezing my heart until I thought I would pass out. I couldn't speak and there was nothing but air between me and Zane.

"Look, believe what you wanna believe. If I'm that much of a dirty muhfuckin' snake, why would I call your ass and tell you anything, hunh? Why wouldn't I just let the shit play out?"

"Even Lucifer thinks about the evil he does, before goin' ahead and doing it. So don't give yourself any medals for that." I sighed before asking, "So where is Quin now?"

"Listen, I'm trynna tell you I do not know. All I know is that muhfucka is on the rampage talkin' about he gon' kill every last one of our asses. So if I was you I would call that brother of yours right quick and see how much of a gangsta he really is."

"Zane, the way things are right now, you better pray that calling my brother is all that I do!" And I slammed the phone down hard.

Talking to Earl would have been the first thing I did except that my uncle Jay had called last week and asked Earl to come to Orlando to help him straighten out a few things. No telling when he would get back.

54

Whatever the price I had to pay for all the mistakes I had made, I knew that I had to find Quin before he found me. But maybe that wasn't a good idea. No telling what state of madness he was in by now. And him thinking that we had stolen something, too? No, that idea wasn't going to work at all. Still, I couldn't have him coming to my home looking for me and jeopardize my kids' safety.

No. I had to get my kids away. Had to get them someplace where they would be safe. But where?

I couldn't take them to my mom's; if Quin couldn't find me, family would be the first place he would look. My relationship with Zane had never progressed to the point that we did the "time to meet the parents" thing. I wasn't sure that Quin could find out where Mom lived, but I wasn't willing to risk it.

There was one person who I knew I could trust. One person that neither Zane nor Quin had ever even heard of.

Miss Loretta.

I dialed her number.

"Hey, Samai! Girl, how you doin'? You and the kids haven't been around much lately. What you been up to?"

Miss Loretta peppered me with questions. I knew that I would be asking her a lot, only having sent her birthday and Christmas cards and taking the kids to her house for dinner once in a blue moon, when we didn't have any food, but I didn't have a choice.

"Miss Loretta, I don't know what else to tell you but the truth. I'm in a lot of trouble, trouble that I don't want to bring down on my kids. I was wondering if they could stay with you a few days—just until I can work things out."

Miss Loretta got quiet. I started sweating, waiting for her to say something. I didn't know what I would do if she couldn't help me.

Finally, Miss Loretta blew her breath out and made a noise in her throat.

"I'm not gon' ask you but one question. Samai, if I help you, is trouble gon' show up at my door?"

It was my turn to be silent. I really didn't think that Quin could find out about Miss Loretta if things got to that but I wasn't going to take any chances.

"Miss Loretta, nobody knows about our friendship. I would bet on my life that nothing like that would happen. The chance of them finding you is low. Trust me, Miss Loretta, I'm not trynna have anything happen to my children, so if I thought there was a real chance of trouble finding you, I would take them someplace else. If you help me, I will do everything in my power to make sure they don't find my children. Believe that."

"Lord, child, I don't know what y'all's generation is comin' to. Just shootin' and cuttin' up each other just for sneezin' loud! But I do know one thing, the Lord wouldn't be pleased if somethin' happened to your children because I refused to help. I'm gon' tell you right now, that it's only because of them that I'm sayin' yes, and God help us all!"

Tears came to my eyes. Again someone who wasn't family was willing to help me.

"Miss Loretta, thank you, for my children and for me. I don't want to take any chances that anyone might see me drop the kids at your home, so here's what we can do . . ."

55

I had Miss Loretta come to a park that wasn't located near either of our houses, but was one where lots of children played. There were usually so many children there, that it was hard to keep track of whose children were whose, which is exactly why it was perfect. After we were there a little while, Ms. Loretta took the boys and left. I had already explained to them that they were staying at Auntie Loretta's for a few days. They didn't mind, they loved her and her grandkids.

When I got back to the apartment, I went to work on my plan.

I knew the only way to get out of this mess was to make Zane admit that he was the one who had stolen from Quin, but the only way I could see to do that was to win Natalie Cole over to my side.

I didn't believe for one minute that any woman who knew Quin, not even one as full of game as she was, would deliberately steal from someone like Quin. What I did believe was that Zane had turned up the charm full blast and had conned her into getting involved in his scheme to steal from Quin. She probably didn't even realize what Zane was up to until she was in too deep to get out of it.

When Zane had called to tell me that Quin was after us, a woman's number had shown up on my caller ID box. The name "Gloria Winston" had popped up. I wasn't sure that Gloria Winston was Natalie Cole's real name, but there was only one way to find out.

I had thought about what I could say to her. We had only had one run-in, and that was on the night that I had threatened to "beat her ass" at Zane's house, the night my cousin and brother had come to get me. I knew that if I were in her shoes, I would be the last person I'd want calling me about anything. But this wasn't just anything. With a maniac like Quin, this could be a matter of life and death.

I decided to dial *67 to block my number first. I didn't know whether or not she had a caller ID box, but I didn't want to take a chance that she did. If she saw my name pop up, the chances she would answer would be slim and none. And besides, even though I had a strong feeling that she wasn't in on Zane's plot, I wasn't a hundred percent sure. She could be plotting with Zane to put the whole thing on me. She could have been sitting right there when Zane had called, though I really didn't think Zane would have said all that if she had been there. But you never knew. And what if he was chilling at her place now? I didn't want him to know that I was calling.

A woman answered the phone. I hoped it was Gloria.

"Hello, Gloria?"

"Who's this?" she inquired with suspicion edging her voice.

"Look, don't hang up. You and me are in some real danger and if my instincts are right, Zane has set us up to take a fall," I blurted out in one breath.

"What? Who the fuck is this? And what you mean *we* in danger?" I could hear the disbelief in her voice. Along with what sounded like fear.

"I'll tell you who I am, but first, let me tell you that Zane called and told me all about you stealing from Quin—"

"Oh fuck, no he didn't. That dirty muhfucka is out his damn mind with that shit! I ain't stole shit. And *especially* not from Quin. You need to get your information straight before you put some shit like that out!"

I took a deep breath. This could get ugly. If I didn't win her over, she could add to my problems by going to Quin and telling him that I'm putting lies out in the street about him not being able to take care of his.

"I'm not puttin' nothin' out. Like I said, Zane is the one who told me. He said that you and him was gettin' high and partyin' offa the stash and the money that Quin had told you to hold."

"That lyin' sacka shit! *He's* the one who . . . wait just a damn minute. Who did you say this is?"

"It's Samai—"

"Aw, hell no! You think I'm stupid, don't you? You and Zane are tryin' to put this shit off on me! Y'all ain't gettin' this shit off! I already told Quin what happened and your ass is grass if you in on this shit with Zane, cuz his ass is about to be fertilizer. I know who you are. You that broad who was screamin' that you wanted to get in my ass 'cause your so-called man had stole your shit! Unh-hunh, I remember. Well, his thievin' ass done messed with the right one this time. And if you still want to kick my ass, come on over and we'll see who the bitch is!"

Then I heard a loud *click* in my ear. I had the feeling that the call had been a mistake and I was in even deeper than when I had made the call. But the truth of the matter was that this was never about Zane and Gloria. This was all about Zane and me.

56

Deep down inside I knew it would come to this. I had made up my mind that I was going over to Zane's house and settle this mess once and for all, but first I had to make a phone call. If it was time for me to face the music, then it was way past the time for Zane to face it as well. I knew I needed some back up to do what I had to, and the only way to get it was to tell the truth, from the beginning, and pray that they would believe me. My plan would only work if I could convince them that I needed help.

Driving down the street that would take me to Zane's place, I was more certain than ever that this was how it had to be. I had to be the one to confront Zane, and get him out of my life once and for all. It was that simple. I wasn't sure what I would find when I got there, but I had decided to put it all in God's hands.

I drove past Zane's house and parked down the street a little ways. I had to be careful. I wasn't sure what state of mind Zane would be in so I could at least keep the element of surprise on my side. I wasn't sure if anyone else would be there.

I stepped out of the car, shoved the car keys into my pants pocket, and took a deep breath to calm down. I wasn't going to let Zane weasel his way out of this. The time for playing had been over long ago. This was about life. My kids, as well as my own, and to save them there was nothing I wouldn't do.

I began walking toward Zane's house, repeating and rephrasing what I would say to him over and over in my head. Zane hadn't always been a snake. It was the crack that changed him. Crack had ignited the beast within, and it had grown into a ravenous monster that would never be tamed, no matter how much you fed and pampered it. When you messed with crack, even the strongest players in the game wound up being played like a child's toy, spinning in a vicious circle. Only in this game you never spun out, just down.

I was thinking about all of this when I thought I heard someone groan. I stopped in my tracks, the hairs on the back of my neck rising, as I strained my ears toward the sound. But all I heard in the darkness was crickets chirping, the sound of cars whizzing by on the overpass a few blocks away, and in the distance a woman's voice calling for someone named Max.

Must have been my nerves playing tricks on me. That's all. I paused for a few seconds and then continued toward Zane's house, but after only a few steps, I heard the groan again, only louder this time. I turned toward the sound and as I peered through the shadows cast by the dim light of a streetlamp, I saw a figure lying knees to chest in the grass only inches from my feet.

I bent down and heard her whisper. "Help me, oh God, please help me . . . ," and she began to cry. I knelt down beside her, and instinctively lifted her head onto my lap. My hand became wet immediately and I was afraid to look at that hand for fear the wetness would not have come from the night dew that had settled over the grass. I knew that if it was blood, this girl would be seriously hurt, bleeding like that.

"Look, I'm gonna try to get you some help," I told her. I took off my sweater, and rolled it up before lifting her head from my lap and replacing it with the sweater.

"Noooooo," she groaned. "Don't leave me . . . please . . . don't leave me alone. . . ." And in that moment, fear must have given her strength that belied her injuries, because she gripped the front of my shirt so tight, it scared me. "He could come back! He's gon' kill me if he comes back. You gotta get me out of here!" she cried in anguish, using the front of my shirt to pull herself up and at that moment, the streetlamp lit her bloody face and I was horrified to see that it was Gloria Winston, aka Natalie Cole.

57

"Oh my God! Gloria, who did this to you?" I asked, at the same time knowing that it had to have been Quin. But where was Zane while Quin had beaten this woman like this? We were only a few feet from Zane's front door. Surely he would have heard something. Suddenly, an overwhelming fear gripped me and I felt like I was going to vomit. I grabbed Gloria's hands and began to pry her fingers from my shirt.

"Noooooooo . . . No! Don't leave me, please!" She was getting hysterical.

"Shh, look, I'm coming back, I have to get help!" I whispered, looking around for any sign that Quin could be nearby. "Shhhh-hhh! Someone will hear you, you got to be quiet." I stood. "I'm not gonna leave you here for long, but I have to get you some help!"

I turned, but in that instant, I felt something cold and hard press against the soft spot behind my ear at the same moment I heard a metallic *click*. My heart began to pound against my chest so hard and loud, I thought it was going to beat right out of my body.

And then I felt lips pressed against my ear.

"Ahhhhh, tell me this, sweetheart," Quin whispered. "While you trynna help oh girl, who in the fuck is gon' help your black ass?"

. . .

Quin forced me inside Zane's house.

"Yeah, keep movin', bitch, you know the drill. Go on downstairs. We 'bout to git this here party started." Quin had the gun pressed into the small of my back, propelling me forward.

"Quin, look, that girl could die out there if we don't get her some help. You could go down for murder."

"For real? I ain't losin' sleep, tramp. You just keep walkin' and hope that you have it as easy as that bitch out there turnin' cold. You 'bout to find out that Quin don't play. And if you mess with mine, I'm definitely gon' fuck the hell outta yours!"

At the foot of the stairs, I could see Zane tied to a chair, his face a bloody pulp, his lips puffy and bleeding, and his right eye was bright red and swollen shut. His head was flung back and I couldn't tell if he was still breathing. But then I heard something that made my blood run cold.

"Mom! I'm sorry, Mom, please don't be mad at me. . . ."

My eyes turned toward the tearful voice laced with terror, and I silently begged God to make it not be true.

There huddled on the floor, hugging her knees, crying her eyes out, sat my baby.

58

"Jadyn!" No longer caring for my life, I ran over to my child to make sure she hadn't been hurt. "Are you all right? Did he hurt you?"

"Mom, he came to the house lookin' for you! I didn't know, Mom, I needed to talk to you, me and Nickie . . . she dropped me off . . . she was going to come back . . . we . . . I didn't open the door, Mom . . . I didn't open the door! He kicked it open, Mom, he kicked it open . . ." Jadyn's words came out in a jumble and her eyes stretched wide, tears streaming down her face. The fear in her eyes was reflected in her voice.

"Shhhh, it's OK, don't cry, baby, it's not your fault! But why were you there? You were supposed to be at . . ." I caught myself before I said my sister's name. Whatever happened here, I didn't want Quin to have a clue about who or where my family was. I held Jadyn close, trying to dry her tears.

"It's going to be all right, baby, I promise."

"You ain't exactly in a position to make promises, now are you, bitch? I ain't touched that young pussy . . . yet," Quin said, giving me a most evil grin. "I been waiting for the rest of the boys to get here!"

I shrank away from Quin's evil and held on to Jadyn's trembling body. *Dear Merciful Savior! Anything, anything but this. The price is too high to pay for what I've done. Please God, not this. . . .*

"Don't be sittin' over there all pitiful now, bitch, cryin' and shit! You brought this shit on yourself. Messin' around with oh boy here. Y'all shoulda' known you couldn't fuck with Quin without havin' to deal with reprecussions. This shit ain't my fault, so don't go bitchin' up now," he said, walking toward us.

I rose to my feet taking a protective stance in front of my daughter.

"Quin, this is between you and me now." I jabbed my finger into my own chest as I spoke. "Just you and me." I inched toward him trying to put distance between him and Jadyn. I pointed back toward her. "She ain't got *nothin'* to do with this. You can do whatever you feel you need to with me. But she ain't got *nothin'* to do with this."

"The fuck she don't! I told you . . . up there," Quin said pointing over his shoulder with the gun to emphasize his point, "you mess with Quin and he gon' definitely fuck yours! I told you that shit, didn't I? So don't be actin' surprised." Quin started laughing. And I froze in my tracks.

"Oh, this shit is funny as *hell*. When I told you I would fuck yours, I bet you never in a million years thought I was talkin' about your daughter."

"No!" Jadyn screamed. "Mom, don't let him hurt me!"

"Quiet, Jadyn," I shushed her. "Not as long as I'm breathin'." I needed her to become invisible. I needed to make Quin focus on me.

"That can definitely be arranged!" Quin threatened, his face darkening. "Who you thank you is, bitch?"

"Quin, you right, you right, you absolutely right! Whoever messed with your stuff *should* have to pay. But that's me, right? Right, Quin? You got those other ones good. Now I'm ready to take my medicine. I deserve everything I get. I mean, you already got Gloria and Zane, right?" I nodded my head toward Zane.

Quin looked over at Zane. "Yeah, stupid muhfucka! I definitely got his ass. We go way back, fool! Why did you try to fuck me? We was brothers! And you let somethin' I was puttin' the rod to fuck with your head like this?" Quin strode up to Zane and grabbed him by his hair, pulling his head back. "This what you get, nigga! This is what you get when you try to step to me! I woulda *gave* you the shit you stole, you bitch ass punk! If you'da asked for it! But yo' bitch ass gone try to steal from me? Hunh, bitch? Don't nobody fuck with King Quin! You hear me, muhfucka?"

Quin slammed Zane's head down so hard I thought his neck would break. And after all of that, Zane still didn't utter a sound.

"Naw, you don't hear me. You can't hear a muhfuckin' thang!" Quin glanced from me to Jadyn and back to Zane. I eased backward trying to make sure my body was between Quin and Jadyn.

"I'm gon' handle the rest of this shit! Then everybody gon' know that Quin ain't nothin' nice and I ain't nothin' to be played with!" Quin took a few steps toward us. But before he could reach us, there was a loud knock at the door, stopping Quin in his tracks.

"Open up, this is the police!" one of them called loudly.

Quin's face became a fierce mask of purple rage.

"What the fuck! You called the police?" Quin raised the gun and cocked the hammer. "Say yo' goodbyes, bitches! If I'm goin' down for murder, two more dead bodies ain't gon' make a damn bit a difference!"

The pounding on the door upstairs got louder. Quin locked eyes with mine and I stared into the crazed eyes of a maniac intent on murder. Everything seemed to go in slow motion after that. Quin bared his teeth and began turning the gun toward Jadyn as his finger squeezed the trigger and I did what any mother would do. I stepped in front of the bullet and traded my life for that of my child.

I heard a booming crash as a red-hot poker pierced my flesh and splattered blood into the air in a spray that splashed my face. I began to fall backward, and a collage of pictures moved freeze-framed, before my eyes. Jadyn screaming and running over to cradle me in her arms; a policeman's voice yelling something as loud footsteps clattered down the stairs; Quin's evil grin as he took aim at Jadyn once again; Quin's face becoming a mask of pain and confusion as the policeman's bullets ripped into his body; Jadyn's soft cool hands gently stroking my face; Jadyn's tears splashing my face and her voice pleading with me not to leave her. I tried to speak and felt a thick, warm bubbly liquid spurt from my mouth, and dribble down my chin, and then everything started fading to black.

EPILOGUE

I opened my eyes and saw all kinds of tubes running in and out of my body. There was a needle in the back of my hand and a mask over my face. My chest hurt and felt like a ton of concrete was laying on top of it, restricting my breathing. I lifted my head from the pillow a little bit and outside of a window I saw the faces of everyone I loved. My brothers, my sisters, E, Devon, and Jadyn were there. Jadyn! *You're safe . . . thank You, God . . . I love you, my babies, I love you all soooo much . . . I'm sorry . . . I'm so sorry for all that I've put you through . . .* Doobie was there. Doobie? What was he doing out there? Miss Loretta. Good old Miss Loretta. *I love you Miss Loretta, thank you for saving my kids' lives . . .* Aunts, uncles, and cousins I hadn't seen in years. Hey, was that Bennie? *Hey, Deacon Bennie.* I tried to lift my head higher to get a better look at him but it was no use, someone had tied a lead bandana around my head and it was too heavy for me to lift.

Mom was sitting beside my bed, stroking my hand, looking as if she had been praying or crying or both. I wanted to ask Mom if I was dying because all those people must be here for a funeral. I couldn't speak because something was stuck in my throat. Maybe I was already dead and this was all a part of being that way. Sure is nice having all of these people here while I'm dying . . . or dead. I looked over at my mom, and a tear rolled down her cheek. Aw,

292 | Mari Walker

Mama, don't cry, it's OK, I tried to say. Mama, I'm thirsty . . . and everything went black again.

I stayed in the hospital for five weeks. They moved me out of intensive care where I had been the first time I woke up and into a regular room after about two weeks. The bullet I had taken for Jadyn had grazed my heart and pierced one of my lungs. That lung had collapsed, which is why I had felt like I couldn't breathe. The doctors said that I was lucky, that if the bullet had struck even a tiny millimeter to the right, I wouldn't have made it, but I knew that luck had nothing to do with it. It was only because of the divine intervention of God that I was still here.

I asked my mom why all of the people had been outside my room before.

"All what people, child?" Mama tenderly stroked my hand. I tried to name all the people I had seen that first time I'd awakened, but she interrupted me before I could finish.

"Hush, child. You need your rest. You musta been dreamin' or something 'cause ain't nobody been upstairs near your room, but me, your brothers and sisters, and your children. Now go on back to sleep, you must be tired."

I learned that Zane wasn't dead but he was in a coma. His brain had been without oxygen for so long that he had suffered brain damage and was probably going to have some paralysis below his waist if he woke up. The doctors weren't sure if it was going to be permanent or not but they said chances were good that Zane would never walk again.

Gloria hadn't been hurt as badly as it seemed. She had to have some stitches in the back of her head. The scalp bleeds quite profusely when injured even slightly, according to the doctors. She also had to get a cast for her broken leg, but she basically got to go home that same night.

Quin had died of the gunshot wounds before the ambulance got to Zane's house. I was glad that I had called my friend, Officer Bennie Howard, and told him the truth about Quin's insane threats, that night. I also told him all about my plan to confront Zane, which he tried to talk me out of, but I wouldn't listen. It was Bennie who had made sure that a unit had been dispatched to Zane's house to take a felony menacing report. That call had probably saved our lives.

"Mom!" Devon yelled as he ran over to my bed. "Mom, the doctor said that you can come home today! Didn't he, Jadyn? Didn't he, E?"

Jadyn and E walked up to my bed, grinning from ear to ear. "He sure did. In fact, he's out there signing the discharge papers right now," Jadyn said, sounding much older and wiser than her sixteen years.

"Ma," E said, taking my hand in his. "I'm the man of the house and you ain't allowed doin' nothing when you get home. Me, Jadyn, and Devon are gon' take good care of you until you are well."

"Yes, sir!" I said smiling and rubbing the top of his head. When had he gotten so tall? They had all grown up during my time in the streets. A time that was definitely over.

Devon grabbed my other hand. "Get up, Mom. Jadyn's gon' help you get dressed. Me and E is gon' wait out in the hall with Uncle Earl. Hurry up, Mom!" he said before leaning close and whispering, "We got a surprise party waitin' for you when you get home. Grandma made you a cake, and Uncle Lee and Aunt Lynn and—"

"Devon!" E and Jadyn chimed together.

Devon put his hands over his mouth. "Oops! Sorry, Mom!" He grinned and E pulled him out into the hall, slapping him on the back of his head as he did. I smiled as I heard them arguing in the hall.

"Boy, how you gon' ruin Mom's surprise party like that with your big o' mouth? You can't keep nothin' a secret."

"Stop hittin' me, man! You better be lucky I ain't tell Mom about the D on your report card . . . now!"

"What?"

"All right, all right, that's enough outta both of y'all! Your mom don't need to be hearin' all that noise. Now be quiet." I heard Earl's voice trying to keep the peace between my two little men.

"Come on, Mom, let me help you. Do you think you can make it to the bathroom?" Jadyn's face was a mask of concern, although she tried to hide it for my sake. I marveled at how well she seemed to be handling all that had transpired. Only time would tell how much she had been affected by it all, but she was not going to have to handle it alone. I would be right by her side making sure she had all the love and support she needed to make her healing complete. We would heal together.

"Think I can make it, with your help," I said, dangling my legs over the edge of the bed. Our eyes met and she smiled.

"You know I'm here for you, right, Mom?" she declared. "Always."

I said a silent prayer that she'd make it through this and she'd be fine. I prayed that, with the Lord's help, we all would.

DISCUSSION QUESTIONS

1. Zane and Samai are total opposites when they reunite at Samai's job. Samai is quiet and reserved but Zane is outspoken, rough around the edges, and, at times, downright vulgar. Why do you think the attraction between the two of them was so immediate and intense?

2. When Samai went to Zane's houseparty, why wasn't she turned off when Zane informed her that some of his guests would be doing drugs?

3. What kept Samai at the party after she saw a different side of Zane?

4. The sex between Zane and Samai was explosive and mind blowing. If someone could satisfy you that way, would you lose yourself in him? Why or why not?

5. Once Samai realized that she was addicted to crack, why wasn't the love for her children enough to make her seek help right away?

6. How did Samai's addition affect her and her ability to care for her children?

7. What kind of man did Zane reveal himself to be?

8. What do you think made Zane behave the way he did?

9. Do you think that Zane ever loved Samai? Did Samai love Zane?

10. Do you think that turning to God is the only way to truly cure addiction?
11. Why did Quin react the way he did when he found out that Zane had stolen from him?
12. Did Samai truly find redemption at the end of her struggle?
13. What long-term effects do you think Samai's lifestyle will have on Jadyn, E, and Devon?
14. Which characters, if any, would you like to read about in another story?